# PRAISE FOR THE SPIRITS OF CHAOS SERIES

"In this endearing origin story, Conway (Harbinger, 2018, etc.) hits the high notes for YA romance readers and superhero devotees alike... The author keeps her tale fun and nerdy, luring fans toward an epic finale but also creating characters readers would love to see grow throughout a series. This fantasy delivers a bright tsunami of hormones and heroism."

—*Kirkus Reviews*

"... a fun superhero themed book that younger teens are going to love. It's light, fun, has great characters, and was overall, a joy to read." —Amanda J. Evans, author of *Hear Me Cry*

"...everything you want in a superhero story that you did not know you needed." —J.R.'s Book Reviews

# WINGS

## Nicole Conway

Owl Hollow Press

Owl Hollow Press, LLC, Springville, UT 84663

Wings

Library of Congress Cataloging-in-Publication Data
Wings / N. Conway. — First edition.

Summary:
While Koji attempts to balance high school and family life with herowork, the dark secrets of the scales begin to unfold and Koji realizes that his epic superpowers might not come as freely as he first thought.

ISBN 978-1-945654-60-2 (paperback)
ISBN 978-1-945654-61-9 (e-book)
LCCN 2020942190

*To Marie & Rylee*

*Don't give up, ladies!*
*The world needs your stories!*

# CHAPTER 1

Adrenaline roared through my veins, making my palms grow slick with sweat as I held my controller in a white-knuckled grip. This was it. The moment of truth.

Sitting on the floor of the computer lab where the Saint Bernard's robotics team had their meetings, I fought to slow my pulse and steady my breathing. I could do this. No big deal. Only seven hundred hours of late-night practice on my game console at home and countless cans of Red Bull, Code Red, and Dr. Pepper had led up to this moment—my inevitable victory. I just had to stay calm. Cool. Collected.

Now was not the time to freak out.

Next to me, my best friend and current reigning school champion of the new game *Alien BotPit 2: Reign of the Battlemaster*, Drake Collins, yawned as he made the final selections to his mech suit. He always went for a medium armor and ranged weapon combo. Today, that was going to be his downfall.

Today, Saint Bernard's Catholic School would have a new champion: Koji Owens.

"Ready to lose?" He flicked me a sarcastic grin as he adjusted the color settings on his mech's armor to pink. Was that a taunt? Adding insult to injury?

Harsh.

I stuck a hand out toward him to shake. "Honor code—no glitching."

His mouth scrunched unhappily, light amber eyes narrowing through shaggy platinum bangs. At last, he gave a dramatic sigh and shook my hand. "Agreed."

"And we're using the map randomizer," I added before letting his hand go.

"Fine, fine," he groaned. "Paranoid much?"

"No," I snapped. "I'm just wise to all your crap, Collins."

He chuckled. Or maybe that was a maniacal, evil genius laugh. I wasn't sure. "Terms of victory are: winner destroys opponent's bot by whatever game-original means available. Sound fair enough for you?"

"Deal," I agreed.

"You guys are seriously lame, you do realize that, right?" Drake's girlfriend, Tabitha Hunt, grumbled. I could practically feel her rolling her eyes from where she stood behind our chairs.

According to Tabitha, she and Drake had been dating seriously since… well, basically right after the Winter Ball last year. He would neither confirm nor deny that status, though, and I couldn't tell if it was because he wasn't into commitment or he just wanted to annoy her. Probably both, knowing him.

Whatever they were, they texted *constantly* and Tabitha always waited in the hall after class so she could walk with us. She'd even started sitting with us at lunch sometimes, plopping herself down confidently right beside Drake. Whether I liked it or not, Tabitha had officially demoted me to third wheel. Ugh.

At least Drake had forced her to start calling me by my name now instead of "sneakers guy" like before. So, I had that tiny bit of my dignity back. But still…

She seemed to treat everyone like they were filthy commoners in her perfect kingdom. Not to mention she clearly didn't understand the significance of video game dominance. This match was the most important thing in my life. Well, you know, except for being Noxius, protecting New York, trying to track down my sort-of girlfriend Madeline, and passing the Chemistry final.

Hmm. Maybe I should have studied for that instead of playing video games. Hmm. I'd taken that exam first thing this morning and, honestly, I barely even remembered going into the classroom. Yikes. Had I even taken the right exam? Oh well. Too late now.

Tabitha probably wouldn't have insisted on hanging around us so much if Claire Faust was still around, but after the incident at the Philharmonic, things had gotten complicated for her family. It didn't take long for the press to get wind of the scandal between the Fausts and our former school headmaster, Mr. Ignatius. They took those rumors and ran with them, and suddenly Claire's terrified face was on the front of tabloids all over the city with a big bold caption: HEIRESS TO COMRIDORE-FAUST FAMILY TO INHERIT EMBEZZLED CHARITY FUNDS.

Not good.

Things had gone downhill pretty fast after that. Now lawyers were involved, a criminal investigation was underway. Some of the online news articles theorized that—if there was any truth to the rumor that the Fausts had indeed tried to frame Madeline's mom for stealing a bunch of money from the Philharmonic's charity fund—they could be brought up on some serious charges. Not that any of it was Claire's fault, of course. She'd been a little kid when all of that happened. But the press seemed more than happy to drag her name through the mud anyway. Bunch of jerkwads.

No one was really surprised when she didn't come back to school after spring break. Apparently, her family's lawyer had advised her to finish out the year at home by taking classes online, just in case there were any weirdoes out there with bright ideas about harassing her while she was at school. Drake thought she must have gotten threats for the family lawyers to insist on something like that.

Just considering that possibility put a lump of raw fury in my throat, like I was trying to swallow a red-hot piece of charcoal. But I hadn't worked up the nerve to call her again. Rotten, I know. But the first time I tried, she hadn't answered, and I'd been forced to leave a stammering, idiotic attempt at a voicemail asking if she was okay. Duh. Of course she wasn't.

Tabitha still talked to her some, although their friendship seemed to have cooled considerably now that they didn't see each other at school every day. Tabitha insisted it didn't bother her, but my super-dragon third eye senses told me otherwise. Each totem scale, like the one I had fixed to a bracelet on my wrist, came with a bonus secret power called a "third eye." Mine was being able to tell whenever someone wasn't being 100 percent truthful. Cool as that sounds, it sort of sucked to realize how often people lied to me.

For instance, I now knew that my dad had no intention of ever letting me drive his car in the city. The art teacher, Mr. Molins, secretly thought my last attempt at still life painting was horrendous. Oh, and Drake had definitely lost the *Dragonball Z* graphic novel I loaned him.

Uuuugh.

Anyway, it seemed like Claire was distancing herself from everyone, most likely afraid one of us might turn on her. But, come on, she should have known better than to think that about me, right? I'd *never* betray her. Some twisted thing her parents had done years ago didn't change anything. Claire was still my friend, and I knew, without a single shred of doubt, that she was a good person. In fact, I probably knew that better than anyone.

Well… except maybe for her fiancé, Damien Blount.

Passing him in the hall was still painfully awkward—for me, anyway. He didn't have a clue that his supposed-to-be-future-wife was in love with me. Damien didn't know a *lot* of things about Claire, though. And even if the whole love thing wasn't mutual for me, I couldn't deny that somewhere deep down, I still liked her a little. Not like in a major way. Nothing like before. But I couldn't push down the rush of furious, protective wrath that rose in my chest whenever I heard people spreading more rumors about her. That was different, though, right? Not love. Or at least, not the romantic kind.

Despite all the rumors flying and the nasty news headlines, it was Damien's place, not mine, to defend her honor. Too bad he seemed too busy yucking it up with all his judo team buddies, laughing and carrying on like nothing had changed. Never mind that his fiancée was probably miserable, confined to her house like a prisoner, and carrying a huge secret about how she'd been spending her spare time. If they were really going to get married, then she should have been able to trust him with a secret like that, right?

Basically, Damien was a clueless jerk. I might've told him that to his face if not for the fact that he could probably put his fist straight through my head with one punch. I liked having all my teeth, so I wasn't about to start anything with him.

Tabitha began whining again. "This is the dumbest thing I've ever—"

"Shhh," someone else hissed. "If you're gonna keep whining then just get out."

We had a pretty decent sized audience. Most of the robotics team and a few of my art class friends crowded behind us, leaning into the glow of the screen that filled the dim computer lab.

"You better not cry when you lose," Drake sneered as we both hit the start button to begin the battle.

"Hey, after I win, maybe I should run for robotics club president next year. They'll be wanting someone with actual battling skills, right?" I fired back.

Whispers and quiet laughter stirred in the crowd.

"Nah, they want someone who can actually do math without having to Google all the formulas."

I set my jaw, thumbs primed on the joysticks as the loading screen showed beautifully intricate artwork of the humanoid robots locked in combat. Then the screen flashed, fading to black before the countdown began.

*3... 2... 1... FIGHT!*

The instant the screen lit up again, presenting us with a map of a rocky, rugged terrain riddled with steep canyons and cliffs, I whipped my mech into action. My fingers tingled, flying over the controls as I threw up my perimeter shield projectors and readied my long-range heat-seeking missiles. Drake hit the boosters on the back of his mech, looking to make his first assault. My heart throbbed against my ribs like there was a miniature man in my chest, punching me from the inside. My left foot bounced as explosions bloomed on the screen and the sound of gunfire mingled with the cheers of our classmates.

Normally, playing video games at school would have earned us all a few days in detention. But special circumstances prevailed today. First of all, it was the last day of the last official week of school. Final exams were almost over, so everyone was just coasting to the finish line—especially if they'd already finished their day's exam and had nothing to do except wait for a parent to pick them up. Second, Drake was the president of the robotics club, so he had his own key to the lab and could let us in whenever we wanted. Not to mention the teachers liked him enough to look the other way. And third, we had a lookout outside the door, just in case.

Couldn't be too careful when it came to breaking school rules on electronics.

Locked in our epic mech battle to the death, I bit down hard against a sudden twinge of tingling discomfort right in the arch of my left foot. No—not now! I couldn't get an itch now!

I squirmed my toes around, curling my foot inside my stupid, starchy uniform socks and black dress shoes. It was all in vain. The itch had taken on a life of its own. It was becoming self-aware, creeping up my whole foot. But if I took my eyes off the screen or my hands off the controller for even a second, Drake would obliterate me. Seven hundred hours and me spending every night and weekend locked in my room like a smelly, soda-hoarding hermit—wasted.

Drake whipped his mech into an aerial assault with both thrusters at max power. I surged after him, determined not to let him fall back to optimal range with those long-range beam cannons. I had him on the run. Perfect. Just a little closer and then—

Out of nowhere, Drake's mech changed trajectory, diving down to meet my bot head-on. I tried to evade, but it was useless. Our mechs collided, and I flailed to swap weapons over to my close-combat plasma sword.

An instant before it should have materialized, Drake's mech began to glow red, then orange, then electric yellow as though it were growing hotter and hotter. An explosion bloomed across the screen with a blinding white light that filled the whole computer lab. Two words faded into view, emerging from a smoky background riddled with hunks of charred metal debris:

*GAME OVER.*

I sat frozen in my chair, staring at the screen. No one in the crowd said a single word. What the heck just happened? Had he… self-detonated his mech?

"We did agree that whichever mech destroyed the other is the victor, right?" He chuckled darkly. "I believe the game is mine."

"You just—but that—you can't—" I sputtered, too angry to put together a full sentence.

"It's called strategy, Koji," he purred.

"It's called *cheating*!" I roared, slamming down my controller. "That's not fair play! Your mech was destroyed too! It's a draw!"

The room erupted into arguing as people began taking sides, converging around us in a shouting mob. Some agreed with me—self-detonation was a slimy tactic and shouldn't count as a win. Others firmly believed I had won since, technically, Drake's mech would have been destroyed first and mine, only as a secondary casualty of the blast. The rest claimed that since the detonation was intentional, the effect of destroying my mech was all that mattered, so Drake should be the winner.

Despite all the commotion and Tabitha declaring that we were all nerds who were going to die alone in our parents' basements, the buzz of something in the back pocket of my school uniform slacks made me tense. My normal phone sat on the ground beside me. This one had a completely different purpose.

Through the crowd of our friends, Drake met my gaze. His hand darted down to his own pocket, eyes wide as he gave me a slow nod. We were getting the same call.

Time to get to work.

I left first, faking an enraged storm out of the computer lab and slamming the door behind me. Okay, so maybe it wasn't completely fake. But we would settle that argument later.

Keeping a casual pace, I headed for the stairs as I slipped the sleek, credit-card-sized black cell phone out of the main fold of my wallet. Drake and I each had one, and we weren't supposed to show them to anyone, make calls on them, or try sending messages.

One missed call from an unknown number flashed on the screen. No big deal. I wasn't supposed to answer those calls anyway.

They were just my version of a superhero signal—my spotlight in the sky.

No sooner had I tucked the phone back into my wallet, returning it to my pocket, than Drake appeared at my side like he'd materialized from thin air. "No message, just a call," he whispered. "I checked news headlines. Unrest in the Middle

East, another missile launch out of North Korea, blah blah blah. Nothing out of the ordinary, though. Any idea what this is about?"

I shrugged. "We'll just have to wait and see."

We kept our casual pace and our voices hushed as we made our way through the school, heading straight to the headmaster's office on the first floor. The secretary sitting behind the broad mahogany desk looked up at us as we entered, smiling through the thick, square frames of his stylish glasses. He was new. Actually, all the office staff had been swapped out after the whole evil-headmaster-tries-to-murder-people-and-destroy-the-city incident four months ago. The uproar among the parents and faculty had been pretty impressive, but now the dust was settling. The new headmaster had smoothed things over, and Secretary Josh was a big hit with the moms. That probably had something to do with his textured, high-fade haircut, obnoxiously perfect teeth, and athletic physique displayed in tightly tailored suits. Drake joked that he looked like a version of me from an alternate reality where I'd been bitten by a radioactive Calvin Klein model. Great.

Josh stood as the door closed behind us, sidestepping when we passed to lock it. "So, who won?" he asked.

Someone must have told him about our gaming match. That, or the FBI had the whole school bugged so they could watch and listen to everything that went down. Probably that.

After all, Josh, the headmaster, and several of the custodial staff were all undercover FBI agents, charged to be our glorified babysitters as we went on about our normal, civilian daily lives.

"I don't want to talk about it," I grumbled as I crammed my hands into my pockets, glaring at the floor.

Drake grinned smugly. "Don't be a sore loser."

"I didn't lose! That did *not* count!"

Josh laughed as he showed us to the headmaster's office and held the door open to let us inside. "Good luck, boys." He closed the door behind us, sealing Drake and me inside the dimly lit room.

Standing there made my stomach flip and wrench. I remembered all too clearly the first time I'd come here and met Headmaster Ignatius. Part of me still expected to see him appear from the shadows, laughing maniacally and brandishing his golden-tipped scepter. Fortunately, the only other person in the room was basically the opposite of Ignatius.

Instead of a grim cave stocked with ancient artifacts, the newly refurbished headmaster's office was painted a soft, soothing blue. The lit bookcases were stocked with hardback thriller novels, succulents in natural stone planters, and dozens of hiking snapshots from around the world. An oil diffuser filled the room with the ambient aroma of lavender and chamomile, and a large oil painting of a rocky Washington beach hung on the only empty wall.

Agent Carrie Bates sat behind her desk, her black hair pinned into a neat, no-nonsense bun on the back of her neck as she flipped through a folder. She was young-ish, too—probably somewhere in her late twenties—with a round face and warm eyes that made her seem deceptively soft and feminine. That totally didn't fool me, though. She was FBI, so I had no doubts that she could have folded me like a lawn chair and left me in a handcuffed heap on the floor in about two seconds if she wanted to.

Still, she was pretty. Her smooth umber skin had a lovely flush of deep rose along her cheekbones, and her long lashes framed her dark eyes as she looked at us over the top of the folder. "So? Who won?" she asked, an eyebrow arched expectantly.

I rolled my head back and flailed my arms like an angry Muppet. "Come on! Why does freaking everyone know about this already?"

"'Cause I tweeted it," Drake replied, like it wasn't a big deal.

I shot him a glare. "Stop tweeting about my life!"

Agent Carrie laughed musically as she put the folder down and motioned for us to sit in the two open leather chairs in front of her desk. "Let's get to business, shall we? Agent Kirkland just contacted me. There's a training exercise planned for this weekend and a request was sent to have the *asset* involved."

My insides fluttered as I sank into my seat, half excited, half terrified. Ellison Kirkland was the FBI agent in charge of handling all the cases involving dragon totems as well as organizing all interface between me, the "asset," and, well, basically everyone else. Our first few times crossing paths hadn't been pleasant. He'd scared the crap out of Drake and me by following us around New York while investigating the secret identity of a certain anthropomorphic dragon monster, ultimately arresting my dad when he thought he'd figured it out. Eventually, when the FBI finally figured out who I was, he had been assigned to keep tabs on us.

All the other agents here at the school, Carrie and Josh included, worked for him. They were a lot more approachable, honestly. They'd asked us to call them by their first names right off and actually seemed interested in trying to keep our lives relatively normal.

Well, normal for an undercover dragon superhero and his tech-genius sidekick, anyway.

"I don't suppose you could persuade your... female counterpart to participate?" Agent Carrie's voice had a hopeful edge.

I didn't have to ask who she was referring to. This was about Oceana—another totem-wielding dragon superhero like me. She'd been the first to discover me in my own dragon-form and had taught me all the basics of flying and using my totem right after I'd found it. We hadn't gotten off to a great start, but I had no doubts about where her loyalties were now. Just like I had no doubts about her real identity beneath that powerful, scaly disguise.

Like an idiot, I'd let it slip to Agent Kirkland that I knew who Oceana really was. My bad. Now they were dying to figure it out, and I'd had to warn my dragoness ally to be extra careful. No way was I giving her identity up, though. She was my partner, so I was duty-bound to have her back no matter what. When it came to revealing that kind of sensitive, personal information—even to the FBI—that was her choice to make.

"Not a chance." I smiled weakly. "She's not into the whole military scene. Sorry."

"Do you have any details about the exercise?" Drake pressed, leaning in closer with an expression of intense excitement I could only compare to a velociraptor spotting wounded prey out in the open. "I get to go too, right? I mean, I *am* his tech expert. And my new devices are ready for an official test." He'd been dying to strap my dragon form into some of his weird inventions for weeks now. Lucky for me, Agent Kirkland had strictly forbidden testing that kind of stuff over the city. Just in case, you know, it exploded.

"Yes, Mr. Collins, you'll be going. Your parents have already been contacted. As far as they are concerned, you are both attending an invitation-only science camp at University of Arizona this weekend." Agent Carrie slid the folder across her desk toward us. "These are the details, as well as the documentation proving the event is valid, in case there are any… lingering suspicions."

I snorted. "Uh, and my dad actually believed I'm going to an exclusive science camp?"

She leaned back in her seat with a knowing smile. "Of course. The headmaster gave you both a glowing recommendation, after all."

I sighed. As long as it worked, I couldn't really object. I'd just have to let Drake do all the lying when it came to what we actually did at this made-up camp.

"Civilian plane tickets have been purchased, so you'll need to arrive at the airport early next Friday afternoon," she instructed. "Pack light. The entirety of Saturday will be spent training, and you'll be flown back home Sunday. Any questions?"

From across her desk, I met Agent Carrie's stare for a second before staring back down at the folder on her desk. She always seemed to sense my unease, like she had sixth sense about it. A Koji sense.

I quietly took the folder and shook my head.

"Nope, all good," Drake agreed.

"That's all I have for now, gentlemen," she said as she stood and gestured to the door. "Oh, but Koji, would you mind sticking around for a minute? I need to go over some of the notes Agent Kirkland sent for you."

She was lying. My third eye gave her away immediately, like a tingly heat in the back of my mind.

Drake and I exchanged a quick look. Then he nodded and swiped the folder out of my hands before starting out the door. "Sure. I'll meet you outside."

Only after the door to her office closed behind him and the sound of his footsteps faded did I dare to lift my gaze to meet hers again.

"Is everything all right?" she asked softly, sounding genuinely concerned.

Sitting alone before her, I rubbed at the back of my neck and racked my brain for the right way to bring this up. "I... I just wondered... did Agent Kirkland say anything about Madeline? You know, like if they'd found any new leads or had heard anything from her?" I hated how pathetic and scared I sounded. But it had been four long months since I'd spoken to her. I didn't even know if she was alive.

My last memory of her, cradling her limp body in my arms in the bottom of a smoking crater after her dad basically tried burning the whole city down to avenge her mother's death, was still scorched into my brain. What came after—how I'd managed to get out of there with my identity and totem scale intact—I still couldn't remember. But I remembered the look in her eyes, the touch of her fingers on my cheek, and the smell of her hair. It put a sting of fresh pain through my chest, centering around the gnarled, hand-shaped burn scar over my heart.

I swallowed hard. "I know it's complicated and... and you guys probably still want to arrest her, but..." My voice caught, dying in my throat before I could finish.

"Oh, Koji." Agent Carrie's tone had that hushed, maternal softness—like someone comforting a frightened child—as she stepped quickly around her desk to crouch in front of me. She put a hand on my arm. "No. We still don't know where she is. Agent Kirkland has chased down hundreds of leads worldwide, but Madeline's a ghost. Someone trained her well, and I doubt we'll find her a single second before she wants us to."

Well, at least she was telling the truth about that.

I worked my jaw, trying not to let that little spark of annoyed anger go nuclear. They still believed Madeline was a threat, even though I knew she wasn't. Maybe she had fought alongside her dad, at first. In the end, though, she'd come around. She'd been the one to bring his big monster down, and she had knocked the scepter from his hand, ending our final fight. Madeline had saved New York—not me.

"I miss her," I heard myself admit in a broken voice.

"Of course you do." Agent Carrie gave my arm a reassuring squeeze. "Just between you and me, I don't think you've seen the last of her."

"You really mean that?"

The corners of her eyes creased slightly as her lips curved into a secretive little smile. "Call it woman's intuition. She'll be back."

All I could do was bob my head. It hurt too much to try to talk about it, even to Drake. Besides, it's not like he could relate. He and Tabitha had their own version of a normal dating relationship going strong. They talked every day. Sometimes, if she forced it, they even held hands in the hall.

I would've killed for just a tiny taste of that with Madeline. To hold her hand. To take her out somewhere for dinner. To sit and watch a movie together. To kiss her again.

"For now, let's just worry about the things we can control, okay?" Standing again, Agent Carrie tipped her head toward the door. "Now, you get out there and demand a rematch because that stunt Collins pulled was *definitely* cheating."

I managed a hoarse laugh. "You think so?"

"Oh, without a doubt." She grinned. "We'll be in touch. Good luck next weekend, Koji."

# CHAPTER 2

"So... *science* camp? Am I hearing that right?" Dad eyed me from across the dinner table like he suspected I might be a shape-shifting alien that had been swapped out for his only son. Or maybe I had suffered some kind of stroke and completely changed personalities.

While he was perusing the paperwork Agent Carrie had given me as evidence, I was busy sweating bullets. Crap. I should have known a call from the headmaster wasn't going to be enough to sell him on this. I'd never been good at science or math. Or basically anything that involved numbers. No way was he going to believe I had been invited to attend an exclusive science camp at a college.

I forced a thick, cracking laugh. "Y-yeah, well, Drake has been tutoring me and I guess I'm getting a little better."

His eyes narrowed. "Is that so? How'd that Chemistry final go this morning?"

Crap. Ducking my head, I stared down into my plate of the spaghetti Ms. Collins had brought over for us. She'd gotten into the habit of delivering us one of her incredible home-cooked meals at least twice a week—something I appreciated since between school and superhero stuff, I didn't have much time to meal prep these days. Well, that and practicing for the video game match. That had soaked up every minute of my free time.

I went back to twirling the long noodles around the prongs of my fork, trying to think of what to say.

"Be straight with me, son." Dad used his no-nonsense parental tone. "Did Drake arrange this just so you two could hang out on a college campus for the weekend?"

"O-oh, um, well, I… uh." I couldn't do anything except make a string of uncertain, panicked noises for a few seconds. "Maybe?" That seemed like the safest answer.

He sighed, rolling his eyes with a chuckle. "Figures. You two are thick as thieves now. Just promise me you won't get into trouble, okay? No drinking. I mean it."

My shoulders dropped as I sank back into my chair with relief. He believed me. I managed an only slightly mortified smile. "Sure, Dad."

"And another thing—there seems to be a stench coming from your room. I went in to check it out and noticed you've basically started your own landfill in there. How about cleaning that up?"

I nodded. "Oh, yeah, sorry about that."

When I was sure he wasn't looking, I let out a shaking breath. That was it. My alibi was set. I hurried to shovel my last few bites of spaghetti into my mouth before I stood to put my plate in the sink.

"Actually, son, there's… something else I wanted to talk to you about." Dad cleared his throat and shifted in his seat. Uh-oh. Something in his voice was off. "It's about Amelia." He shifted again and wouldn't even glance my way.

I jerked to a halt, accidentally dropping my plate in the sink with a clatter. My stomach swirled as I stared at him. "Drake's mom?" I swallowed hard.

He nodded. "Yeah. So, you know we've been seeing each other for a while now and, well, things have gotten a little more serious here lately."

Oh no—God, please, no. I'd only seen Dad act like this one other time. Anything but *this* again.

"Dad, I, uh, we, err…" I wheezed, fumbling for words to try and stop it before it even began. "We already studied human reproductive anatomy stuff in Biology last year and, uh, you pretty much covered everything when we discussed it a while back. So, you know, I'm all good." My voice squeaked like the desperate squeal of a guitar string before it snapped. I was ready to tell him I was Noxius if it would change the subject and spare me from this humiliation. I was sixteen, for crying out loud! Did he seriously think I didn't know how all *that* worked by now? And what would make him think I needed to know what he and Ms. Collins were doing? Gross.

Dad cringed back, his gaze snapping up with his eyes wide and face flushed bright red. "N-no, Koji, that's not what I—!"

We both jumped as his phone began to vibrate and ring, inching across the table with every buzzing spurt. Ms. Collins's name along with a smiling snapshot of her from our spring break trip to Savannah lit up the screen.

Saved—I was saved!

As Dad answered his phone, he held up a finger in my direction like he wanted me to wait. Was he really asking me to hang around so we could continue this discussion?

Umm. Nope. Not happening.

I darted out of the kitchen and made a mad dash for the stairs, ejecting myself from the conversation like a pilot with his engines on fire. He could be angry about it later—that was fine. Parental wrath I could handle. Attempting to keep a straight face while he gave me some insanely awkward refresher on intimate relationships and dating. No. That was like being slowly bathed in acid. He would have to catch me first.

And maybe pry my door open with a crowbar.

I decided to spare Drake the unspeakable horror of how I'd almost gotten the gruesome details of the relationship brewing between our parents. But after tiptoeing around Dad for a week, dodging any and all attempts to have that conversation, which was bound to be the most embarrassing one of my life, I didn't know how know much longer I'd be able to avoid it. Just thinking about it made my skin crawl as Drake and I sat in the backseat of Dad's car, headed for the airport. Next to me, Drake was slumped against the door with his gaze fixed on his phone screen. The fast beat of a bass-heavy techno song thumped through his big earphones as he scrolled.

Had his mom had ever tried to corner him and talk about the same thing? Probably not. Man, I envied his ignorance.

My dad and Drake's mom, Amelia Collins, had started dating about six months ago, and based on everything I'd seen, things seemed to be going well for them. But that didn't mean it wasn't excruciating to watch them together. The flirty, dewy-eyed glances. The constant hand-holding. The pet names. It was fresh agony. Somehow, Drake managed to act like he didn't care what our parents were doing—even when they were doing all of that shamelessly right in front of us. I wondered if he really didn't care or if he was just determined not to look directly at it, kinda like the flash from a nuclear explosion.

Not that I minded them dating. Ms. Collins seemed really nice. She went out of her way to talk to me and ask how things were going with my art classes, which was nice since Dad tended to treat my interest in art like a weird fetish I'd eventually grow out of. Yeah, right. Ms. Collins worked long shifts as a nurse at the Presbyterian Hospital but always tried to carve out enough spare time to cook a few meals and hang out with us a few nights a week. Sometimes it felt like she and Drake spent more time at our place than they did at their own apartment. I couldn't decide how I felt about that.

We'd gone on a weeklong trip together for spring break to Savannah, Georgia. To my relief, she and Drake had slept in a separate bedroom in the small, historic house we'd rented. See-ing her and Dad exchanging those dreamy looks and carrying on like a couple of middle-schoolers gushing over their first crush left me with a painful knot in my chest. Things were obviously getting more serious between them. But exactly *how* serious were they now?

And what would that mean for me?

Dad and I had always been a team—just the two of us. Now it seemed like the only time he remembered I existed was when I did something stupid or the school emailed him my report card. Honestly, I didn't know how to handle this. Every blog and article I'd read about what to do basically said the same thing: I needed to talk to him about it. But that was the whole problem. We'd never had a conversation like that before—about dating and feelings and all that crap. Dad had never dated any-one this seriously before. I was in uncharted waters. Part of me knew those articles and bloggers were right. I should try talking to him about it. That was the mature thing to do, right? It was just... *so* awkward. Too awkward. I'd gone over it in my head a hundred times, and yet everything I wanted to say seemed pa-thetic, selfish, and whiny. Like a desperate cry for attention.

I sighed and looked back out my window as we cruised up to the airport terminal. Maybe after this training exercise I could muster the courage to talk to him about it. Yeah. That was a bet-ter idea. He'd be home for a few weeks because of the college's summer break. Perfect time for a heart-to-heart chat.

It took about six eternities for Drake to unload all of his luggage from the car. Calling this little excursion a science camp was shaping up to be an even better excuse than I'd first real-ized. It gave the perfect excuse for why he would want to bring six suitcases packed full of all his electronics. He'd painstaking-ly packed each piece in layers of black foam and wrapped all the bags with bright yellow tape with the word FRAGILE spelled out in bold letters. TSA was going to have a field day with that.

"Looks like that's about it, boys. Watch out for one another, all right? Buddy system." Dad patted Drake's shoulder and ruffled my hair. "Shoot me a text when you land. And Drake, remember to call your mom."

We both nodded and stood on the curb outside the airport terminal's sliding glass doors, watching Dad get back in his car and drive away. Once he'd vanished into the dense current of taxis, shuttle busses, and other cars, we exchanged a look. Drake grinned. I couldn't resist smirking back.

Time to go.

Grabbing a couple of his bags, I led the way into the terminal where check-in gates stood along the far wall. Before I could figure out which one we were supposed to go to, a familiar figure stepped into our path with a thin, bemused smile.

In a nondescript black suit, skinny tie, and polished dress shoes, Agent Kirkland's dark eyes glanced quickly between us before he tipped his head, gesturing for us to follow. "Right on time. Let's get going."

We followed along behind him, weaving through the crowds standing in line to check in, get their boarding passes, and unload their bags. I kept expecting him to stop in front of one of the desks. After all, I'd flown all over the country dozens of times. I knew the drill.

But Agent Kirkland took us straight to security. One discreet flash of his FBI badge to the bored, foggy-eyed officer manning the ID check counter at the first security checkpoint got us through without even so much as a second look. My smirk widened. Top security clearance? Why, thank you, Mr. President. Don't mind if I do.

We made our way through the bustling airport at a brisk pace, stopping only long enough for Kirkland to swipe a keycard so we could pass through a private locked door. The hallway beyond led away from the main concourse and down through the employee service corridors, then out onto the tarmac. Hundreds of passenger airplanes hummed and roared around us, parked at their gates, loading or unloading passengers, or slowly rolling toward the runways, lining up for takeoff.

Waves of heat rolled through the air in gusts off jet turbine engines, rustling in my hair and mingling with the smell of jet fuel and hot asphalt. Now there was a smell I knew all too well. Dad liked to joke that fighter pilots' kids, like me, practically had jet fuel in our veins. Maybe he was right about that.

"Step lightly, Mr. Owens," Kirkland shouted over the noise as he slid his signature black sunglasses over his eyes and motioned to one of the aircraft parked off by itself, away from the rest of the airport's traffic.

My jaw dropped.

Drake let out an excited sound somewhere between a bark, a scream, and a laugh.

We were riding in a freaking C-17.

# CHAPTER 3

"I love my life," Drake yelled as he forged ahead of me, rolling his bags as fast as humanly possible toward the gray behemoth parked on the tarmac.

I chuckled and shook my head as I jogged to catch up. As a career F-16 pilot, Dad would have been wholly insulted to have Drake so impressed by what they called a "heavy" in the pilot community. Still, it was hard to look at that robust metal giant and not be impressed. And this one had been sent here especially for us?

Okay, fine. So that was pretty cool.

We handed off Drake's baggage to a few of the ground crew before we climbed inside the aircraft's massive interior. C-17s were usually meant to haul big pieces of equipment or lots of people at one time. Today, however, Drake, Agent Kirkland, and I were the only ones strapping into the seats that lined the outer perimeter of the jet's wide cargo bay. There were a few other crewmembers, sure, but that was it. I grinned until my cheeks hurt. The only reason they'd be shipping a few people around in a plane like this was for an epic, top-secret transport. Drake and I were officially precious cargo.

Once our luggage was strapped down and the huge rear door was closed, the low, idling hum of the engines bellowed to life with an ear-splitting fury. Kirkland handed us both a pair of specialized protective earmuffs. Drake seemed to find this especially awesome—right up until Kirkland also gave him a stack of the little plastic barf bags. His face paled a little and he looked over at me as though hoping for an explanation.

Granted, I'd never ridden in the back of a heavy before either, but I'd heard enough pilot-speak around the squadron bars to know what this was about. The inside of the cargo bay didn't have windows… or air conditioning. Puking was pretty much a given for people who weren't used to being shaken around in a hot tin can for a few hours.

Drake would never hear me over the roar of the engines, so instead I just made a wincing face and held my hand out for him to share a few of those bags. Then it was time for takeoff.

Five hours and a couple of barf bags later, the jet shuddered and lurched as we touched down. The familiar, oppressive desert heat flowed in like a blast from a furnace as the massive bay door opened again. Ah—now there was another familiar smell. It put an excited spring in my step as I unbuckled from my seat and started down the ramp and out of the jet. Were we in Arizona? Or Nevada? Both had huge Air Force bases where we'd lived for Dad's job, so either way, I was back in some of my old stomping grounds.

An incredibly long runway stretched out before me. I frowned, panning my gaze across a few sparse, unfamiliar buildings clustered nearby. Were those hangars? Dust swirled in the dry air, kicked up by the C-17's four huge engines, as the glare of the setting sun cast long shadows over a wide horizon crumpled with bare rocky mountain peaks. All my confidence fizzled. I didn't recognize any of them. Where the heck were we?

Before I could ask, a big armored truck rolled onto the runway before me and snarled to a halt. Agent Kirkland didn't waste any time. As soon as the back doors opened, he grabbed a few of Drake's bags and ordered us to get inside. Once we were all loaded up, a couple of soldiers in full body armor shut and locked the doors from the outside. I couldn't even see where we were going because the small windows in the back of the truck were blacked out.

My stomach did a nervous backflip. What was going on? This was a lot more intense than Agent Carrie had made it sound.

"This is Area 51." Drake spoke up suddenly, his expression wild with delight as he stared at Agent Kirkland. "Isn't it?"

Kirkland sighed, almost like he knew what was coming. "I can neither confirm nor deny the specifics of—"

"I KNEW IT!" Drake screamed like a preteen girl at a boy-band concert. He gave a maniacal laugh and a victorious fist pump in the air.

"Try to contain yourself, Mr. Collins. We won't be giving you the grand tour. There are very specific rules about your behavior while—"

Drake wasn't listening. He turned to me with his light brown eyes sparkling with ideas, most of which were probably highly illegal and sure to get us locked up in some federal, top-secret prison. "This is... the coolest thing that's ever happened to anyone. Do you have any idea how long it took me to hack their databases here? *Months*, Koji!"

Agent Kirkland frowned, slipping off his sunglasses and tucking them in his breast pocket. "Yes, which then led us to refortify all our firewalls and security systems, costing the taxpayers millions of dollars."

"Well, if a sixteen-year-old kid can hack through all your databases from a crappy basement apartment, maybe you should've had better ones to start with." Drake sat up straighter, crossing his arms over his chest proudly. Once again, I was reminded that my best friend was potentially a criminal mastermind. Scary.

Little wrathful fires flickered in Kirkland's eyes. Uh-oh.

I swallowed hard and forced a cringing smile. "I'll, uh, I'll try to make sure he doesn't do anything illegal."

Drake gave a snort and rolled his eyes. "Really, Koji? You seriously think you can keep an eye on me like some kind of babysitter? Your dad doesn't even trust you to keep a goldfish alive."

I pursed my lips and glared at him too. I was beginning to figure out why he hadn't made many friends before I'd arrived at Saint Bernard's.

If the two of us scowling at him intimidated Drake, it didn't show at all. He remained smug, kicked back in his seat with one of his bags—a black canvas backpack—resting casually in his lap. We rode for a good thirty minutes in silence until, at last, the armored truck came to a halt.

As soon as the doors opened, Kirkland bailed and began barking orders to the four or five soldiers waiting outside. They took our luggage and left in a hurry, gone even before Drake and I had climbed out of the truck.

Besides Agent Kirkland, the only person who stayed behind wasn't just some common soldier.

A tall, clean-cut man about Dad's age stood waiting, his grim, chiseled features set in a hard frown. The chest of his blue dress uniform was covered in medals and ribbons, and I recognized the insignia—a silver eagle—on the shoulders. He was a colonel, just like my dad.

A cold sweat prickled on the back of my neck as I studied him, pangs of terror surging through my gut. Oh no, this was bad. *So* bad. What if this guy knew my dad? What if he recognized me?

I cringed, waiting to see recognition dawn on his features as his icy blue eyes appraised Drake and me with speedy precision. But it never did.

"Welcome to Groom Lake, gentlemen. My name is Colonel James Cook, and I'll be your handler for the duration of this exercise. I trust I don't need to stress to you the seriousness of this occasion." The colonel's tone was anything but welcoming. Actually, it sounded like a veiled threat—don't screw this up for everyone by acting like a couple of delinquent tourists or we'll feed you to the alien we've got caged in the basement.

"N-no, sir," I answered, my throat dry. I couldn't tell if that was from the desert air, the fact that I'd just spent the last few hours puking in the belly of that airplane, or sheer terror.

Drake gave a nod.

"Good. Follow me. I'll be going over the rules for your stay here, so listen up." Colonel Cook turned sharply and began walking toward an enormous hanger.

Drake and I exchanged a glance. Looks like I wasn't the babysitter after all. Poor guy. He had no idea what he was in for.

"Please note that this facility is under extreme twenty-four-hour surveillance. No one goes anywhere without us knowing about it, so when I tell you that you are *not* permitted to leave this hangar under any circumstance—I mean it."

The colonel guided us into the massive hangar. The metal building was tall enough you could have parked a jet inside with plenty of wiggle room, and closed off on both ends so that you couldn't see outside. But a glance around the massive interior and all I saw were soldiers and official-looking people in lab coats walking by in small groups, talking in hushed voices, and ignoring us completely. Most of the space was empty. Weird.

"Accommodations have been set up for both you, meals will be provided, and supervised contact with your parents back home will be allowed twice a day," Colonel Cook explained as he led the way across the hangar to a metal door on the far side, pausing long enough to swipe an ID card through the lock by the handle. A green light blinked, and he entered a code that made the door's locking mechanism unlatch. He held the door ajar so we could go in first.

Beyond the door, a narrow hallway led away from the hangar into in adjacent building. I went through first, making sure not to hold eye contact with Colonel Cook any longer than necessary—just in case he recognized me. As we made our way down the hallway, we passed more people in lab coats and doors locked with the same card-access system as the first. Heavy security like that wasn't a surprise, though. This was supposedly the most secure military installation in the country. And while my dad insisted they didn't have actual aliens here... I guess you could say I still wanted to believe.

Occasionally the hallway walls opened onto wide glass windows, and I glimpsed dark rooms filled with the glow of dozens of computer screens. Some spanned the entire wall, like mission control from a sci-fi movie. Wicked cool.

Colonel Cook stopped before one of the windows that showed a computer lab filled with personnel and glowing monitors. "We will begin our mission brief tomorrow morning at oh six hundred hours. Let me be perfectly clear: as long as you are here, you are to behave professionally. This isn't a joke. It isn't a game. The men and women you'll be working with for this exercise have trained their entire lives to be a part of something like this, dedicating hundreds of hours of intense preparation for this moment."

He spoke sharply, pinning me under a harrowing gaze as though he expected me to be the one causing problems. "That said, your identities are still highly classified, so many of the individuals you'll be working with don't know your real names. For your personal safety and that of our country, it needs to stay that way. We've come up with two code names for you to use instead of—"

"I already have a codename," Drake interrupted with a confident grin. "But I'm guessing you knew that."

The colonel's eyes narrowed, glinting ominously. He didn't reply.

I, on the other hand, stared at my best friend in shock. He had a codename? For what?

Before I could ask, Colonel Cook unlocked the door to the lab. It swung open with a rush of super-cooled air, probably meant to keep all those fancy computers from overheating. All around the room, men and women in lab coats stopped or turned in their rolling chairs to stare at us. No one said a word.

Awkward.

"Your equipment has already been unpacked and prepared in the adjoining room. You'll work in here for the duration," the colonel said, still giving Drake a hard look. "Ms. Yamamoto will be assisting you—she's one of our leading tech experts."

A younger lady with slim glasses and long black hair pinned neatly into a bun on the back of her head stepped forward with a smile. "It is a pleasure to meet you both." She gave a slight bow, making the ends of her long white lab coat swish around her knees.

Drake returned the bow. "Just call me Cloudmaker."

Nearby, one of the lab workers choked. *"Cloudmaker?"* he wheezed in disbelief. "You're him? No way!"

"None other." Drake stood a little straighter, chin tilting up and chest puffing with pride.

"But you're just a kid!" someone else sputtered.

He arched a brow, cognac eyes smoldering dangerously as he stared around the room like an eagle surveying its turf for any possible challengers. "And Braille was invented by a fifteen-year-old. Pascal wrote his first theorem at thirteen and invented the calculator at eighteen. So, what's your point? That I'm too young to be smarter than you?"

No one said another word.

Drake smirked again. "Thought not. Now, if you're finished boring me with your inferiority complexes, let's get to work."

I shouldn't have been surprised that my codename, Noxius, got a similar response. I guess no one had expected the city-saving draconic superhero to be a kid in Converse sneakers and a vintage Star Wars T-shirt. Oh well.

Unlike Drake, however, I didn't have any snappy comebacks primed for the scoffs and eye rolls. Some of the scientists just stood there staring with their mouths hanging open. Others laughed, almost like they thought it was a joke, and I got horrible flashbacks to the time Dad forced me to join the middle school football team. What a nightmare. Thankfully one practice and a dislocated elbow was all it took to convince Dad that maybe contact sports were not my thing. Or at least, not one where all the other players outweighed me by a good fifty pounds.

After finishing the colonel's painfully awkward tour, Agent Kirkland reappeared to hand us both a brown paper sack with some dinner packed inside. A couple of sub sandwiches, a bag of chips, a cookie, and a couple of bottles of water were all we got before we were shown to our "temporary living quarters" near the hangar. Kirkland went on again about our behavior and not trying to sneak anywhere as he confiscated our cell phones. Thankfully, Drake had uploaded some auto-reply software to both of them so if either of our parents texted, they wouldn't think we were blowing them off. That kind of thing was pretty essential after all my disappearing acts earlier in the year. Hopefully it would keep me from getting grounded over that again.

Agent Kirkland showed us around our tiny suite and gave his own version of a brief warning that we were not supposed to leave this spot until tomorrow. Then he left.

I let out a heavy sigh of relief as soon as the door clicked shut. The rest of the night was supposed to be low key. We could settle in, get some sleep, and prepare for the exercise tomorrow. Honestly, it was just nice to stand in a room without some official government guy breathing down my neck.

"Cloudmaker?" I finally asked as I crunched up my empty dinner bag and tossed it in the trashcan by the door. I'd never heard Drake's codename before, although apparently everyone else here had.

Kicked back on the top bunk in the cramped room we'd been given for the weekend, Drake had already set up shop and was hard at work. He had a bunch of metal bits, teeny circuit boards, and wires spread out in front of him. His eyes darted over the hardware, hands moving with expert precision as he put them all together with excruciating care.

"It's my hacker tag," he replied without looking up.

Well, duh. I'd figured that much out on my own. I was more interested in what it actually meant. "Why'd you pick it?"

"'Cause it's the name of a bomb. The T-12 seismic bomb, to be precise. They used them back in World War II to blow up bunkers and stuff buried too deep underground or too resilient for normal bombs to touch. Back when I first started dabbling in hacking secure databases, I used that handle. I've since expanded my skillset, but the name stuck. Although, some of the cyber circles I ran in started calling me a red hat. Mostly crackers. I guess they thought it was an insult." He yawned and sat back for a moment, rubbing his forehead with the heel of his hand.

I frowned. Absolutely none of that made sense.

Drake must have noticed the steam coming out of my ears as my brain overheated trying to figure out what he was talking about. He laughed and leaned back on his hands. "Look, Koji, a true hacker abides by a certain code—sort of like a pirate code. There's some etiquette involved. And among hackers, there's a bunch of different types depending on what you specialize in and what your motives are. The most common are black hats, who are the ones you hear about getting into security systems and stealing data. Then there are white hats, who do the same thing, only they don't steal it—they show the system owners where the holes in their programs are and how they can be fixed. Grey hats are... somewhere in between that, I guess."

"Okay, so what's a red hat, then?"

"Nothing, really. Someone made it up as a reference to an old video game called *Where in the World is Carmen Sandiego*. They were saying I was just hacking systems and leading the cops on wild goose chases for the attention. Like it was just a big ego trip for me or something." He shrugged like that wasn't true, but that wicked grin flickering over his features made me wonder. "Like I said, Probably a bunch of crackers. They've always been jealous of my mad skills. Some even tried breaking into my software. Couldn't do it, of course. Amateurs."

I tried to ignore the glaring fact that my best friend was in fact a borderline evil genius. "So, uh, what's a cracker then? Is that different than a hacker?"

"Crackers are usually just a bunch of jerk pranksters. They can do remote hacks, but they like to do it by causing software to fail, destroying data, or just generally being stupid. They're like little kids playing with fireworks—just blowing stuff up for fun. No art to it. No style or etiquette." He yawned again and shook some of his shaggy, surfer blond hair out of his eyes. "Ugh, I can't think when I'm hungry. Would it kill them to toss a pizza or a few burgers in here? I mean, come on. *One* sandwich? Really? I need brain food. Someone bring me some Doritos."

"No kidding," I agreed as I sat on the bottom bunk, my stomach still grinding away. Not that the food they'd given us was bad, but Kirkland had greatly underestimated my appetite. I'd have given anything for a large, extra cheesy pizza and a chocolate shake.

I had to change the subject. Thinking about food was giving me a headache. "So those guys in the lab knew who you were as Cloudmaker?"

"Yeah. They're still kinda sore about me hacking the FBI files for totem information." He shrugged and leaned back over his spread of electronic gadgets. "They'll get over it, though. Or not. Doesn't matter either way."

He was probably right about that. We were all on the same side now anyway, right? "I think I'm gonna take a shower and get some sleep," I said as I rummaged through my bag for my shampoo, deodorant, and toothbrush. Our personal stuff had been stacked in a corner—probably after they got done searching it for hidden cell phones or anything against their long list of ridiculous rules.

This was beginning to feel less like a cool training exercise and more like an excuse for these government goons to study us up close. Even our room seemed like a prison cell. It was smaller than a cramped hotel suite, with a set of bunk beds against one wall and an attached bathroom about the size of a closet. No windows. One door. All it was missing was a slot near the floor for them to shove trays of gruel through.

Not exactly the VIP treatment I'd kinda-sorta been hoping for.

"Okay, yeah, sure," Drake murmured, already bent over his electronics again. I got the feeling that was a default response for when he wasn't paying attention.

By the time I finished showering, combing the knots out of my hair, and changing into an oversized sweatshirt and mesh athletic shorts to sleep in, the lights were off and Drake was out cold. It didn't take me long to do the same. Settled into the bottom bunk, I stared around the strange room. Voices and footsteps echoed down the hall outside. The distant hum of an engine droned in the background. Or maybe that was just the AC. My hand drifted to the thick leather bracelet on my opposite wrist. I traced my fingertips over the smooth surface of the scale fixed there. To the untrained eye, it didn't look like anything important—like maybe something I'd picked up as a vacation souvenir.

But it wasn't just some trinket. I wasn't just some kid who'd lucked into finding an ancient artifact. And tomorrow, I'd show all those stuck-up lab nerds what I, Noxius, was truly capable of.

There was a storm coming—*my* storm.

# CHAPTER 4

I swaggered into our mission brief early the next morning like a legit rock star.

They'd rolled open one of the broad bay doors at the far end of the hangar, letting in the scarlet glow of the sun rising over the mountains. Heat rippled on the horizon as the light shimmered off the black scales and horns that mottled my half-dragon form. Standing at seven feet tall—not counting my wings, of course—I towered over everyone else like a menacing, scaly, black giant. I still had a humanoid shape in this form, but my lizard hind legs, lashing tail, and wings made for an interesting mix of reptile that got a lot of attention as I prowled by. The rippling contours of my body were covered in small black scales that shone like dark glass, and my neon blue eyes flickered with primal, ancient power as I glanced around at my captive audience.

For a second or two, all motion inside the hangar seemed to lurch to a halt. Soldiers, officers, and scientists stopped to stare at me.

"Who's laughing now?" Drake snickered next to me.

I couldn't resist a satisfied, toothy smirk as I rolled my rippling shoulders, flexed my corded arms, and fanned my leather black wings out in a quick stretch—just for show. Nothing wrong with reminding them who they were dealing with.

Near the open bay door at the far end of the hangar, Colonel Cook was already waiting for us. He was the only one in the hangar besides Drake and Kirkland who didn't seem afraid of me. Walking straight out to meet us, he stared up at me with the same steely, calculating expression he'd worn the day before.

"I'd hoped we could conduct this meeting before you changed forms."

"That ship sailed when you put reconnaissance devices in our room," Drake retorted, tossing his head to get his lengthy bangs out of his eyes. "You even bugged the bathroom. Nice try, by the way. But I guess you forgot who you're dealing with. And here I thought we were pretty clear about the whole no peeking thing."

The colonel choked, his face turning a disturbing shade of red as he glared between us and finally settled a smoldering glare on Agent Kirkland. "These are punk *kids*, Agent. You can't expect us to just give them free reign of—"

"I expect you to follow orders, Colonel," Kirkland snapped, cutting him off with a frosty glare. "This exercise was requested by the president himself. I carry out his orders, which means you are to follow my instructions down to the very last detail."

"One look at him while he's transforming and he loses all his power," Drake added, his tone ominous. "You ready to bet innocent lives on Oceana being able to bring down another giant monster by herself? I'm guessing not."

Colonel Cook's mouth snapped shut, his nostrils flaring with rage like an angry bull about to charge. At the last second, he sank back on his heels, let out a deep breath, and seemed to recompose himself. "Very well, then. We are already behind schedule. This way."

He motioned toward an area of the hangar sectioned off by big metal partition screens. Inside, a wide array of computer equipment and some familiar rolling cases were arranged on long folding tables. All of Drake's gear had been delivered and was waiting for his assembly.

Drake's eyes lit up as he assessed the scene. "Good thing I work fast. Go ahead and get the guys in the lab ready to go live in seven minutes. I want full video, audio, and bio-monitoring systems online when I get in there." He shrugged out of his backpack and rolled up his sleeves. "And someone get me a Mountain Dew and a Snickers. I can't work under these conditions. I need junk calories pronto."

I cruised over to take a seat on a heavy-duty metal bench right in the middle of the partitioned space, wiggling my dragon toes as my best friend got to work. Right on cue, the pretty scientist lady from yesterday, Ms. Yamamoto, appeared and began helping Drake unpack the instruments from where he'd neatly arranged them in the packing foam. She smiled at me when she passed, somehow managing not to look terrified at my monstrous appearance.

Drake's attempt at making a high-speed surveillance drone to follow me around in combat had gotten him into some trouble a few months ago—mostly 'cause he'd almost pulled it off. Turns out, flying something like that around the city was illegal on more levels than I could count, so he'd been forced to go back to the drawing board. And thus the IMF Suit was born. Drake dubbed it that as a clever play on the classic Mission Impossible movie, which he claimed was what inspired him to start building his own electronics when he was a little kid.

IMF actually stood for "Interfacing and Monitoring Feedback" and was basically a way for him to communicate with me while I was in this epic, half-dragon form. Not only that, he could also track my physical condition through a network of sensors stuck to my scales at various points on my body. And last, but certainly not least, he could see what I was seeing through live video feed coming from a collection of tiny cameras, each about the size of a pencil eraser.

"How did you manage to shield these devices from the effects of his electrical powers?" Ms. Yamamoto asked as she leaned in close to my head, carefully positioning one of the cameras on my right temple. It stuck to my scales with a rubbery adhesive Drake had concocted himself.

"It wasn't easy," Drake replied. He was busy gluing one of the small microphones into my scaly pointed ear so I could hear him. "He fried my stuff a lot in the beginning. But I found the right mixture—the same stuff that's in that adhesive—that keeps the electronics insulated from most of his lightning. The cameras are a little more sensitive, though, so if he shifts into his full dragon form, I'll almost certainly lose the vid-feeds."

"And the bio-monitors?" she asked as she crawled all around me like a kid on a piece of playground equipment. One of her hands grazed over my chest, fingertips brushing the hand-shaped scar that warped the scales right over my heart. My scales had healed better than my delicate human skin, but the handprint was still plainly visible.

The contact made my face tingle. My stomach clenched and I couldn't bring myself to look Ms. Yamamoto in the eye until she'd moved to a different area. I didn't want to run the risk of her asking about it.

When she leaned in close to me, I caught a whiff of her perfume, magnified by my sensitive dragon nose. She smelled good. Man, I really hoped she wouldn't be able to see me blush in this form. I'd never had a girl—woman—basically anyone female touch me this much. Besides, it tickled. I had to bite down to keep from laughing as she stuck more monitors on my side, right under my arm.

Drake was still talking as he worked. "They're nothing astronomical, really. Not too different from some of the cutting-edge hospital tech that tracks pulse, respiration, blood pressure, brain activity—stuff like that." He stood back a moment, glancing me over with a critical furrow in his brow before he picked up a headset and slid it over his ears. "Testing. Testing. You hear me okay?"

His voice crackled at first, then came through my earpiece crystal clear. I nodded and gave him a thumb's up. "You hear me?"

He grinned. "Loud and clear." Slipping off the headset again, Drake did a slow walk-around to recheck the positions of all sensors and cameras before he finally let out a satisfied sigh. "Looks like we're ready. Remember, the insulation on the devices should protect them from impact, but if you crash land too hard, we're likely to lose some of them. The communication devices are the most important, so just... try not to land on your head, got it?"

I snorted and twitched the end of my tail, standing to flex my wings again. "Sure. I'll keep that in mind."

"Good." Drake snatched up the headset and one of his many Frankenstein-laptops he'd built and nodded to Ms. Yamamoto. "Are the guys in the lab ready?"

She looked a little breathless, her mouth open and eyes widening in awe as she backed away from me. "Y-yes. We're standing by for the mission brief."

Drake's grin broadened, glinting with impish mischief as he petted his laptop like an evil genius stroking his favorite cat. "Excellent. All right, Noxius. Time to be awesome."

"You got it, Cloudmaker."

"Copy, all systems are live and tracking. We've got visual and audio feed." Drake's voice rambled in my pointed, scaly dragon-ear. "You still hear me, Nox?"

"Yep." I strode forward, wings spread to the heat of the sunrise as I stepped out of the hangar and onto the open tarmac. I breathed in the dry desert air, my dragon senses primed to every sound and smell. Soldiers in armored trucks gathered around, marking off an area to keep the rest of the onlookers back. Only a few of them were allowed to get closer, taking photographs and more video feed.

"Radio channels are now open. You receiving us, Colonel?" Drake said.

"Affirmative." The older man's stiff, dissatisfied tone made me want to roll my eyes. Thankfully, Drake was the one who'd be doing most of the communicating on my behalf, so I wouldn't have to deal with his attitude.

"All right, guys and girls, we're treating this like the real thing, so try not to suck." Drake chuckled over the radio. "Go with mission specs."

I could practically feel the colonel seething as he started laying out the scenario for our training mission. Pissing him off was apparently Drake's new favorite pastime. Sticking it to the man. It made me smile.

"We've got a Big AL—that's one confirmed alien life-form. Requesting asset assistance at the following coordinates," the colonel began, finally dropping the disdain as we got down to business. He rattled off a series of numbers, none of which had any meaning to me whatsoever. I was counting on Drake to translate. "We've got six Hogs and one Spooky already en route, ready to intercept. Asset needs to rendezvous with the forward air controller in the first formation."

Okay, that last part I got—but only because I'd heard Dad and his pilot buddies throwing around that kind of jargon basically since I was born. Hogs were a type of fighter jet otherwise known as the A-10 Thunderbolt II. Some people called them "tank-killers" because their specialty was blowing up pretty much anything they pointed their massive gun at.

And a Spooky?

My body shivered with delight at the thought. I'd never actually seen one of the massive gunships in action before. But the idea that I might actually get to watch them fire their insanely huge cannon was enough to make my dragon tail wag.

"Got it," Drake answered sharply. "Noxius, whenever you're ready."

"Born that way." I laughed in a deep, throaty growl as I crouched low. My powerful legs coiled, wings snapping out wide as I called on the ancient power thrumming from a single glowing scale on my wrist—my totem scale. Wild energy sizzled through me, and I took to the air with a roar like thunder, streaking skyward with a rush of wind.

Drake's voice was still crystal clear in my ear, even over the rush of the wind. "You need to fly north until you spot the Hogs. One of them is in charge of the actual attack plan. He'll give you instructions. Got it?"

"Uh, maybe," I answered, hovering for a moment a few graceful beats of my wings while I tried to get my bearings. "Which way's north again?"

"Just fly straight, dummy."

"Oh. Right. On it!"

It didn't take me long to find the formation of two gray fighter jets cruising low through the rugged terrain. They looked a lot different than the ones my dad had flown—more robust and heavy-duty. Made sense, though, since they were built for blowing stuff up on the ground than whipping around in high-speed aerial dogfights.

That was my job this time. Well, maybe.

I dipped in close, easily matching the speed of the aircraft and cruising alongside them until another voice came over the radio.

"Asset, this is Misty 25." The younger-sounding male voice came in a little crackly. "Big AL is located on the north end of a dry lakebed shaped like a dog bone. Game plan is for asset to contain Big AL while A-10s do gun runs. I have a Spooky standing by."

"Got all that?" Drake asked.

"Got it," I confirmed. I gave the pilot a thumb's up for good measure.

"Copy that, Misty 25, this is Cloudmaker with ground control. Asset is ready to intercept." Okay, so it really wasn't fair that Drake seemed to breeze right through all that cool, official-sounding lingo like he'd been doing it for years.

I'd have to work on that.

"So, where's the dog bone valley?" I asked.

Drake was quick to reply. "Just keep going straight. You'll see it. Any ideas on how to deal with the faux monster?"

"Yep." A confident smile curled over my dragon lips as I pumped my wings faster, rocketing forward and leaving the A-10s in the dust.

Part of me wondered what Dad would have thought if he could see me right now. He'd been flying fighter jets for twenty years. What would he think about me acing around with them as a draconic superhero? Would he be proud of me? Or would he be angry because I was doing all this—risking my life and fighting giant monsters—without telling him the truth?

My stomach turned and my heart twisted painfully in my chest because deep down, I already knew the answer. No way would Dad ever be okay with this. And if he found out...

Crap, I didn't even know what he'd do. Lose it, probably. Ground me for the rest of my natural life. Never speak to me again. Try to take my totem away.

That last thought shot through my brain like a molten arrow, making my jaw clench and a growl kindle in my throat. A feeling like a sudden wildfire of rage jarred my mind. I'd never experienced anything like it. It didn't feel like me.

But the mere thought of anyone trying to take my totem... The words were like a fiery sword rising from the inferno in my soul: no one was ever taking this power away, not unless they killed me first. This totem scale was mine; it had chosen me. I'd never give it up to anyone without a fight.

The blind rage focused me, making all the black spines along my back, arms, and calves prickle. Every muscle burned with strength. My pulse cracked like thunder, and overhead, dark clouds gathered over the rocky, barren landscape. This wild fury felt so primal. So unpredictable. So strange.

Strange—but unbelievably *good*.

# CHAPTER 5

Okay, so there wasn't an *actual* giant monster for me to fight in the valley. That would have been cool, yes, but this was just an exercise so the military could get used to fighting alongside me in case there was ever another attack. For the sake of training, my enemy was... a giant stack of metal shipping crates filled with rocks. Yay.

So lame.

When the valley came into view, I swooped down to do a wide circle around the northernmost end where the stack of crates stood out against the rocks, prickly shrubs, and miles of rust-colored dirt.

"You see it?" I asked Drake, wondering if his cameras were working.

"Yep. We've got eyes on Big AL," Drake announced. "Asset going in."

"Copy that," the colonel replied.

I could hear the smirk in Drake's voice as he added, "Oh, and tell your boys to watch out for lightning strikes."

That was my cue.

With a rush of wind, I pulled upon the power of my element. Storm clouds gathered over the valley, blotting out the sun with rumbling thunderheads that swirled slowly like a miniature hurricane. Lightning sizzled and popped, arcing from cloud to cloud and occasionally tagging the ground below. The raw, crackling power surged in the sky and winds around me—I could feel it all as though that storm were a part of my innermost self.

"Hey Noxius, you okay? I'm getting some weird feedback from your bio-monitors."

My eyes popped open. Wait, when had I shut them? My mind was hazy as I glanced around at the stormy chaos raging around me. Where was I? What was I doing here? For a second, I couldn't remember.

Then it all came back. Right. I was supposed to be containing the "monster" down below.

"Oh, uh, sorry. On it," I replied and dove closer. But even as I turned all my focus to the training exercise, something itched at the back of my thoughts, like someone was tickling my brain with a feather.

Something wasn't right. I just couldn't put my finger on what.

The rest of the training exercise filled the valley with the crack, pop, and boom of battle. I broke in hard with my elemental power, stinging the stack of crates with my lightning bolts and even calling down a mighty vortex of wind like a massive tornado. It threw up dust, rocks, and debris in every direction.

But once the Hogs arrived, I had to back off the storm a little. No need to fry my allies inside their highly conductive metal aircraft. Soaring back to give them space, I watched as the fighters did gun runs, lighting up the ground with fire from their massive front-mounted gun in an ear-splitting *brrrrrrrrrrrrt*. Stuff exploded. More fire bloomed in the air with a teeth-rattling *boom*. It was glorious. By far the coolest thing I'd ever done.

Right up until the Spooky arrived.

When people say "Time to bring in the big guns," they're talking about the AC-130—even if they don't realize it. I wasn't sure how it'd gotten the name 'Spooky,' but I did know that it had the absolute biggest, most awesome, kill-pretty-much-anything gun mounted inside. It wasn't even a gun, really. It was a freaking cannon. And when the massive dark airplane began turning in slow circles overhead, wheeling above us like a gigantic metal buzzard, I grinned from one pointed dragon ear to the other.

"Are you seeing this?" I couldn't help myself.

Drake laughed. "Fanboy much?"

"It's a howitzer cannon, for crying out loud! Don't act like you're not geeking out too."

"Not over the radio," he countered. "Now shut up. Game face, remember?"

Right. I had to keep my composure. Cool—I had to stay cool. Superheroes did *not* fanboy.

Oh screw it.

I laughed like a maniac as the cannon began to fire out of the side of the huge airplane. Each round punched through the stack of metal containers with a sharp, concussive *boom*. More fire. More clouds of dirt and debris.

"Dra—er—Cloudmaker, did you see that?"

No response.

Oh no. Had I broken the earpiece? Already? I tapped at it just for good measure. "Anyone there? Can you hear me?"

Nothing.

Pumping my wings, I hovered long enough to glance back in the direction of the base. My heart stopped. My blood went cold. Panic rose in my chest, squeezing every bit of breath from my lungs.

There was smoke rising from the base.

Oh God. Drake!

I whipped into action, a feral snarl of terror bursting from my throat as I surged back the way I had come. What was happening? Who would do this? Why?

I drove my wings harder, willing my storm to rise with a flurry of wind that sent me rocketing forward. The ground blurred past below as I ducked through canyons and raced along the mountain peaks.

Faster—I had to go faster. I had to get there *right now*.

"Koji!" A familiar voice boomed in my ears so loud it made my vision spot.

I flapped erratically, shaking my head and trying to clear my sight. I glanced down toward the ground just in time to see a blurred figure standing on a cliff edge below.

Dad?

No. That couldn't be—that wasn't—

Without warning, everything suddenly went dark.

Someone was calling my name.

"Koji? Koji, can you hear me?" The person sounded close, like maybe they were leaning over me. Why did I recognize that voice?

"D-Dad?" My voice came out as a weak, rattling groan.

"It's Kirkland, Koji. You need to open your eyes. Look at me." He sounded worried. But why? What had happened? Where was I?

Slowly, I forced my eyes open. My head throbbed as though someone was pounding on it with a giant mallet like in the old cartoons. I blinked drowsily, squinting into the glare of the sun at all the unfamiliar faces staring down at me. They all wore similar expressions of wide-eyed shock and concern. Who were these guys? Where was I?

Agent Kirkland appeared over me, looking worried as he snapped his fingers right in front of my nose. "Look here, Koji. Can you see me? Do you know who I am?"

"J-Jerk... FBI... agent babysitter," I managed to croak.

His mouth flattened and he sank back some, seeming annoyed and relieved all at the same time. "Tell them we'll be there in five minutes. Get the medical bay prepped."

"W-What...?" No matter how hard I tried, I couldn't force out the rest of the question. My brain was foggy and sluggish, like all my thoughts had been packed into a blender set to liquify.

"You flew straight into the side of a cliff," Kirkland explained as he moved back, making room for the paramedics. "Your physical injuries seem minor, but we still want to get you checked out. Just lie still."

It wasn't like I had much of a choice. Somehow, I was back in my human body again, and every muscle felt tingly and strange. I couldn't even lift my throbbing, aching head. Geez—what had happened to me?

I was flying, going... somewhere? Ugh. Nothing made sense. It hurt too much to try to focus.

Lying back, I tried to let my frazzled brain relax as the paramedics strapped me onto a stretcher and loaded me into the belly of a helicopter. It was no use, though. Something wasn't right. I could feel it deep inside—a creeping fear that took root in my heart. I'd used my totem dozens of times, but this was the first time I'd ever blacked out like that.

My eyes rolled closed again. Why was I so tired? Why did my head hurt so much? It only took a minute or two before I drifted off, lost in the rhythmic *thump-thump-thump* of the helicopter's rotors.

I woke up back at the base—or so I assumed. I sort of doubted they'd take me to a generic hospital considering, you know, I'd crashed during a top-secret test of my awesome superpowers. Propped up in a narrow hospital bed in the medical bay with an IV drip of fluids in my arm, I had no idea how I'd gotten there. How long had I been out? Hours? Days? Nah, surely not. Or at least, I really hoped not. My dad would absolutely lose it if we didn't come home on Sunday and no one told him why.

The longer I lay there, the more things began to slowly come back into focus. I remembered seeing smoke rising from the base. Clearly that hadn't been real. Nothing was on fire here. Then I'd seen Dad while I was trying to race back. He'd called out to me a few seconds before...

I shuddered, clenching my teeth as I stared across the empty hospital room. Kirkland had said I crashed into the side of a cliff—or was it a mountain? It didn't matter, really. I'd crashed and then somehow reverted back into my human form. Lucky for me, I hadn't gotten seriously hurt. Just a few bumps, scrapes, and bruises.

Nothing that warranted a hospital bed and IV drip. Or so I thought.

"Koji!" Drake burst through the door. He rushed to my bedside, face flushed and brows crinkled up in concern. "Are you all right?"

Agent Kirkland was right behind him, scowling disapprovingly as he murmured a quiet conversation with the tall woman in a long white lab coat walking alongside him. She was close to my dad's age, with wavy brown hair pulled back in ponytail. I'd never seen her before. A nurse? Or a doctor?

"What the heck happened?" Drake whispered as though he didn't want them to overhear. "Your vitals went berserk and then you totally freaked out. It was like you couldn't hear me at all."

My face burned with embarrassment as I bowed my head slightly, fidgeting with my hands in my lap. "I don't know," I admitted quietly. "I thought... I thought I saw..." My throat closed up when I dared to look up and found Kirkland and the woman staring down at me expectantly.

Great. I had an audience.

When I didn't finish, Agent Kirkland walked over to put a hand on Drake's shoulder. "I'll take it from here. Why don't you and Doctor Jamie go pick out something for him to eat?"

Drake shot him a poisonous glare. "Don't patronize me. I'm not five years old. If you want me out then just say it," he snapped.

"I-I, uh, I would really like a soda, actually." I rubbed the back of my neck, casting him a pleading look. I didn't want him to be angry with me, but if there was something Kirkland needed to talk about in private, then I wanted to hear it.

"Fine. Whatever." Drake snorted and rolled his eyes, muttering under his breath as he stormed out.

The tall woman smiled, something faintly sympathetic in her gaze as she handed Agent Kirkland a large paper folder before following my grumpy genius best friend out into the hall.

The door closed behind them and suddenly, the silence was crushing. I held my breath, watching Kirkland's expression crease along his forehead and the corners of his eyes as he held the file in quiet reverence.

"Give it to me straight, doc." I tried to laugh, although it sounded squeakier and more panicked than anything else.

"Koji, there's something I haven't told you," he admitted, his tone quiet and unusually genuine. Not even a hint of superiority. Uh-oh.

I gulped. This was bad.

"Gerard Ignatius, your former headmaster, is dead."

The words hit me like a punch to the chin. I stared at him as my body slowly went numb. Madeline's dad was dead? "H-how? When?" I stammered.

"He awoke from his coma a few months ago, but it was clear that his mental state was... not good. He was deeply disturbed. We attempted to interview him several times, but every exchange was erratic, nonsensical, and ultimately useless. He deteriorated rapidly."

"Went crazy, you mean," I clarified.

He nodded. "At the time, we were unsure of what was caus-ing the sudden deterioration in his mental state. He talked a lot about the totems—and you—but it was unclear how much of what he said was useful or just the ramblings of a madman. We ran a battery of tests, trying to discern if internal brain trauma from the battle might be the cause."

Kirkland paused for a moment, seeming to hesitate on whatever it was he wanted or needed to say next. His gaze tracked down to the folder in his hands. With a sigh, he simply tucked it under his arm. "In the end, we had nothing definitive to explain his state, although the question was raised about what the side effects of exposure to the scepter and totems might be."

"You think my totem is making me go nuts?" I guessed. Glancing down at the leather bracelet on my wrist, my stomach twisted as the scale fixed to the center gleamed under the fluo-rescent lights.

"I think we don't know what exposure to these items might do to people—to you, in this case. And until we figure that out, I think we should try to limit the amount of time you spend as Noxius," he said, stepping over to stand at my bedside. That folder was still tucked under his arm, and I could see sheets of black plastic-y paper tucked inside. X-ray films? "We're still gathering information, running tests, and doing everything we can to paint a clearer picture of what these artifacts even are. Until we have some concrete answers, let's play it on the safe side, all right?"

I sucked in a deep, steadying breath. "Yeah. Okay."

"Good." He smiled, but it was painfully forced. I got the prickly feeling that maybe he wasn't telling the *whole* truth.

I narrowed my eyes a little. What else did he know? What wasn't he telling me?

Looking down at my totem again, I swallowed against the tightness in my throat. I'd never really considered what using this power might do to me. Had my scale's power made me hear and see things during the training exercise?

Would it happen again? Would I hurt someone else? Or myself?

Suddenly, a new worry rose in my brain and I blurted it before I could even give it a second thought. "Hey, uh, can I ask you something?"

Agent Kirkland paused, his hand on the doorknob. "Yes?"

My mouth quirked uncomfortably as I tried to think of the best way to ask. "So, I, uh, I still haven't told my dad about any of this. About me being Noxius or anything." I stole a glance up at him. "Do you think I should?"

"That's always been your choice, Koji. If you want to tell your dad, then I'm more than happy to go with you to do it. I understand that this will be difficult for him to hear." His tone carried the faintest hint of sympathy. "But if you're asking for my personal opinion, then ... no. I don't think it's time yet for him to know. Maybe once we have some real answers as to where these totems came from and what their lasting impact will be on you and anyone else that's come into contact with them."

I groaned and rubbed my forehead. He was right. Dad had already lost Mom. How could I tell him I was a government-protected, dragon-shifting superhero? As if he would ever be okay with that. I mean, how many times had he called the cops last year whenever I went missing for a few hours? Like fifty? Okay, so not that much, but still. Overprotective did not even begin to describe it.

Fear sank into the pit of my stomach like a cold knife whenever I tried to picture telling him. I couldn't do it. Not yet. Dad was finally happy now. He had Ms. Collins and things were going great with them. He finally got to be home more often and didn't have to worry about deploying. After years of hard work, he was spending more time relaxing and enjoying life than I'd ever seen before. I didn't want to ruin that.

I didn't want to ruin his life... again.

"Okay," I decided firmly. "We don't tell anyone about Ignatius. Not even Drake. Not until we know for sure what's happening."

Agent Kirkland nodded in agreement, though his brow furrowed. "If that's what you want."

It wasn't. But it was what everyone else needed. So, it would have to be enough for me too. I would be fine. I had to be.

"I have to ask," Kirkland spoke up again. "Why not tell Drake? You two are close, aren't you?"

Yeah, we were. And that was the whole problem. If he even suspected something was happening to me because of my totem, I shuddered to think what he might do. Freak out? Tell my dad? Or his mom?

I wasn't ready to deal with any of that. Not yet. Everyone was counting on Oceana and me to be the first means of defense in case something else totem related went wrong again. I mean, sure, the military might be able to handle it. But the final totem was still unaccounted for, and I seriously doubted they could stand against a full-blown totem wielder and the scepter without our help. Not to mention, who knew what else might be out there that we didn't even know about.

I just had to keep my head as clear as possible. I had to focus. No more losing my mind and flying into cliffs.

Then it hit me. What about Oceana? Should I warn her that using her totem might be messing with her head? She'd been using hers a lot longer than I had. And what about Madeline? Did she even know about her dad?

"Sorry about screwing up the exercise," I said as Agent Kirkland opened the door.

He jerked to a halt, flashing me a confused frown like he wasn't sure what I meant. "You did well today, Koji. I daresay you even impressed Colonel Cook. And as far as he knows, what happened at the end can be attributed to you being under-fed and dehydrated before the mission began."

A smile tugged at the corner of my mouth. "So, what you're saying is we're on a need-to-know basis and he doesn't need to know?"

Agent Kirkland just rolled his eyes and shook his head. "Try to get some rest, Mr. Owens. We'll have you boys on the first flight home tomorrow morning. First class, this time." He stepped out of the room without another word, closing the door behind him.

I had too much to think about to get excited about the up-graded flight. All Agent Kirkland had was theories. They didn't know what had happened to Ignatius, and they didn't know what was happening to me. The only person who might know anything about it was Madeline, and she'd vanished months ago.

I wondered if texting her about her father's death might get her to finally call me back.

No—that was a jerk move. If she didn't know, then she deserved to have someone who cared about her tell her face-to-face.

I rolled over in the stiff, starchy sheets and closed my eyes, struggling to get my mind to stop racing long enough for me to doze off. It didn't work.

My thoughts circled back to Madeline. Where was she? Was she alone? Was someone helping her dodge the FBI? Why wouldn't she text me back just one message, so I knew she was alive? I couldn't even decide between being worried about her or being angry that she'd basically ghosted me. Didn't she know what this was doing to me? How it was eating me up inside? Didn't she care?

Uuugghh, no—that was a stupid thing to think. Of course she cared. She'd been looking out for me from the beginning.

And now she was steadily becoming little more than a phantom in my mind, her words haunting my memory and sending chills of anxiety through my fingers and toes. Just the thought of her alone out there somewhere in the world, grieving over the death of her only remaining parent, made my breath catch and my hands curl into fists.

Our last words to one another—the very last thing she'd said to me as I cradled her in my arms in the smoldering crater left by our battle with her father—had sounded like goodbye. But I wasn't going to accept that. It wasn't over. I *would* see her again. I had to believe that.

Because anything else was more than I could take.

# CHAPTER ～6～

Drake was pretty annoyed that I'd broken several pieces of his IMF Suit on the first real test run, and I spent most of the flight home apologizing about it. He grumbled that it was fine, he could fix it, but I could tell he was still pretty pissed. So much for not landing on my head. It wasn't like I'd done it on purpose though.

Dad and Ms. Collins were waiting for us at baggage claim after we landed. They walked up to greet us, holding hands and smiling brightly. I hesitated as soon as I spotted them, my mouth scrunching and my stomach turning a little. Seriously, it was like they did *everything* together now. For whatever reason, that was starting to get on my nerves. How was I supposed to talk to Dad about all this if he was always with her?

I tried to suck it up and smile. No point in complaining, right? It's not like it would make any difference. Dad was smitten. Maybe after a while, things would cool off between them and he would remember I existed.

Or not.

"I realize this is a stupid question, but are you boys hungry?" Dad chuckled. "I thought we could stop somewhere for dinner on the way home. Sound good?"

"Sweet! Yeah, I'm starving." Drake was already wheeling some of his luggage toward the exit.

"How about that new seafood place?" Dad beamed at Ms. Collins. "I've been craving it ever since we left Savannah."

Really? Didn't he remember that I absolutely *hated* fish? I'd spent that entire trip scouring the menus for anything that wasn't seafood and ended up eating mediocre cheeseburgers and chicken fingers the entire time like some picky little kid.

"Hey, uh, could we maybe go someplace else?" I tried, hoping he'd remember.

Dad shot me a puzzled frown. Then realization dawned over his features.

My shoulders relaxed. Whew. That was a close o—

"Oh, don't worry about it, Koji. I'm sure they'll have something else on the menu you'll like. Maybe a burger or some chicken. Sounds good, right?"

It took me a second to blink away my shock. Then I looked down at the tops of my sneakers so he wouldn't see me frown as I mumbled, "Yeah. Great."

Not cool, Dad. Not cool.

I trudged along after them out of the terminal, silently wishing I could just get a cab and go home. It would've been nice to have some time alone in my room to clear my head. Or just take a nap. Maybe that's why everything was getting on my nerves. I hadn't slept well either night at the base. Yeah, that had to be it. I was just tired.

Dad's trunk was full of a bunch of junk he'd cleaned out of his office at the university, so I had to sit crammed in the backseat next to Drake with one of his suitcases in my lap. Closing my eyes, I let my head rest against the cool glass of the window as we left the airport and cruised slowly through the New York City evening traffic. The low hum of the car engines, horns honking in the distance, and the whir of the air conditioner made my body sag against the car door.

I'd almost nodded off when Dad spoke up. "So, how was the camp?"

I waited, hoping Drake would take point on this since science wasn't really my thing.

He didn't.

Leaning up enough that I could peek over his suitcase, I scowled when I realized Drake had his headphones on and his music up full blast. He was lost in his own social media world, scrolling his phone to the thump of some heavy techno beat.

"Fine," I grumbled as I leaned back against the door.

"Learn anything new?" Dad asked.

"Not really."

I didn't have to see Dad's face—I could hear his signature frown of parental disapproval in his tone. "Koji, is something wrong? Did you boys have a fight?"

I sighed. "No, Dad."

"Oh, honey, I'm sure they're both just exhausted. It was a long flight after a busy weekend." Ms. Collins's voice was a soothing balm to the growing tension in the air. "I'm sure after everyone gets something to eat and rests, they'll be ready to tell us all about it."

Well, I officially owed her one. Dad let it go and I got to spend the rest of the ride drifting in and out of consciousness with my cheek mashed against the window.

I must have passed out cold by the time we got to the restaurant because Drake rapping his knuckles on the other side of the glass made me snort awake. He laughed, holding up his phone so I could see the picture he'd taken of me. I'd drooled a big smudge onto the glass. Fantastic. I wondered how long it would take him to hack into my sad excuses for social media accounts to make that my profile picture.

Probably like five seconds.

The instant we got inside, I got the vibe that this wasn't just some casual dinner spot. The waiters were all wearing pressed slacks, button-down shirts, and gold nameplates. Smooth jazz played through the dim, rustic-styled dining rooms. All the tables had white cloths and candles flickering in little glass globes in the center.

I glanced at Dad. What were we doing here? Was he up to something? This place was kinda fancy, and none of us were really dressed for it. I mean, I had on wrinkled jeans, my sneakers with my lucky laces, and a black shirt with "HAN SHOT FIRST" written on the front in bold white letters. Not exactly spiffy dinner attire. Before I could ask, we were shown to a table and one of the waiters put down a basket of freshly baked rolls right in front of me.

Mmmmm... my curiosity could wait.

Drake and I descended upon the bread like piranhas. Especially when someone set a dish of warm, whipped cinnamon butter between us. We went through two baskets of rolls like it was nothing, which got a chuckle from our waitress as she made her way around the table to take our orders. Of course, I was the only one who didn't order any seafood or fish. Hooray for another burger. I would've given anything for a slice of pizza or a big cheesy calzone.

Oh well. Burgers weren't a bad alternative. I could deal.

"And just some fries on the side," I said as I handed the menu back to her.

"Of course. Our burgers are excellent—I think you'll enjoy it," the waitress said as she scribbled down my order. "And how nice of your friend to bring you out to dinner with his family."

Uhh... what?

I stared up at her with my mouth hanging open, too shocked to say anything before she briskly walked away to put in our orders. Um. What the heck just happened? Did she actually think Dad, Drake, and Ms. Collins were a family and I was just some *tagalong* friend?

My throat went stiff.

Slowly, I turned my gaze around the table to where everyone else was sitting around the table, talking and laughing like a perfect, happy family. They hadn't even noticed what that wait-ress said.

A sharp pain twisted right in the center of my chest. It squeezed at my heart until I could barely breathe. My thoughts tangled and suddenly, the fluttering prickle of fresh anxiety rose slowly up my spine. All the warmth seemed to seep out of my face.

Why would that waitress say something like that? Didn't I look a *little* like my dad? At least enough that people would know we were related?

"Everything okay, son?" Dad called from across the table.

I jumped, realizing I'd been staring straight at him without blinking during my silent mental breakdown. "O-oh, uh, actually I need to go to the bathroom. Be right back."

I got up and left the table, speed-walking around the tables and chairs to the restaurant's fancy bathroom. Locking myself in a stall, I leaned against the door and tried to take a few deep, steadying breaths.

What the heck was with me today? Nothing felt right. My brain was a haze of racing thoughts—my totem randomly going haywire, Mr. Ignatius dying, my sort-of girlfriend still missing, and now being slowly shoved out of my Dad's life by my best friend and his mom. It was too much.

I rubbed my eyes. Somehow, I had to pull it together. If I kept letting little stuff like this get to me, I'd drive myself nuts and make everyone else miserable. Besides, things had to get better soon, right? This was just a run of bad luck. It would pass.

It had to.

"Koji? You there?" Drake's voice echoed through the bath-room. "The food's here."

Geez, how long had I been in here? "Sorry. Coming."

He was already gone when I left the stall. I paused long enough to wash my hands and rinse my face before I went back to the table. The sight of a huge gourmet burger, loaded down with a generous helping of mayo, pickles, and cheese, instantly lifted my spirits. I sat down and prepared for battle, unfurling my napkin and tucking it into the collar of my shirt.

Dad cleared his throat. "Before we start, there was something I wanted to share with you guys."

His serious, somewhat nervous tone made me freeze. Next to me, Drake wasn't moving either.

Now what?

"After how well things went on our spring break trip, I decided to take a little leap of faith." He blushed, shifting in his seat as though he were trying to wrestle something out of his pocket.

OH NO.

Dad pulled out a thick, glossy envelope and opened it—proudly placing four big, colorfully printed tickets in the middle of the table.

Ms. Collins gasped and covered her mouth with her hand.

Drake leaned over to get a better look, then snatched up one of the tickets and held it up with a wide grin. "Are you serious? We're going on a *cruise*?"

"Yep. As long as your mom doesn't mind, that is." Dad leaned back in his seat, practically glowing with satisfaction and pride as he looked over at her. "What do you say? Does five days in the Caribbean sound like a good summer vacation?"

I dropped my fork. It hit my plate with a noisy clatter.

"B-but this is... this is too much!" she protested shakily as she picked up one of the tickets to read the details. "I don't even know if I can get that much time off work."

"I already took care of that." Dad waved a hand dismissively. "I hope you don't mind, but I called your boss last week and explained everything. He said it was fine."

"Yes!" Drake did a victory fist pump.

"Oh, Danny." Ms. Collins gave my dad a teary-eyed smile as she leaned over to kiss his cheek. "Thank you so much. But, please, you have to at least let me pay you back for—"

"Absolutely not. This is my treat. I insist." Dad shook his head with a sly smile.

They went back and forth like that, dewy-eyed and crooning to one another for a few painfully embarrassing moments while I just sat there, still frozen to my chair, and stared at the two remaining tickets in the middle of the table. One for Dad. One for me.

I swallowed hard.

The picture printed on the front showed a sleek, pristine white cruise ship sitting amidst a sparkling, turquoise ocean. It had everything you might want—waterslides, huge pools, surfing simulators, hot tubs.

But I wasn't going to be able to do any of that. I still couldn't swim. I couldn't even sit in a bath without having a panic attack that left me totally helpless.

And apparently my dad had completely forgotten about that, too.

School was out. The days were warm and sunny. Somehow, I'd managed to pass my Chemistry exam and escape that nightmare with a C+ average. I should have been dancing in the street.

Except Drake wouldn't shut up about the stupid cruise.

For four weeks, that was all he talked about. Ms. Collins worked her usual long shifts at the hospital, so he spent most days and nights with us. He slept on the floor in my room, used my bathroom, ate my bags of Doritos, and even borrowed some of my clothes. Dad joked about us basically being brothers. If that's what it meant to have a brother, I was not okay with it. I had no personal space anymore—not with him moving all his computer and electronic stuff onto *my* desk, eating *my* favorite snacks, and getting to pick every movie or TV show we watched because he was the "guest."

It didn't help that Dad was off for summer break, too. He was home almost every day, and they egged one another on constantly about the cruise, chatting about how they wanted to go snorkeling or on one of the dolphin tours, or try their hand deep sea fishing.

Finally, I couldn't freaking take it anymore. I had to get away. I needed some room to breathe and be alone in my own head. So I packed some of my art supplies—my case of Copic markers, sketchbooks, and headphones—into my school backpack and ducked downstairs.

"Going somewhere?" Dad called from the couch where he and Drake were watching *Parks and Rec* reruns.

I didn't stop. "I need to pick up something from the art room at the school. Be back in a few."

Okay, so it wasn't a complete lie. Mr. Molins, the school art teacher, had been hounding us to come by and pick up our projects and journals from last year. He'd probably be up at the school now. He did some private tutoring in the summer and had asked me if I wanted to join in on a mini-class he was offering for anyone interested in cartooning. Normally, I would have given my right arm to take a class like that. But it conflicted with a certain wonderful, super-awesome *cruise*. Ugh.

Dad and Drake didn't ask any more questions as I left the house and started for the school. We were leaving in two days, taking a flight down to Miami so we could board the ship. My stomach churned with every step, flipping and spinning as I made my way along the sidewalks. What was I going to do for five whole days? Just the thought of setting foot on a boat and heading out into the open ocean made my breath catch. If I had a panic attack, got seasick or, you know, *drowned*, then it would ruin the whole trip. Dad would be furious. Drake would probably be pissed too. Ms. Collins would be disappointed.

And I'd be the epic loser outcast who had messed up a perfect vacation.

I sighed as I stomped up the steps to the front of the school. The doors were unlocked, and the lights were on. Good. I wouldn't be the only one here.

On the top floor of the school, the art room door stood open like it was welcoming me home. The airy hallway was lined with windows that let the midday sun pour in. The fragrant aroma of fresh paint wafted past my nose and soothed my stressed-out soul.

But that feeling didn't last.

Standing in the doorway, I stared at the arrangement of artwork from last year. Mr. Molins had positioned everything along the far wall where we could grab it and go. My stomach gave another painful twist. Madeline's stuff was arranged in a neat pile off by itself. I guess he knew she wasn't going to come back for it. No one had seen her since the Philharmonic incident.

Not even me.

"Koji?"

I startled, almost jumping out of my sneakers.

Turning, I stared down into Tabitha's suspicious, frowning face. Her sharp eyes scanned me, as though trying to figure out what I was doing here without actually asking. I couldn't help it—I did the same thing. For a different reason, though.

Sporting a flashy, emerald green sequin dress that hugged her petite body in a way that was definitely a violation of the school dress code, Tabitha cocked her hips and arched a brow expectantly. I guess she wanted an explanation for why I was here alone, but I couldn't pry my eyes away from her fancy black heels and that skimpy, sparkly dress. It was kinda blinding. I'd never seen her wear anything like that before. Or that much makeup. Her lips were painted deep ruby red and there was dark, smoky eyeliner around her eyes. Even her deep auburn hair was pinned into a neat bun on the back of her head and studded with a matching emerald pin. What was she doing here dressed like that?

"I-I, uh, you look..." I tried to pick a safe, friendly word. "Nice?" I decided at last. I didn't want her to think I was trying to hit on her or something.

She huffed and rolled her eyes. "We have a ballroom competition tomorrow. I'm participating in the Argentinian tango and the rumba. Today is dress rehearsal," she explained, waving a hand dismissively.

"Oh." Well, that explained the outfit. I knew Tabitha was on the school's ballroom dancing team, but hearing they were practicing and competing over the summer was news to me. I wondered if Drake knew. Did he go to watch her practice? Or to any of her competitions?

In the interest of survival, I decided not to ask. Tabitha and Drake had a weird relationship and I'd already wasted enough brainpower trying to figure it out. Plus, bringing it up usually made her angry.

And Tabitha was seriously scary when she got upset.

"I saw you going up the stairs. What are you doing here? Mr. Molins left for lunch with some of the other teachers a while ago." She leaned around me to glance into the art room, as though checking to see if he'd gone in ahead of me. "Where's Drake?"

I rubbed the back of my neck. "At my house. I just came to get some stuff. And maybe draw a little."

Her eyes narrowed, appraising me again. "So what you really mean is, you came to get away from him."

Great. How was it that girls could always see straight through me? It was incredibly unfair since I had no skills at reading female behavior whatsoever.

"Kind of, I guess." I tried to sound indifferent as I turned away and went to put my bag down by one of the long drafting tables.

It didn't work.

"Did you guys have a fight or something?" Tabitha followed me inside, her fancy heels clicking over the floor.

"No, nothing like that. It's... complicated, okay?" I didn't want to talk about this—especially not with her. Nothing against Drake, but Tabitha and I hadn't exactly gotten off to a great start last year. She'd made fun of my shoes, my geeky interests, and basically everything about me whenever my back was turned. Sometimes, she'd even done it to my face.

Now that she and Drake were an item, I had to admit she had backed off a lot of that. Not that she was friendly or anything, but she seemed to tolerate my presence with only mild disgust now.

Still, I didn't quite trust her not to plant a dagger in my back as soon as I let my guard down.

Wandering to the far wall of the art room, I gathered up a few of my projects from last year—folders packed with some of the sketches I'd done. I could work on tweaking old designs. Surely that would get my mind off everything, right?

I almost crashed right into her as soon as I turned around. Geez, why was she following me like that?

With her hands planted on her hips, she pursed her lips and made a thoughtful clicking noise with her tongue.

I tried to brush her off. "Look, um, I... I don't think Drake is gonna come here, so—"

"When I'm done with practice, we're going to get coffee," she announced.

I froze. My mind went completely blank—like the little hamster who'd been sprinting for his life on the wheel in my head suffered an immediate heart attack and died.

"Th-that's, uh, there's no way I can, um... I mean, I'm not really looking for, uh..." I sputtered and choked like an idiot.

Tabitha tipped her head back with a loud, exasperated groan. "Oh my God. Not like *that*. Don't be such a perv. You're so not my type. No offense, but ew."

I couldn't figure out how, exactly, I wasn't supposed to be offended by that.

"I just mean just as friends. So if you want to talk about stuff or whatever, then let's go."

It took a second for my brain to reboot. My totem sense verified she was telling the truth. Tabitha wanted to talk to me. On purpose.

No. No way. Third eye or not, there had to be a motive hidden there somewhere. This was *Tabitha*. So, what was her angle?

When I didn't answer right away, she shifted uncomfortably. "It's just, you know, Claire doesn't come around anymore. We text some. But her parents made her shut down all her other social media accounts. And it sounds like you could use a break from the genius. So…" She let her sentence trail off with a shrug as she looked away. For the briefest second, her expression dimmed and she actually seemed uncertain. Sad, even.

Hmm.

"Okay," I agreed.

She blinked up at me in surprise, staying quiet for a moment before she finally gave a nod. "I'll be done around six."

"Should I invite Drake?" Backup would have been nice in case she suddenly sprouted fangs and tried to devour my soul or something. Also… I wasn't sure how he would feel about me going out with his sort-of girlfriend by ourselves. Not that it was a date or anything.

And oh, sweet mother of God, it was definitely *not* a date.

She shook her head and turned to leave. "No. It's not like he'd actually want to come, right?" With the wispy ends of her shimmering dress trailing behind her, Tabitha left me standing in the art room alone. She didn't even say goodbye.

This was beyond weird. But I had a hunch that Tabitha was only asking me to hang out because she was lonely. Claire Faust, her best friend and my former vision of love and perfection, was gone. Drake didn't take her seriously and had made ignoring her his favorite boredom cure. I couldn't think of a single good reason for anyone to ever sit with Damien—and not just because he was in a relationship with Claire.

Was I really the only option left here?

Yikes.

Not that I had any room to talk, really. Without Drake, I was alone too. Maybe it made sense for us to hang out some?

I couldn't decide how I felt about that as I went back to gathering up my art projects and packing them into my bag. When I finished, I sat down and spread out one of my sketchbooks and pencils. With my headphones on and one of my favorite playlists blaring, I settled onto a stool at the drafting table and got to work.

Hours passed and I barely noticed until my music paused as I received a string of incoming texts from Drake and my dad. They wanted to go out to dinner with Ms. Collins and then to see a movie. I frowned, staring down at the screen. Dad wanted me to come home. Drake wanted to know if he could borrow a clean shirt.

My mouth scrunched as I slumped forward, resting my elbows on the table as I tried to decide what to say. I didn't want to go out with them again. What if another waitress assumed I was the outsider? What if Dad heard this time and just laughed it off like it wasn't a big deal?

Before I could second guess it, I typed out a reply to Dad and hit send.

```
KOJI:
Hey Dad. I've got a headache, so I'd ra-
ther stay home if that's okay.
Gonna finish packing up here and head
back in a few. You guys will probably
already be gone by the time I get there.
Don't wait up.
```

My heart felt like a small, frozen block of lead buried deep in my chest. I'd never lied to my dad before. Well, not like this, anyway. Sure, I'd fibbed about some stuff when it came to hiding my superhero alter-ego. But I'd never just outright lied to him for selfish reasons. We'd always been a team and that was part of our agreement—we were both supposed to be 100 percent transparent about stuff. Don't hide anything. Be honest. Get it out in the open so we can fix it.

I hated myself instantly. Why? Why had I done that? Drake would figure it out. He always did. And then he'd want to know why, too. Stupid, Koji! Mega stupid!

My phone chimed, announcing Dad's reply:

DAD:
That's fine. Be safe walking back. Text me later so I know you're okay. We'll be home around midnight.

For whatever reason, reading that made my heart feel even colder. He really didn't care if I went or not? He was fine just going out with Drake and Ms. Collins without me? Didn't he want me around anymore?

I scowled and crammed my phone into my pocket. A toiling, churning mixture of confusion and rage boiled in my brain. Anger like a million white-hot needles seemed to prick at my insides. It didn't make sense. I had no right to be angry. But knowing that only made it worse.

Packing up my stuff, I stormed through the art room to gather the last few pieces of my pathetic attempts at pottery from a shelf in the back. Suddenly, my hand jerked to a halt. My fingers trembled, only inches away from the lopsided, mushy-looking pot I'd made during my very first attempt at ceramics.

That was the one Madeline had helped me make.

My expression skewed. Everything went blurry for a second and I shut my eyes tightly, bowing my head as I stood alone in

the shadows between the shelves of student-made art projects.
Where was she? Where was Madeline? I… I needed her. I needed someone to see me right now, and she'd always been there to
see me whenever I felt invisible.

I swallowed hard against the tight aching stiffness in my
throat as I pulled my phone out of my pocket again. I could send
her another text—beg her to come back or to contact me. Deep
down I knew it wouldn't matter. It wouldn't make one speck of
difference. Madeline wouldn't answer. She never did. And once
again, I'd feel the sting of rejection.

So instead, I scrolled down to another name—one I'd sworn
I would never text again except maybe in a life-and-death situation—and quickly typed out a message. My heart hammered in
my chest as I hesitated, finger poised over the send button. This
was a bad idea. I knew that. But right then, I didn't care.

So I hit send.

```
KOJI:
I'm sorry if this is weird, but can we
talk? I'll be at the usual place to-
night. Midnight. It's not about your
parents. I just need to see you.
```

I swallowed hard. I hadn't sent anything to Claire Faust in
months. Now, all I could do was wait and see if she replied.

# CHAPTER 7

Tabitha emerged from the school a little before six. I'd left her a message letting her know I would be waiting out front. Sitting outside on the steps, I kinda hoped the evening air would help to clear my head some. It hadn't, of course.

Maybe this weird coffee outing would fix that, though. Or she'd wait till I wasn't looking and push me off the curb in front of a car and I'd die. Win-win.

Tabitha had already changed out of her sparkly ballroom dancing costume and into some more casual clothes: dark skinny jeans and a stylish white shirt that was cropped short to show a hint of waistline. Like Claire, she dressed fashionably whenever we got to wear street clothes. Granted, her style seemed a little trendier and boho than Claire's, who usually wore understated and much more modest outfits, but this suited Tabitha.

Or, I thought so, anyway. Okay, so maybe it was a little weird to notice what Tabitha and Claire liked to wear. But my artistic brain always picked up that kind of thing. Not that I personally had any sense of fashion. And I definitely wasn't checking her out. It was sort of like sizing up potential subjects for future characters in my comics.

Villain characters, in this case.

"Is there somewhere nearby you want to go?" I asked as I stood, collecting my backpack and an armful of my paintings and sketches that wouldn't fit.

"There's a place that has good lattes a few blocks that way." Tabitha shouldered her own duffel bag as she fell in step beside me.

Together, we left the school and started down the sidewalk side by side. Awkward? Oh yeah. Should I make small talk? That seemed like the nice thing to do. But I'd never actually tried having a casual conversation with her before. What could I even say that wouldn't be moronic?

"So, uh, how was practice? Er—I mean, rehearsal?" That seemed like a safe question.

She shrugged, staring straight ahead as some of her wispy bangs blew over her face. "Fine, I guess. My partner is an idiot. But Drake won't join the team so I'm stuck with whoever the instructor pairs me with."

Memories of last year's Winter Ball flickered through my mind. Drake had made quite an impression with his tango dancing skills. Apparently, he'd taken ballroom dancing as an elective once and proven that he had some pretty killer dance moves. Despite that, he'd refused to join the team and didn't seem interested in taking part even if his girlfriend was there, dressed in skimpy outfits and dancing all over some other guy.

I wondered if that hurt her feelings. Wait, did Tabitha even have feelings?

The coffee shop was tucked into the corner of a busy intersection, and by the time we ducked inside, the traffic had picked up as everyone left work for the day. The shop made for a nice reprieve from the gridlocked streets and noise. It had a cozy, modern feel to it with sleek, minimalist furniture made of dark wood and natural stone. Tall windows spanned the entire storefront and overlooked the traffic that rolled by. I paid for our coffees while Tabitha picked out a small, high-top table right next to one of the windows.

She didn't even look up as I set the tray of drinks down between us and eased into the chair across from her. The thoughtful crinkle right between her eyebrows intensified as she fidgeted with a stack of bobby pins she must have pulled out of her hair.

I tried to think of something else to say that might diffuse the weird tension in the air. But before I could come up with something, Tabitha cut straight to the chase.

"I guess Drake is basically living with you now, huh?" She didn't even look up from her neat stack of hair pins.

I frowned down into my coffee cup. "Yeah. Pretty much."

"'Cause your parents are dating?"

Slouching back in my seat, I rubbed the back of my neck and tried to decide how to answer. "I guess so. I don't know. He was around a lot before that started. But now that they're officially together, it's like he never goes home. And he's great to hang out with and all—that's not the problem. I just... I don't know. Maybe I'm being a jerk about it. It just seems like whenever they're around—Drake and his mom—Dad forgets I'm even there."

Her brows pricked up for a second with a knowing expression as she went on avoiding eye contact. "Yeah. I know what you mean." She sighed quietly.

I waited for her to explain. Somehow, that felt like a lead-in to what might have been the reason she'd insisted on hanging out with me like this.

Finally, Tabitha puffed another exaggerated breath and brushed her bobby pins into her hand, dumping them all into her bag before she reached out for her coffee cup. "My stupid sister moved back in. She's doing all this research and thesis work getting *another* PhD, so of course Mom and Dad just let her do whatever and take over the whole freaking house."

"I didn't realize you had a sister."

"She's way older. We don't talk much," Tabitha mumbled. "Every time she comes home, it's like Mom and Dad just fall at her feet and worship her. And once again, I'm just the dumb kid they had by accident. The mistake. They don't want me around. No one does." She stared into her mug. "Now even Claire has basically dropped me."

Wow.

Staring at her from across the table, it took me a few seconds to process all that. No wonder she was constantly bugging Drake, wanting them to do couple-y things. She was... lonely.

"I'm sure that's not true. I mean, you and Claire seem like really close friends. You've known each other for a long time, haven't you?" I tried to sound comforting.

She still wouldn't look up as she sipped at her drink. "Have you even talked to her lately? Her family's a hot mess—way more than the news even knows about. They don't have all the gory details, not that they wouldn't love to know."

I leaned in closer, my interest sparked. "And you do?"

"Um, yeah? Of course? We've been friends since kindergarten. But I'm not saying a word to them. They'd just use it to go after Claire again and none of it's her fault."

"I haven't heard from her in a while. Things were kind of tense after the Philharmonic incident." My mouth quirked as I forced myself to admit it out loud.

"'Cause she feels guilty about dragging you into it." Tabitha cast me a meaningful look over the rim of her cup. "But honestly, it's not her fault. She didn't even know all of their nasty secrets until recently. I guess the lawyers are airing all the old Faust scandals now. It's all she went on about the last time we actually got to talk." Her expression steeled slightly, a hint of cold aggression smoldering in her eyes as she stared me down. "I'll tell you, but you have to swear not to tell anyone else. Not even Drake. Got it? This is best friend only privileged information. I wouldn't be sharing except... I dunno, she's always acted different around you. Maybe you can get her to open up a little more about it. She's kept everything inside for so long. It felt like a little more of her was dying inside every day. But she never talked about it at all until you came here. She's changes when you're around."

"She, uh, she does?"

"Yeah. She's happier. More relaxed. More like her old self back before her family locked her in with Damien. I guess that was when she started to hold it all in. She was a different person after that—more private. It was like she walled herself off from everyone else in her life. There was always this distance, even between us. She wouldn't show anyone her true feelings about anything anymore. She just went along with whatever her parents wanted her to do."

My heartbeat skipped. Could this really be true? Claire was... different around me? I hadn't noticed anything like that. In fact, it had seemed more like she had always made a diligent effort to keep her distance from me. Every smile and word seemed so guarded.

Well, except for that one time after the Philharmonic. It had only been a brief conversation, just a few minutes or so, but her smile—I couldn't get it out of my head. It was the first time I'd ever seen her smile like that.

"The last time I really got to talk to Claire, she was freaking out because her mother admitted that she'd faked her whole pregnancy," Tabitha said, her voice a cautious whisper.

I nearly dropped my cup. "W-What?"

"Yeah. She couldn't get pregnant. You know, kept having miscarriages and everything. So she and Mr. Faust approached Laura Ignatius, Madeline's mom, about being a surrogate. They offered to pay her some crazy huge amount of money if she would do it and keep it all secret. She agreed, but at the first ultrasound, they found out Mrs. Ignatius was pregnant with twins—*fraternal* twins. Meaning, she'd conceived again after they implanted the Faust's embryo."

I stopped breathing. No way. That... that couldn't... I mean, it wasn't possible that Claire and Madeline were really... *sisters*?

Tabitha read my mind. "They're twins. Claire and Madeline have different parents, so they aren't technically biologically related, but Mrs. Ignatius carried and gave birth to both of them at the same time." Tabitha's gaze drifted back to the tabletop again. "Things started to unravel between their families even before they were born. The Fausts were paranoid about Mrs. Ignatius going public with the truth that she had been the one to have Claire. Mrs. Faust put on a real show, making it look like she was pregnant the whole time. It was a huge cover-up."

"But why? Why would it matter if she had to have a surrogate or not? Who would care about that?" I blurted—a little too loudly, I guess, because Tabitha shot me a scorching glare.

"You obviously don't get how things are in these social circles," she grumbled. "It's not enough to just look perfect. You have to *be* perfect in every way, all the time."

No. I didn't get it. But that didn't matter. This must have been what kicked off the rivalry between the two families all those years ago. Nothing else made sense.

"Mr. Faust was so worried about Ms. Ignatius going public about the fake pregnancy that he began paying her with charity funds from the Philharmonic to make it look like she was stealing. He blackmailed her and said if she ever told anyone, then he would make sure she went to prison." Tabitha's expression dissolved into sorrow. When she looked at me again, there was genuine concern crinkling her brow. "It's been so hard for Claire. I'm worried about her, Koji. Now her parents are trying to cut her off from the rest of the world—trying to keep her in this cage of lies while they scramble to cover it all up before it gets out in court. You've got to try to see her. You've got to make sure she's okay. Maybe she'll open up to you."

I bit down hard on the inside of my cheek. Claire hadn't responded to my text. Or maybe she couldn't? There was no way to know for sure.

All I knew I had to see Claire as soon as possible. Tabitha was right—I needed to make sure she was okay. Whatever stupid issues I was having with Drake and my dad paled in comparison to this.

"Okay," I replied. "I'll try to get her to talk to me."

Tabitha's smile was half-hearted. "Sorry to drag you deeper into this. Despite the fact that you are probably the biggest dork that has ever walked the face of the earth, you seem like a nice guy."

"Uhhhh, thanks, I think."

"Plus, it only makes things more awkward that you and Madeline were an item before she and Claire both disappeared," Tabitha went on as she sipped at her drink. "What was the deal with that, anyway? Were you dating like officially or was it just a fling?"

I hung my head a little. "I... I honestly don't know." Crap, it hurt to admit that. "I liked her a lot. And she seemed to like me. We kissed once and didn't even go on a real date. So, I guess, we weren't actually a couple. I'm not sure it qualifies as a fling either, though."

"Oh." Tabitha sounded surprised. "I thought it was more serious than that. You hung around her all the time."

"Well, like you said, I'm a huge dork and so finding girls that are willing to be seen in public with me is kinda hard. She was one of those girls," I grumbled, casting her a sulky frown.

Tabitha's mouth mashed up like she'd tasted something sour. "Sorry. It's not a *completely* bad thing—being a dork, that is."

"How?" The way she said it made it sound like an incurable disease.

"It's like you're really innocent, I guess. Totally inexperienced. Which is kind of embarrassing but at the same time... weirdly refreshing. You don't have the usual ulterior motives, and you don't seem to care about your social image. I mean, no one who did would be caught dead wearing those shoes out in public." She nodded toward my favorite sneakers. "It helps that you're cute, though."

Heat tingled through my cheeks as my brain churned into overdrive, trying to sort out if she was actually being nice to me or not. There was probably smoke coming from my ears as I stammered, "I-I'm... cute? Girls actually think that? About *me*?"

She cracked a smirk. "Don't let it go to your head. You clearly don't have the fashion sense or social skills to get smug about it."

Fair enough.

"Just promise you'll let me know if she's okay," she added quickly. "And... if you remember... maybe you could let her know that I really miss her. Okay?"

I couldn't hold back a smile. "I will."

# CHAPTER 8

The house was dark and empty when I got back home. Dad, Drake, and Ms. Collins were probably still enjoying their dinner together somewhere, talking about the cruise, and not even wondering where I was. Or maybe they were already at the theater, sharing a big bucket of popcorn.

Fine by me. I had bigger problems to deal with at the moment, and I didn't want anyone else getting in my way.

Tossing my bag and art projects onto the floor by the front door, I went to the kitchen to make myself a couple of ham sandwiches, choke them down with a glass of milk, and leave a convincing amount of dishes in the sink and crumbs on the counter so Dad would think I'd spent some time there.

Taking my stuff up to my room, I quickly arranged my pillows and blankets on the bed to look like a Koji-shaped lump was sleeping there. It wasn't Ferris Bueller–level perfection, but it would do. I typed out a few quick texts—one to Dad to let him know I was home and going to bed and the other to Drake to let him know what I was really doing. Then I turned off the light. At least Drake would know I was out flying as Noxius and not sell me out to Dad. My alibi skills were improving, at least.

I glanced at the clock on my desk. 11:30. Excellent—I had a little extra time.

I'd gotten a lot more careful about when and where I transformed. I couldn't risk anyone seeing me leave my house as Noxius and figuring out my secret. Cracking my circular window, I crept onto the sloped roof before I scurried to the back of the house. It was easy hopping from one rooftop to another, and I managed it without making much noise. Once I was several blocks away, I spotted what I was looking for—a private terrace covered in old forgotten bicycles, rusty lawn equipment, bedframes, and giant plastic tubs. Perfect.

Dropping onto it, I placed my hand over my totem bracelet. I sank back into the darkest corner I could find and let my eyes roll closed. A twinge of hesitation tugged at my heart. Agent Kirkland wouldn't like this. We'd agreed that I should take it easy and not use my totem—not until we knew more about what it might be doing to my head.

I set my jaw. It was just for a few minutes. And I wasn't going to be fighting or even using my elemental power. I was just flying a little—nothing like last time. I'd be fine.

Probably.

"Awaken," I murmured, and immediately the thrum of power hummed through my body like ocean winds filling a ship's sails. My chest heaved, arms and legs flexing as tingling energy shivered over my skin. When it was over, I emerged from the gloom with my dragon wings spread and my senses primed.

I didn't know for sure if Claire would actually show up tonight. I had never asked her to meet up with me like this, and she'd never replied to my message. But one thing was certain—I needed to feel the strength of my wings a little. My soul craved it. The release. The total freedom.

Yeah. I needed a lot of that right now.

Leaping from the terrace, I dove into the open air. One flex of my shoulders pumped my wings wide and sent me rocketing up into the clear night air. The skyline sparkled below as I soared higher, bolting for the heavens like a scaly missile. The

wind teased through my shaggy black hair and combed sooth-
ingly over my sleek black form. After a few minutes of flight,
the ominous shape of an abandoned power plant with big
smokestacks beckoned in the distance. That was where Oceana
and I liked to meet. Or it had been, at least.

I sucked in a steadying breath and steered for it, taking my
time to wheel and soar high above the sleeping city where the
dark of the sky would hide my shape. No need to give away my
position. A quick, stealthy descent was the safest, so I picked
one of the larger smashed-out windows—wide enough for my
half-dragon form to pass through without shattering anything—
and zoomed in fast and low. When I touched down inside the
power plant, it barely made a sound. The wind off my wings
stirred up the dust, sending it drifting in the air and sparkling
through the shafts of moonlight that poured through the windows like a million microscopic fireflies.

"You're getting pretty good at those landings," a quiet female voice said.

I turned, peering into the dark where a slender silhouette
stood waiting. My chest tightened, seizing up as her name left
my lips as a soft, growling exhale. "Claire."

It was her—she'd actually come to meet me. And she
wasn't even wearing her totem form as Oceana.

"If you keep looking at me like that, then I'm going to assume you just called me here because you missed me," she
teased as she stepped out of the shadows.

It wasn't until she was standing before me, looking up at
my towering dragon form, that I could see how forced those
words were. She was smiling, but it wasn't real. Her eyes were
empty, as though all the light inside her had been snuffed out.

And now I understood why.

Crouching down so that we could look at one another eye to
eye, I watched her move in closer. I held perfectly still. I'd been
around her as a regular human while she was wearing her
Oceana form and, honestly, it was terrifying. So I knew my size,

strength, and general strangeness might be a little unnerving. Her smile faded as she reached out to brush her hand along the side of my face.

Her hand felt tiny and fragile in mine as I moved slowly to grasp it and gently pull it away. "Close your eyes," I said.

Her head tipped to the side curiously. "You really trust me that much?"

I nodded.

Her smile was real for an instant. Then she closed her eyes.

I stood back and put a hand over the glowing totem scale on my wrist, commanding it to sleep. All the ancient draconic power seeped out of me, draining away until I was left standing before her as my true self—regular, dorky, unfashionable Koji. The guy who, until she found out my secret identity, had never been enough. She'd fallen for Noxius long before she ever felt anything for me. Or at least, that's how it seemed. Tabitha didn't know about her crush on my alter ego, or that Claire and I had anything to do with Noxius and Oceana. She only knew half the story.

Or maybe I was the one who'd only known half the truth about what was going on with Claire. Tabitha's words still tangled my brain as I watched Claire, standing only inches away, with her eyes closed and her expression riddled with anxiety. Her long golden hair fell in spools of perfection around her face, over her shoulders, and down her back. I hadn't seen her in months, and she took my breath away.

What if Tabitha was right? What if she had just been putting up those walls between us to protect herself? Or maybe friend-zoning me back then was her way of trying to spare me the scandal and drama of being caught up in her family's mess. They expected—no, they *demanded*—so much from her. It was way more than just some overprotective parental concern. They were even trying to force her to marry Damien.

But did knowing that change anything?

I heard her breathing hitch. From a few feet away, the shadows from the cool moonlight painted her beautiful face in bold relief, but they didn't hide the tears that started to run down her cheeks. Her brow quivered and she bit down hard on her lip.

"Claire?" I took a step closer.

She looked up, shaking her head and trying to wave me off. "I-I'm sorry. It's not you. I'm fine." Those walls were coming back up. "Just give me a second. Really, I'm fine."

Nope. Not this time. I wasn't going to let her hide. Hiding like that was going to kill her. And she didn't have to hide from me.

Surging forward, I snagged my arms around her and dragged her into a tight hug. "Stop that. It's... it's okay." My voice caught because I knew, deep down, it wasn't. Nothing was okay for either of us right now.

Claire let out a desperate sob as she wrapped her arms around me and squeezed me back like someone gripping a life preserver in a stormy sea. She buried her face against my shoulder and trembled, gasping in frantic breaths while she cried. "I'm so sorry, Koji."

"For what? You've got nothing to be sorry for." I put a hand on the back of her head in a way I hoped was comforting.

"I could feel it in your message," she whimpered against my shirt. "Your anger, frustration, and pain. I never meant for any of this to hurt you. Everything about my parents, I don't even know what to believe anymore. It's so much worse than I thought. They're... they're *terrible* people, Koji. And I'm one of them! I can only imagine what everyone's been asking you about me. I just—God, I am so sorry."

I blinked and pulled back enough to look in her eyes. "You're not terrible. You're nothing like them. I know that better than anybody. It's not fair for everyone to blame you for anything that happened with Mrs. Ignatius."

Her expression wavered, riddled with uncertainty. Then realization settled over her features like the weight of the world had just been dropped on her head. Her beautiful, sea-green eyes seemed to dim. "Tabitha told you."

"Well, yeah, kinda," I stammered. "She's not telling everyone, though. Just me."

Claire shook her head like that didn't matter. "I can't stop thinking about Madeline. I let them convince me that she was my enemy, that she wanted to slander our family because of jealousy. But all of it was a lie. And now she's gone." Her voice wavered, eyes welling again. "I can't even apologize to her! How can you not hate me, Koji? After the way I treated her? I know what she meant to you."

I grasped her chin, forcing her to look me in the eye. "Claire, seriously, I'm not upset with you. Not even a little."

She gave a quick, humorless laugh as she wiped at her eyes. "I'd never picked up emotions like that from you before. I just assumed," her voice caught and she took in a deep, unsteady breath, "I assumed you found out about everything and were angry."

"Nothing like that. I—well, I needed someone to talk to. Someone who knows all my big, bad superhero secrets." Arching a brow, I tilted my head to the side as I studied her. "Umm, not to jump topics here, but how could you sense all that from a text?"

She bowed her head, mouth screwing up as she looked away. "It's my third eye. I can sense emotion in other people. Some are much clearer than others. You are, by far, the clearest. I guess because you're a totem-wielder, too."

"Oh." I couldn't help sounding surprised. She'd never told me about her third eye—probably because she was still trying to decide if she was going to trust me or not. Then bigger, wyvern-shaped fish to fry distracted us before we could talk about that kinda thing again.

A sudden rush of realization and total humiliation made my whole head flush. Oh God—did that mean she'd known about my crush on her the *whole time*? Great. Just great. No wonder she'd kept her distance. I'd probably seemed like a lovesick creep, fawning after her right from the start.

"It's okay," she said quietly. "You don't have to be embarrassed."

I swallowed hard, struggling to force my voice to stay steady. "L-Listen, Claire, I wasn't upset with you when I sent that message. I swear."

She peered at me in confusion. "What is it, then? I've never sensed anything like that from you before."

I hadn't asked her to come here so I could dump all my issues in her lap. She had enough going on in her own life, and doing that would've been the most selfish thing ever.

"It's not a big deal, really," I deflected, rubbing the back of my neck. "Just some crap with Drake and my dad... and a cruise. Don't worry about it."

Her eyes narrowed slightly as though she were daring me to try brushing her off again. "Don't be like that. I could feel everything you were feeling. I know it was a big deal," she scolded. "So spill it, Koji. Otherwise, I'll be forced to transform and make you."

One corner of my mouth quirked into a half grin. "*Make* me? Really? I've been training, you know. With the military. Hardcore stuff. I think I could probably take you now."

Claire stood on her toes long enough to flick the end of my nose. "Bring it on, Owens."

It didn't take long for Claire to talk me into confessing pretty much everything about how things were getting weird and awkward at home. She sat next to me on a fallen steel beam, listening as I rambled on and on. I told her about Dad dating Ms. Collins and always fawning all over her. I ranted about my dad being all buddy-buddy with Drake, who apparently was going to be living with us for the foreseeable future. And then there was the cruise—my literal vacation hell.

It wasn't until then that I realized I'd never actually told Claire about how my mom died, and why I couldn't swim. She knew about that last part, of course. She'd almost drowned me a few times—once on purpose and other times during the throes of our epic battles with giant monsters. But we hadn't spent a lot of time discussing our personal lives during those intense moments.

She sat quietly, watching me with her lovely sea-green eyes seeming to absorb every detail as I explained how I'd almost died as a toddler in the accident that had killed my mom. When I was finished, she didn't say anything for what felt like an eternity. We sat silently in the dark of the abandoned plant, staring at one another. At last, she dropped her gaze to where she was fidgeting with her hands in her lap.

"I had no idea." She spoke so quietly I could barely hear her.

I shrugged, looking down too. "It was a long time ago. I know I should've gotten over it by now, it's just... I can't help it. Every time I try to go swimming or even just sit in a hot tub or something, there's this panic that comes alive in my blood. I can't resist it. It takes over everything and I can't even think. I can't move. I can't do anything."

"And your dad doesn't know about this?" she asked with a disapproving frown. "That you still can't swim, I mean."

Running my fingers through my shaggy black hair, I leaned forward to rest my elbows on my knees. "I don't know. I thought he did. Maybe he forgot. Or he's just assuming I grew out of it. We didn't exactly have a lot in the way of bodies of water in Arizona before this. In Korea, no one really swam in the ocean and pools were kinda hard to come by where we lived. I mean, there was one on the base but it had really weird hours.

Anyway, it's not like I have a choice now, right? We leave in a couple of days."

"Yeah," she agreed. "I wish there was something I could do."

I flicked her a glance and waggled my eyebrows. "Oceana could come kidnap me."

Claire giggled and nudged me with her elbow. "From a cruise ship in the middle of the Caribbean? And why would she do that?"

"Oh, you know, maybe she has a thing for me? Like she couldn't wait to whisk me away back to New York so we could spend the whole time watching all the Marvel movies in chronological order."

Okay, fine, so that last part was kind of a test. Drake asked me once if I really knew anything about Claire—what she liked and didn't like. He'd asked what I would do if I found out we had nothing in common. Well, except for being totem-wielders, of course. At the time, I hadn't had a good answer for any of that. Now I just wondered if liking her back then had been doomed to be an epic disaster or not. We'd gone to the same school, had a lot of the same classes, and had been around each other for almost a year now, but I still didn't know much about her.

"Are we counting *X-Men* in this lineup? Or only the *Avengers* films? Because that might take more than a few days." She arched an eyebrow.

My heart stopped and my soul left my body. I gaped at her, unable to make a sound. Claire Faust knew about *X-Men*?

"What's that face for?" she asked when she noticed my mouth hanging open.

"I-I just didn't figure you liked that kind of thing," I admitted, ducking my head slightly.

She pursed her lips unhappily. "Because I'm a girl?"

"No! No, it's not that at all." I raised my hands in surrender. "You just... don't really give off that kinda vibe, I guess."

Her eyes narrowed. "Because I'm blond, my parents are wealthy, and I go to a private school?"

Okay, this was bad. And everything I said was making it worse. My face was probably glowing like a stoplight as I bowed my head lower and grimaced. "Th-that's, ummm, I-I…" Crap. Why? Why did I have to say stupid stuff like that? "I'm really sorry. I suck at talking to girls and—"

Claire burst into a fit of laughter. "Oh my God, Koji! I'm just teasing you!"

My whole body went slack with relief. "Seriously? That was cruel."

"I like action movies. I've never been much into comics, but I read a lot of fanfics." She grinned sheepishly.

Okay. Two could play the teasing game. "Fanfics, eh?" I eyed her dubiously. "You mean like *naughty* fanfics?"

"What? No! Not those kinds!" Her face flushed bright pink.

"Suuuure." I chuckled. "I bet you read all the dirty ones."

Claire wrinkled her nose and crossed her arms. "Not fair, Koji. I'm not really one for romance novels. Or sappy movies, either. Tabitha always drags me to romantic comedies but, I hate them. The endings are always the same—happily ever after, blah, blah, blah. So boring."

I wondered what kinds of movies Damien took her to see. Did he let her pick? Or did he make her go along with whatever he liked? I couldn't bring myself to ask. Just the thought of that guy made me want to hurl.

"So, uh, then what's your favorite one? Movie, I mean," I asked.

"Old? Recent? Or of all time?"

"Of all time."

She paused, her mouth pursing thoughtfully. Then a soft, distant smile brushed over her beautiful features. "*The Iron Giant.*"

Whoa. Seriously? Claire Faust's favorite movie of all time was… a cartoon from the 90s? I couldn't help it. I had to ask—I needed to know why.

Before I could get the question out, Claire stood up and gave a loud sigh that made her shoulders drop. "Maybe I should do this more often," she mused as she pulled her phone out of the back pocket of her jean shorts.

"Do what?"

She shrugged. "Sneak out at night to meet up with a guy."

"Th-that's…" I couldn't do anything except choke and stutter. Geez, the way she said it made it sound like I'd arranged a romantic rendezvous. Like we were just slinking off to find a place to make out or something.

"Speaking of which, I need to head back. My parents will freak out if they check on me and I'm not there." Her whole demeanor seemed to droop. With the glow of her phone screen lighting up the near dark, I got a good look at the dark circles under her eyes.

"I'm sorry. I shouldn't have kept you for this long." I stood up too.

"No, it's okay. I needed this." She glanced up at me, her smile soft and genuine under the glow of her phone's screen. "I'm really glad you messaged me. We should do this again. It's nice to have someone to hang out with a little and talk to. You know, someone who doesn't already assume they know everything about me."

I shifted, trying not to blush like a total idiot. Her smile still sent a jolt through me like I'd licked an electrical socket. It was stupid, really. Why couldn't I just get over her? Madeline was *somewhere*.

"Hey, uh, I'd be a major jerk if I didn't ask this. Do you think you could call Tabitha? Or message her or something? She's really worried about you."

Claire's smile faded. She gave a small nod. "I know. I miss her, too. But the press has been relentless, and I don't want her to get dragged into it, too. It's bad enough that Damien—" She halted suddenly, lips pressing together into a tight, uncomfortable line.

That's when I noticed—she wasn't wearing her giant engagement ring anymore. Whoa. When had that happened? I mean, I'd just assumed everything was still peachy with them. He'd seemed fine at school. And she hadn't mentioned anything about him. Sooooo... what did this mean?

Before I could make up my mind about whether or not it was safe to ask her about it, my phone buzzed in my pocket. I took it out, glancing at the screen long enough to see I had a new message from Drake. He wanted to know where I was and if everything was okay.

I sighed and texted him back, letting him know I was heading back now. "Looks like I gotta go too."

The touch of warm, soft lips on my cheek made me freeze solid. I stared down at Claire, my eyes wide as all the blood seemed to rush to my face and ears. She—had she—was that a kiss? It was, right? I hadn't imagined it? I wasn't hallucinating again?

"Message me again sometime. I want to hear all about the cruise," she said, her smile as cryptic as it was dazzling as she waved and turned away. "See you later, Noxius."

# CHAPTER 9

Uuugh. This was bad. *So* bad. I could *not* start falling for Claire again. Sure, talking to her had been great. And now that we knew each other's secret identities, things felt less tense and awkward. Being around her had even been calming to my frazzled, overstressed brain.

But nothing about our... situation had changed. She was still in a relationship with someone else. Er, well, maybe. She'd taken off her engagement ring. That didn't necessarily mean it was over, though, right? Maybe she just hadn't wanted to wear it or had already taken it off for the night. Yeah. That made way more sense. No sense in jumping to wild conclusions over nothing.

Not to mention, I wasn't ready to give up on Madeline. I knew if I saw her again, if I could just hold her hand or talk to her for a few seconds, I wouldn't even be thinking about Claire that way. Right?

Right.

So stop it, Koji. Just knock it off. Move on. That ship sailed long ago and I wasn't even in the same universe when it left.

So why couldn't I stop thinking about it? About her? Three days later, my mind was still a tangled wreck. Ugh. Maybe I should just give up dating indefinitely. Clearly I wasn't any good at dealing with relationships, anyway.

Staring straight ahead while I sat on the back seat of Dad's car, once again scrunched between suitcases and pieces of luggage, I silently wished I could miss this ship, too. Or plane, rather. We had a flight booked from New York to Miami where we would board our cruise. All the way to the airport, I debated opening the door and executing a tuck-and-roll bailout to escape. I imagined myself flailing over the gravel on the shoulder of the road, tumbling to a halt, and getting up to dust myself off before I made a mad sprint back toward the house. I could totally pull it off. Might break a rib or fracture something, but that was a risk I was *almost* willing to take.

At least I wasn't alone. Drake was smushed against the door on the opposite side of the car. I couldn't see him because of all the luggage. That is, until his arm appeared around one of the suitcases. "Hey, check this out." He waggled his phone in my face.

I took it with a frown. The screen showed headlines of trending stories, and the one he selected was something about doctors being held hostage in South America. I tapped the story and read on. A team of volunteer medical doctors from all over the world had traveled to aid impoverished towns and villages in South America. A small, unidentified group of armed men had abducted them. Terrorists? My stomach fluttered at the thought. Why would anyone take doctors hostage like that? What could they possibly gain?

If everything in the article was true, none of the doctors had strong political ties or influence. A weird choice of victims, for sure. Something was off. It didn't add up. There had to be more to it than what the article said.

"Looks bad," Drake whispered, his voice barely audible. "Think we'll get a call?"

I frowned and handed his phone back around the suitcase. "I doubt it." As bad as it was, stuff like that happened all the time. Besides, this was probably political on some level, even if the news wasn't reporting it that way. Agent Kirkland knew I didn't want to get involved in anything like that. I wasn't going to be the government's proverbial fist. If more totem stuff, like giant reptilian monsters attacking major cities or crazed headmasters wielding ancient power, started happening then I was all over it. I'd be the first one there, ready to throw down and brawl. But I didn't want to be a glorified soldier.

Not that I had anything against soldiers. Dad was one, after all. But taking on that role meant I'd also have to start taking orders—mostly from people who might not have the best of motivations. I'd be giving up my right to choose when and how I used my totem's power to potentially serve someone else's agenda.

I was not okay with that.

We arrived at the airport early enough to check in, grab a quick dinner in the terminal, and sit around for a few minutes before we boarded. Drake sauntered along beside me, his eyes never leaving his phone screen and his earphones blasting fast-tempo techno.

Dad had opted for red-eye plane tickets so that we could arrive on the day our cruise was supposed to depart and avoid spending the night in a hotel. Luckily, that meant the flight wasn't very full and there was extra room to spread out in our own rows and sleep. I dozed as our plane took off for Atlanta, tossing and turning as dreams of Madeline, Ignatius, and flashes of fire blurred through my mind. My dreams were like that a lot now—something between a nightmare and a memory.

In Atlanta, we changed planes and headed for Miami. Our jet touched down just as the first rays of the morning sun bloomed over the horizon in warm hues of soft purple and deep scarlet. We took a cab to a Waffle House for breakfast and sat around, killing time and munching. For some reason, flying always left me ravenous, so I didn't hold back. I wolfed down three waffles, bacon, eggs, hash browns smothered in cheese and chili, and a glass of milk while Ms. Collins watched from across the table, suppressing a smile.

"Hungry or something?" Drake asked, arching a brow at me like he was wondering if I was going to puke.

"Keep that up and I'll have to start taking you jogging with me." Dad chuckled.

"Trying to enjoy the last meal I'm going to get to actually enjoy for a while," I retorted as I licked the syrup off my fingers.

Dad's tone had a dangerous edge. "Oh?"

"Well, you know, between getting seasick and throwing up constantly or possibly dying because someone pushes me into the pool, who knows." I avoided his gaze. I didn't need to see him to know he was staring me down, eyes pinched into that disapproving signature Dad frown. But, hey, he was the one who planned this whole trip without even asking me if I could actually swim now.

"Why would you die if you fell in the pool?" Ms. Collins's asked with a cautious smile—like maybe she thought I was kidding or something.

No one answered.

Beside her, Dad was still glowering at me. I flashed him a quick, semi-defiant glare in return. I wasn't going to test his full-on wrath, but I still wanted him to know—to remind him—what he was about to do to me. A week on a boat was basically my own personal slice of hell.

Next to me, Drake had gone back to eating and was staring into his heap of hash browns like he'd found religion somewhere in there. Probably hoping to avoid getting caught up in this showdown. Good call.

The waitress came to deliver our bill and unknowingly diffused the situation before anyone answered Ms. Collins. Fine by me. I wasn't going to explain myself to her. Not about this, anyway. Dad should be the one to tell her why his *only* child couldn't swim, which he'd apparently forgotten when he decided to drag me on a vacation that involved the freaking ocean.

I didn't say anything else as we climbed into another cab and headed for the port. The instant the massive ships came into view, my stomach dropped, and a cold sweat prickled my skin. I took a deep, slow, steadying breath and closed my eyes. Calm— I had to stay calm. Don't look at the water. Don't think about it. I'd be fine.

Probably.

It took an eternity to board, and we waited in the huge cruise terminal building along with the thousands of other passengers. The whole time I stared down at my shoes, my phone, or one of the comics I'd brought along. Basically, I looked at everything *except* the ocean. It didn't help much. I could still hear it, roaring and hissing whenever the doors opened to let more people inside. I could smell it, too. That fishy, humid saltiness stung my nose and made my stomach roll.

A buzzing in my pocket made me flinch. I took out my phone, glancing at the new message from Tabitha displayed on the screen:

TABITHA:
Thanks.

I smirked. Claire must have called her. Good.

KOJI:
Stop being nice to me. It's weird.

TABITHA:
You're still a major dork.

Grinning, I sent one last response.

KOJI:
That's better.

I put my phone back in my pocket and went back to flipping through my comic.

After hours spent waiting while my stomach cramped from eating too much, I decided I was probably suffering from some kind of waffle overdose induced insanity. That was the only reason I could explain how, for the briefest instant I considered the idea, Tabitha might actually be my friend now. Crap. How had that happened?

Dad had booked two ocean-view cabins right next to one another—one for himself and Ms. Collins and another for me and Drake. Our luggage was already sitting inside the door as we wandered in, staring around at the small, albeit nicely furnished, room. Towels folded into a frog and a monkey were arranged on the beds with complimentary chocolates, and the mini fridge was stocked with snacks and drinks. A flat screen TV was mounted to the wall above a sleek dresser, and a decent-sized porthole window looked out onto the port where people were still boarding.

Hmm. Not bad. Worst case scenario, I'd just spend the next five days kicked back on the bed, watching TV and eating my feelings.

"Hey, uh, Koji?" Drake cleared his throat as he turned to face me, rubbing the back of his neck. "About what you said at breakfast."

Great. I was kinda hoping no one would bring this up. "Yeah?"

"I'm sorry, man. I totally forgot about your water phobia." He sounded genuinely concerned. "Are you gonna be all right?"

Okay, okay. So, I wasn't mad at Drake. Yes, he'd basically moved into my house, taken over my bathroom, eaten my favorite snacks, and left his crap all over my desk. But none of those offenses were friendship-ending. It wasn't fair to take it out on him, or even be angry because he was excited about what would have been an otherwise awesome vacation. He hadn't known me for even a year, so I couldn't even blame him for forgetting about the water thing.

This was on Dad, not him.

"Yeah, I'll manage," I admitted quietly as I sank down to sit on the edge of one of the beds. "Look, just don't let me drag you down, okay? If you wanna go ride the waterslides and all that, it's fine. I'll find a pool chair and read."

His mouth scrunched unhappily. "There's other stuff we can do on the ship. There's laser tag and zip-lining and indoor rock climbing. There's even a movie theater."

"Okay. We can definitely do some of that." I nodded, deciding not to remind him that even being on the ship was kind of a challenge—like a constant, low-key panic attack.

Drake gave me a sympathetic smile. "Your dad really blew this one, huh?"

No kidding. "Yeah. I'm sure the only thing he was thinking about was how to get your mom into a bikini."

His expression skewed with disgust and he pretended to gag. "Agh! Dude—*why*? So gross, man. Super gross."

"Right? I kinda hate myself for even thinking of that."

He flopped down onto his own bed and picked up the remote to scroll through the channels. "I can't believe they're rooming together this time. Guess that charade is finally over." He snorted and shook his head. "I swear, if I even think I hear them going at it over there I will puke my guts up and throw myself off the back of this ship."

"I'll be right behind you," I agreed.

Drake flicked past cartoons, crime dramas, and commercials. The sight of a somber-faced news anchor made him stop. A bold text headline filled the bottom of the screen. BREAK-

ING NEWS: DOCTORS WITHOUT BORDERS HELD BY TERRORIST CELL IN COLOMBIA.

I swallowed hard, watching in silence as a series of snap-shot images showing six people—the captured doctors—flashed across the screen. They all looked middle-aged, maybe in their late thirties. The pictures showed them with their families, holding their children, or wearing wedding attire.

"While we continue to await updates, it is apparent that the situation has not changed. We have reports that all six hostages are being held at gunpoint in a rural area of Colombia and no demands have been relayed in exchange for their release. It is believed at least one of the hostages has been injured, but the severity is unknown." The cool-faced reporter spoke evenly, but the twinge of tension in his brow was a dead giveaway. This was bad—maybe even worse than they were letting on. "Our sources in Washington indicate that the president is in contact with other world leaders concerning this incident, but no public statement has been released."

"Koji." Drake said my name like a warning. "I, uh, I took a peek in the confidential files and e-mails going through the military channels."

"What? When did you even have time to do that?"

He waved a hand like it didn't matter. "They weren't doing anything wrong—they're just a bunch of volunteer doctors. They were over there just trying to help people."

I tore my eyes away from the screen, chewing at the inside of my cheek until I could taste blood. "Do you think I should just fly over there and, what, start ripping terrorists in half like phone books?"

Drake shot me a shocked stare, his mouth open slightly. "Uh. I was going to suggest just getting the doctors out. Wait—can you actually *do* that?"

I rolled my eyes. "Do you even remember me fighting a giant crocodile monster with my bare hands?"

"Okay. Fair enough. But are you really okay with just sitting here and watching this happen? Let's at least ask Kirkland if they need our help, right?"

I hesitated. One the one hand, yeah, I would've loved kicking a little terrorist butt. But what if I lost it like I did during the training exercise? What if I accidentally detransformed again? Those terrorists might take me hostage too. Then the entire world would know my secret, which would be a big problem... if I even survived. Knowing I was the face behind Noxius's power would basically slap a giant target on my back and put my family in danger. Drake and his mom, too. I mean, how long would it take for someone to try to kill me or kidnap Dad and use him to force me to do something bad?

Not to mention, this had nothing to do with totems or giant draconic monsters. It wasn't my fight. And I couldn't just go rushing in like the world police, could I?

My totem bracelet seemed to grow heavier on my wrist. I briefly wondered if I should try to message Claire and ask her opinion. That was a pointless idea. She'd been against us charging off to do heroic stuff from the start. I already knew what she'd say.

"We need to wait," I decided at last. "There's bad stuff happening everywhere, Drake. We can't just jump in every time things look bad. I'm not about to start playing world police with my totem, and I know Oceana would feel the same way. If... if this is bad enough that the military can't handle it, and they truly need my special brand of help to save innocent lives, then Kirkland will contact us. We should give them a chance to settle this without getting us or the totems involved."

Drake stayed quiet for a few seconds, then he nodded. "Okay." He paused again before I heard him mutter, "I've got a bad feeling about this."

I didn't reply—mostly because I didn't want to freak him out.

I had a bad feeling too.

# CHAPTER 10

I made it until lunch the next day before I threw up. Not because of Dad and Ms. Collins—although their level of old people PDA was off the charts and more than enough to make me want to vomit. The stupid water finally got to me. I'd only been on a boat a few times in my life and never one this big or on the open ocean. All my hopes that the size of the ship would make the rocking, swaying motion of the water unnoticeable came crashing down around my ears as I sat on the floor of our claustrophobic little bathroom.

"You okay in there?" Drake called through the door.

"Just kill me, please," I groaned as I leaned into the toilet again and heaved.

The door cracked open just enough for Drake's hand to slip in and put a small packet on the counter behind me. "Here. Mom brought some medicine for motion sickness. She said it'll probably make you drowsy. Better than puking though, right?"

I tore off some toilet paper to wipe my chin. "Thanks."

After a few more sessions of retching, I finally managed to stagger up to the sink and take the pills. Staring at my reflection in the mirror, it felt like everything was sloshing back and forth. I shut my eyes and shook my head, trying to clear my head enough to stumble out of the bathroom and collapse onto my bed.

"You don't have to sit in here," I mumbled as I burrowed under the blankets. "Go have fun. I'm fine."

"You sure?"

"Yeah. I'm just gonna try to sleep some."

"Okay. I'll be back in a couple of hours," he replied, his footsteps retreating toward the door.

"Thanks."

"You know, to make sure you're not dead."

"I'm not that lucky."

He snickered. "Who knows? If you are dead, I'll just roll you out the window. A nice sea burial. The sharks'll enjoy it."

"Win-win."

His laughter retreated to the hall as the door clicked shut. Alone in the quiet of our room, I tried not to pay any attention to the subtle, constant motion that made my head pound. Now would have been a fantastic time for Dad to come and check on me. Maybe if he realized how much misery I was in, he'd apologize for ever subjecting me to this torture.

Of course, he didn't. Dad was probably reclining in a hot tub with his arm around Ms. Collins while they sipped fruity cocktails and played footsy under the water. This whole experience made me extremely grateful that he'd never dated seriously before now. If he'd skipped off with some woman when I was younger, I might've starved to death or wandered out into traffic while he was busy staring longingly into her eyes.

I lay on the bed, suffering silently, until my mind hazed and my thoughts blurred as the nausea medicine began to soothe the spinning, cramping sensation in my stomach. I wondered if I'd have to take this stuff for the rest of the trip. Great. I'd probably be drooling on myself in every photo.

Somewhere in my delirium, a buzzing, humming sound pricked at the back of my mind. I knew that sound. It meant something—something important. But I was too tired to care.

Then the door opened. Dad? I lifted my head to squint as Drake rushed back into the room, his face pale and eyes wide. Geez. What was that look for?

"Get up, hero. We got the call," he said, keeping his voice hushed as he held up his sleek, black super-secret FBI phone.

Oh crap. That was what I heard! I'd totally forgotten to put mine back in my pocket.

Panic shot through me and I bolted upright. Seizing my backpack from beside the bed, I rifled through to find the right pocket. I had one missed call from an unknown. "What happened? Was it Kirkland? What did he say?" I looked to Drake for an explanation.

Drake was already rummaging through one of his bags, hurling clothes everywhere. "They're coming for us tonight. Movie theater. Nine o'clock."

"What? They're coming here? To the ship?" How the heck was the FBI going to pick us up from a cruise ship in the middle of the ocean?

"Yep."

"Is this about the doctors in Colombia? Did something happen?"

Drake looked back long enough to toss me something—a small, hard plastic case about the size of a paperback book. "He didn't say, but probably. What else could it be?"

I caught the box and cracked it open long enough to take a peek at what was hidden inside. "Are these more of those bio-monitor things?"

"Eh, sorta but not really. It's an ultra-light version of your IMF Suit," he explained as he took out his laptop and shoved it into his backpack along with his headphones, a few cables, and a headlamp on a wide elastic band. "No bio-monitors. Just communication and GPS. Thought it might come in handy."

"No kidding." I studied the pair of small devices tucked neatly into black foam inside the case.

"The GPS range isn't as great as the IMF Suit. With this one, I'll need to be within range—roughly a hundred miles. Shouldn't be a problem for this, though." He took out a tackle box and tucked it into the bag, too. "We've got two hours to prep."

Wait, two hours? I glanced down at the clock on my phone screen. Geez. How long had I been out? I'd missed dinner and everything. "What about the lovebirds?"

Drake breezed past with an armful of clothes, heading for the bathroom. "Already took care of it. I said we were going to catch a movie and go play laser tag afterwards. They won't wait up."

My shoulders sagged in relief. "I guess if I get beaten to a pulp, we can just say I tripped and fell at laser tag." Dad would totally buy that, given my history over the last year. As far as he knew, I'd never been in battle with any giant monsters. I had, however, fallen into a dumpster, gotten a concussion from catching a giant clay pot with my face, and been entangled with the terrified crowd of innocent victims at the Philharmonic attack.

Seriously, it was a little astounding he wasn't at least slightly suspicious that I might be involved with Noxius. Buuuut, then again, he had apparently totally forgotten that I might die if someone accidentally pushed me into the pool, so whatever. I guess his mind was so tangled up with this new relationship, he wasn't noticing anything else these days.

Sitting on the edge of my bed, I fidgeted with my totem bracelet. I ran my fingers over the smooth, gleaming white scale fixed to the center of the braided leather band. If this was about those doctors being held hostage—and it probably was—then this was the first time I'd be going into real battle against people instead of monsters. It was one thing to fight a giant creature bent on wrecking the city for no good reason. It was different to know I'd be going in to possibly hurt other human beings. Terrorists or not, I'd never... you know, *killed* anyone. Was I going to have to do that? Kill people? My stomach clenched into knots just thinking about it.

I grabbed my personal cell phone off the nightstand and pulled up my messages with Claire. Should I tell her what I was about to do? I didn't expect her to come help me. Kind of the opposite, really. She wouldn't approve of this at all probably. But if something went wrong, then she needed to know. She needed to be on guard in case something with rogue totem-wielders and giant, city-crushing monsters ever happened again.

I flicked a glance up at the bathroom door before quickly typing out a message:

```
KOJI:
Going to a party in Colombia tonight. No
plus-ones, tho. Wish me luck.
```

I really didn't want Oceana involved in this. I wasn't asking for her help. She'd been dragged into my fights before, but those were different. Those concerned totems and, ultimately, attacks on her family. This wasn't like that. I was just letting her know in case something happened. And whatever happened next was on me.

Agent Kirkland stuck out like a sore thumb. In the throngs of families heading into the movie theater wearing brightly colored vacation attire, he was the only one in a black suit and tie. Was this seriously his idea of being discreet? Good grief.

When our eyes met across the theater lobby, he tipped his head to the side, gesturing for us to follow. We made our way through the crowds, taking a back exit into a quiet hallway. It was getting late. The other passengers were probably heading to bed, attending the late-night entertainment events, or settling into one of the bars or lounges for the evening. No one said a word as we walked briskly through the maze of halls running the length of the ship, Kirkland in the lead.

He guided us to the top deck and to the door of a large suite. Slipping a card key out of his pocket, he swiped it and let us go in first—right into a living room where several other agents lurked. I recognized Agent Carrie right away. She stood at the back of the room, arms crossed and expression tense. As soon as she saw me, she forced a thin smile that was probably intended to reassure me. It didn't. Not with two guys standing guard on either side of the door holding machine guns.

"Really? Now the FBI is stalking my family vacations? What's with the bouncers?" I groaned as I glanced around at the rest of the agents. Some were hammering away on laptop keyboards while others paced and talked quietly on cell phones.

"We're only trying to look out for you," Agent Carrie replied, her tone apologetic. "Things have gotten more complicated."

I bit down against the shiver of anxiety that tingled up my spine. I needed to play this cool. "Right. Well, what's this about? If you're calling us in then I'm gonna assume whatever's going down in Colombia isn't some political thing, right?"

Kirkland motioned for us to join him as he sat down on one of the sofas arranged around a glass coffee table with a bunch of papers and photos spread out on it. I recognized some of the people in the pictures as the doctors being held hostage.

"No. This isn't about politics, religious extremists, or anything we might prefer at this point." Kirkland's tone was ominous. "This is about you."

I froze. "Me?"

"Specifically, Noxius," he clarified.

"What do you mean?" Drake demanded as he scooted to the edge of his seat and grabbed some of the papers off the table to look them over.

"We were approached by the CIA shortly after these individuals first took the doctors hostage from a village near Ciudad Perdida. This kind of situation isn't abnormal for the region. While the area is now considered safe for tourist traffic, there have been kidnappings by extremist military groups in that location before. Initially, it was of no concern to us. This unfortunate event was unexpected, but not something our group in the FBI would be involved in," Agent Carrie explained. She eased onto the sofa next to Kirkland, studying me with her warm, dark brown eyes betraying her worry.

"The CIA quickly informed us that this particular group was not politically motivated. In fact, their motivations are still unknown, but they have made their demands." She paused, taking a deep breath. "They want you and Oceana delivered to them in exchange for freeing the remaining doctors in their custody."

Drake's sharp gaze flicked up from the papers. "*Remaining?*"

Carrie's brow knit unhappily, and she stayed silent when Kirkland clarified. "One doctor has already been executed. We have reason to believe several others may have suffered injury, but with their exact location unknown, it's difficult to be sure."

Horror throttled all the breath from my lungs. Oh God. They were killing innocent people? Because of me and Oceana?

I sat, petrified, staring between the two agents until Drake broke the tense silence. "Well, that part wasn't on the evening news."

"Or in any of the data files you've undoubtedly hacked into," Kirkland added with a challenging arch to his brow. "We can't risk any of this going public. If these people, whatever their intent, seek to obtain control of Noxius and Oceana, we want to find out why."

"Well, you can probably bet that it isn't to give them high fives or invite them over for a barbecue." Drake dropped the papers back onto the coffee table and slumped back, folding his arms.

"No. And we certainly don't want Noxius or Oceana publicly associated with them in any capacity whatsoever," Kirkland agreed. "Even raising the suspicion that you two are somehow affiliated with these terrorists would be enough to set the country ablaze with conspiracy and demands for the exposure of your identities."

I bowed my head. "What do you want me to do?" I couldn't keep myself from sounding defeated.

"Nothing you don't want to do, Mr. Owens. That was the deal, and I intend to honor it." Agent Kirkland's voice softened some—probably more than I'd ever heard before. Was he being nice? Whoa. "But we are asking for your help. This is a rural area with rugged, nearly impassible terrain. It's extremely unlikely that we could get an extraction team on the ground without tipping off these terrorists, and we haven't been able to lock in their exact location to even make an attempt."

He hesitated, taking a deep breath. "If we were to send you in first and give the appearance of surrendering to their demands, then you could gather some valuable intel. We'd get a lock on their location, details about their forces, and try to ensure that no more hostages were injured as we apprehend the people responsible."

My palms went clammy. This was way worse than duking it out with some giant monster. For whatever reason, knowing I'd be facing down a bunch of insane men with guns made my pulse spike into overdrive and a cold sweat run down my back. Monsters were big and scary but were ultimately just animals with simple motives. Usually, they were just following their instincts.

People, on the other hand… they could be just plain evil.

"It's dangerous," I murmured.

"Yes," Agent Carrie replied softly.

"I'm probably going to have to kill someone."

Kirkland's voice held a sense of grim finality. "It's possible."

"But if I don't, the rest of those doctors will get executed."

I took a few seconds to breathe, listening to my pulse roar in my ears as fury like acid burned through my veins. I looked over at Drake, setting my jaw and giving him a nod.

He nodded back.

"Okay, then. Let's do it."

# CHAPTER 11

Since becoming an awesome, lightning-wielding dragon-superhero, the frequency of my terrible ideas resulting in truly awful plans that would probably get me killed had skyrocketed. Tonight, however, I was kicking things up to a whole new level. Oceana wasn't even here and I could still sense her scorching disapproval from half the world away.

It wasn't like I had much of a choice. Not really, anyway. I couldn't stand by and let more innocent people get hurt or killed because of me. If these terrorist jerks wanted Noxius, then I was about to give them more of him than they could handle.

While Kirkland stepped to the side to talk quickly with Drake, Agent Carrie gave me a hooded sweatshirt with the cruise ship's logo on the front. I quickly pulled it on. It looked a little strange when paired with my shorts, but I had a feeling this wasn't a fashion-based choice.

Drake and I followed Agent Kirkland out of the FBI suite and through the ship, navigating passages and hallways marked for employee use only. Stopping before another door, Kirkland turned and nodded to Drake. "Three minutes, Mr. Collins."

"I'll only need two." Drake flung down his backpack and took out the plastic case with the Bluetooth devices tucked inside.

Kirkland opened the door long enough to slip out. Then Drake and I were alone.

"Okay, remember what I said about this. I don't get any feedback on your physical condition and my GPS tracking is limited, but Kirkland thinks I can maintain contact from the ship." Drake went silent as he handed me the devices. "Koji, I get why you're doing this. But try to be careful, okay? If you go out there and get killed, I'll have to spend the rest of my life lying to everyone about how you fell off the back of the cruise ship or something, and I'm gonna be seriously pissed off."

I met his gaze, trying my hardest not to let any of my apprehension or fear reach the surface. "Don't do that. Don't lie about it," I countered. "If this does go south, if I can't get out, then you need to tell my dad the truth, okay? He won't be mad at you, I promise. But he deserves to know what really happened." I forced a thin smile. "Who knows, he might actually be proud of me. Going off to fight terrorists and save people? I mean, he can't say I didn't follow in his footsteps, right?"

"This isn't like that." Drake's expression darkened. "Listen, while you're there, you've got to try to find out more about these guys. Names or whatever you can get. I'll track them down to the ends of the earth. There's nowhere they can hide from Cloudmaker."

I smirked, taking the pair of monitoring devices and offering to bump my fist against his. "Relax, I got this."

He didn't look convinced as I pulled the hood of my sweatshirt up to hide my face and turned away. Throwing open the door, the rush of wind and concussive *thump-thump-thump* of helicopter rotors nearly blew me off my feet. Kirkland waved me over and seized my arm to help me into the unmarked black chopper that was parked on the small helipad at the very top of the ship. Then he climbed in and showed me how to strap into one of the seats.

My stomach flipped, swirled, and churned as I gripped the straps of the five-point harness that buckled me to the seat as the chopper took off. Below, the sleek white cruise ship quickly dissolved into nothing but a faint streak of lights against an endless black ocean. Dad and Ms. Collins were somewhere down there having a great time with absolutely no idea what Drake and I were up to. Once, that had thrilled me a little. It was a cool secret, right? Being a superhero and no one knowing about it except my best friend was like having this unspoken ace in the hole. It felt like a guarantee that I was, in fact, the coolest guy at school even if no one else knew.

Yeah. That luster had worn off pretty fast after that whole mess at the Philharmonic. Er, well, even before that, actually. Lives were at stake. My secret was probably the most dangerous one in the world.

It didn't take long for another point of light to appear on the horizon. Only, this wasn't some tourist-packed leisure cruise ship. I gulped hard against the stiffness in my throat as our helicopter did a quick circle around what looked like a mini version of an aircraft carrier. The front deck was lined with a row of Ospreys, an odd, almost helicopter-looking aircraft that looked like something straight out of a James Cameron science fiction movie. I'd only seen them a few times, usually whenever we were close to somewhere that had a lot of Marines. They were mostly used for transporting soldiers.

Clenching my clammy, sweaty hands into fists, I waited until we had touched down on the ship's landing pad and Kirkland had unbuckled before I dared to move. He stuck close to my side as a few soldiers in fatigues directed us into the ship. As we crossed the deck, I noticed a couple Ospreys were being prepped for flight. Transports for us? Or just backup?

There wasn't time to ask.

As the soldiers led us through the halls of the ship, speeding along the narrow metal passageways until we came to a briefing room. Inside, eight men in black, full-body combat gear sat around a long table. My heart stopped for a second or two, probably cutting a few years off my life, when they all looked up at

me at the same time—the random teenager in a cruise line hoodie.

They were freaking Navy SEALs.

I forced a quick, totally horrified smile and waved.

God. Why did I wave? *Way to go, Koji. If they didn't think
you were a moron before, they definitely do now.*

None of them said a single word to me, even after Kirkland
ushered me into a seat at the far end of the table. I sat in silence,
mentally kicking myself for the stupid wave, while one of the
men stood and began going over our plan. He spread out a detailed map of the area around the compound where the terrorists
had demanded Oceana and I be delivered.

Recon experts believed the terrorists were holding the doctors close by, but the exact location was still a mystery. Their
minimal movements had kept our team in the dark about the real
number of their forces. Basically, the situation was bad all the
way around, and our enemy was playing it smart. They were far
more familiar with the mountainous terrain and rural location,
and they'd almost certainly be using that against us. Guerrilla
warfare at its finest.

Studying the map, I couldn't shake the growing sense of
nausea that swirled in the pit of my stomach. Something about
this wasn't right. But what other choice was there?

I was here now. I had to see this through to the end. What I
did next might be the only chance those doctors had of ever seeing their families again.

"Once the hostages are confirmed secure, we have permis-
sion to engage and neutralize the threat by any means necessary,
including deadly force. Our asset will be assisted by four A-10s
and two CV-22 Ospreys." The man, who must have been in
charge of the rest of the SEAL team, cast me a meaningful look
from the other end of the table.

Oh. Right. *I* was the asset.

"We'd like to take a few of these hostiles alive, if possible,"
he added.

I nodded. "I, uh, I'll see what I can do."

"We'd like to find out who they are, where they came from, and what they intend to do with you," the man continued. "Knowing that may prevent this from happening again."

Using my lightning to fry them up like fast-food chicken might put an end to it too, but I wasn't about to get cocky. Not yet, anyway.

The rest of the meeting passed like a blur. They discussed tactics, worst-case scenarios, and what I was supposed to do once the terrorists took me into their custody. Drake would monitor me remotely, recording everything I saw and heard so their experts could pick it apart later. The hope was for me to be in custody long enough for all the doctors to be released. Once they were safe, I could open up a proverbial can all over their terrorist butts and get out while the military forces cleaned up anyone left behind who managed to escape my sizzling draconic wrath. If things went really bad, then our last ditch, everything-is-spiraling-the-drain resort was for me to go full dragon and basically take out as many of them as I could before making a speedy escape. No way they'd be able to contain me in that form which was a big relief considering the level of reckless, unnecessary danger I was meddling in this time.

All this hinged on the hope that I didn't lose it like I had last time and do something exquisitely dumb. Like crashing into a cliff. Thankfully, the SEAL team didn't seem to know about that, and Kirkland didn't volunteer any information about it.

The brief ended abruptly and the SEAL team got up, leaving Kirkland and me alone in the room so I could change forms and prepare. As the door banged shut, I sat stiffly in my seat, staring at the map that was still spread out on the table in front of me. What had I gotten myself into? Could I even do this? What if I messed it up?

A heavy hand fell on my shoulder, jostling me a little. "I didn't want to ask you to do this, Mr. Owens," Agent Kirkland said quietly. "Regardless of the power that has manifested, you are still a very young man. Too young to be making these kinds of choices. Ultimately it wasn't my decision. For what it's worth, I feel I may have misjudged you initially. You've been unexpectedly responsible with your power."

It was worth a lot, actually. Kirkland was a crusty old fun-killer. I mean, he'd totally shot down my idea of appearing as Noxius to crash the Macy's Day Parade this year. But he seemed genuinely concerned about what happened to Drake and me. At least, he cared enough to not want us getting caught up in international terrorist plots.

"Thanks," I answered hoarsely. "I'll try not to let you down."

"Just watch your back. Trust your gut. And if anything seems off, get out. I don't want to risk losing our greatest asset over this." He'd gone back to that all-professional tone I was beginning to suspect was a façade. Hard to tell with him.

"Right." I twirled my finger in a gesture for him to turn around and leave. "Now if you don't mind, a little privacy while I slip into something more comfortable."

Agent Kirkland cast me one of his signature unimpressed frowns before he sighed and left. Alone in the briefing room, my gaze drifted back to the map as though pulled by gravity. Marked with red ink was the target—the place the terrorists wanted to swap me for the hostages.

I set my jaw and clapped a hand over my totem scale brace-let. I could only guess what these terrorists wanted me for. Did they think they could chain me? Use me like a scaly attack dog? Force me to fight, maim, and kill for them?

No freaking way.

Game on.

The instant I climbed into the back of the Osprey, tucking my wings in and using my clawed toes to grip the metal floor, all eyes were on me. The four SEAL team members sharing my ride stared, mouths open, as I lumbered by to crouch down between them. There was no way my scaly hindquarters would fit in one of their seats. Dragon problems.

Squatting in the middle, I listened as the rotors of the aircraft sped up, their rhythm intensifying as we took to the air. I could have flown to the target myself, but they wanted to keep my presence a secret until we got closer to the Colombian coast.

My heart pounded in frantic pace with the *whump-whump-whump* of the Osprey's twin rotors. Wild energy sizzled along my arms and legs as my dragon senses drank in the sounds and smells. We were getting close. I could smell the humid, musky scent of the jungle. Damp soil. Plant life.

"Two minutes out." Drake's voice crackled in my ear.

His little communication and video devices stuck right to my hide with a strong adhesive—something he'd assured me wouldn't come off even during a fight. I had one mounted by my ear and another at the base of my tail so he could see what was in front and behind me through the tiny cameras.

"How're you holding up?" he asked.

"Well, I feel like I'm gonna puke, so about the usual for when I'm about to dive into a fight."

Drake chuckled. "Copy that. Ready?"

I drew in a deep, trembling breath. "Yeah."

"Go get 'em, tiger."

On cue, the rear loading ramp opened with a mechanical roar, revealing nothing but darkness. Warm, humid wind howled in, stirring my hair and sending shivers of delight through my body. These moist tropical breezes made the perfect storm-making material.

I gave the SEAL guys a thumb's up and sprang forward, diving headlong out of the back of the aircraft. The darkness swallowed me whole. A flex of my shoulders spread my wings wide to catch the rush of wind. It only took a small surge of power to begin calling forth storm clouds. They gathered over the ocean, filling the sky eagerly with tongues of lightning and cracks of thunder.

"Your destination is dead ahead," Drake said, mimicking the monotone female voice of my dad's car GPS. We'd official-ly dubbed it Miss Your Turn Again since Dad had spent a large portion of our time arguing with it during the road trip to Savan-nah.

I snorted a laugh. "Recalculating—please make a U-turn."

He laughed back. "Seriously, though. Look sharp. The CIA guys let the bad guys know you're inbound and ready for the exchange, so they know you're coming."

I grinned. Good.

With a beat of my wings, I surged toward the densely jun-gled coastline. My dragon eyes could pick out every detail—every tree, rock, and hint of movement. I zoomed low over the tops of the trees, following the curve of the mountainous land-scape. I couldn't see much of the ground thanks to the dense forest canopy until the meetup point came into view. Ciudad Perdida. As far as I'd been able to tell from the brief, it was an archaeological site. The ruins of the ancient city were a popular tourist attraction for anyone willing to make the trek to find it. Not easily done.

On the steep hillsides, several pale stone terraces glowed in the moonlight that bled through the cracks of my gathering stormfront. They were just patches of bare rock like terraces on the slope of the steep hillsides, smooth and open. Pretty visible for a meetup point.

Hmmm.

"That's it, right?" I double-checked, wondering if Drake would be able to see what I was seeing through the cameras.

"Yep. You are cleared for landing."

Drawing my wings in, I cruised in a slow circle over the ru-ins before picking one of the higher exposed stone platforms to touch down. No one was in sight. I couldn't even smell anyone in the vicinity. Weird. Where were they?

I glanced up, drawing upon a little more of my power to bring the storms in and blot out the moonlight. Lightning arced from cloud to cloud, sending out flashes of blue and purple light.

And that's how I first saw her.

A tall, slender woman in a tailored business suit and flashy heels appeared from the gloom, climbing the steps to the top of my terrace. My stormy winds blew through her long black hair, and the stark flashes of light cast her stunning features in bold relief. High cheekbones. Thin lips. A wide jaw and vibrant green eyes hooded by dark lashes. Her light brown skin gleamed under the glow of my storm as she stopped before me, staring up with an eerily blank expression.

I hesitated. Who was this woman? Why wasn't she afraid of me? What the heck was going on?

And who in their right mind wore heels like that in the freaking jungle?

"I hear you call yourself Noxius," she said, her smooth, calm voice tinged with a British accent.

I frowned, curling my lip to show her some of my jagged fangs as I growled low. "And I hear you like murdering innocent doctors who came here to help people."

A smile bowed her lips and she tilted her head to the side, as though she were sizing me up. "Pawns in a greater game. Soon you'll understand."

"I doubt it." I flared my wings, sending out a burst of power that made the air boom and shudder with a clash of thunder.

She didn't even flinch.

Geez, who was this lady? Some kind of android?

"Doctor Khepri Nimr Livingston," Drake piped up like he could read my mind. "We're still running background but it looks like she's a pretty famous Egyptologist. Mmmmm. Looks like she's also an expert on Assyrian and Sumerian civilization.

Chief Inspector of the Egyptian Antiquities Department. Studied in England, had a bunch of fancy titles at the British Museum."

That still didn't tell me what she was doing out here. She obviously hadn't walked here—not in those shoes.

"I must apologize for meeting you like this," she offered as she took another step closer. Behind her, flashes of movement betrayed other people moving in. Only, these weren't pretty women in snazzy heels. There were men—*lots* of them—carrying guns. Those didn't worry me. If I could take a blast from another totem-wielder and live, a measly bullet wasn't going to do much. Surely they knew that. So what was the plan?

As they prowled closer, weapons at the ready and eyes fixed on me, Dr. Livingston went on talking in her smooth, concise tone. "Under the circumstances, we felt there was no other way to arrange a meeting. Now that you are entertaining an audience with the American military, our situation has become increasingly complicated. It was most urgent that we make contact with you as soon as possible."

"Oh yeah? Not to burst your bubble or anything, but I didn't actually come here to chat. Either you hold up your end of the bargain and hand over the rest of your hostages—alive—or I'm gonna start breaking things. I'll start with limbs and then move on to spines and necks."

Her smile vanished in an instant. Every feature went hauntingly blank as she stared at me, blinking slowly. "Very well then," she replied at last. "I presume your female ally is lying in wait? The chosen host of the water-spirit—Oceana, she called herself, I believe. I can only assume you hope to use her as leverage to be certain that we honor our bargain?"

I gave a snort. "Something like that."

A knowing smile sparkled in her eyes, as though she knew I had no intention of ever giving up Oceana. She nodded slightly, sweeping some of her long hair behind her ear before she raised a hand to gesture to her pack of gun-toting goonies. "Then let us begin."

# CHAPTER 12

Dozens of Dr. Livingston's henchmen flanked us, dressed in camo-printed body armor and brandishing the same kinds of large guns with long clips as the gate guards at every military base I'd ever been to. They'd certainly come dressed for a party.

I rolled my neck and shoulders, preparing for the imminent showdown. One of the men approached Dr. Livingston carrying a pair of massive metal shackles. My pulse spiked into overdrive. Heat flushed through my system, tingling along my spine and making every muscle draw tight. Was that how they intended to contain me? With ancient-looking handcuffs?

At first brush, the shackles didn't seem like anything special. Mere metal wasn't a match for my dragon-y awesomeness. And yet, the closer they got, the more my chest began to constrict with unease.

What were those things? Were those *markings* engraved on them? Where had this crazy lady gotten them?

"Oh... oh, ummm." Drake's voice squeaked a little. "Uh, Noxius, it looks like she's got some friends we know."

I froze, staring at the shackles as the man slung them off his shoulder with rattling clank. Each circular cuff was more than big enough to go around my dragon-morphed wrists, and all those strange engravings—geez, just the sight of them made my senses prickle. Were they some kind of language? Or something else?

"Noxius, you gotta get out of there!" Drake panicked in my ear. "I'm looking at a picture of her at some museum event a few years ago—she's standing next to *Gerard Ignatius*!"

Oh. Crap.

A growl slipped past my teeth as I sank backward into a crouch and flared my wings. Reflections of my glowing blue eyes flashed in Dr. Livingston's eyes as she stared me down, completely unfazed by my aggression.

"Save your strength. You came here to help others, sacrificing yourself for their freedom," she observed coolly. "Likewise, your activities in New York have always been spurred by your desire to protect others. You value life. You seek to protect it, even against the nature of your totem's spirit." Her expression tightened, focusing on me with a challenging edge. "That is how I know you won't hurt me, Koji Owens."

The wind rushed out of my lungs all at once. I gaped at her, my vision spotting and heartbeat stalling. She... she knew my real name? But how? Had Ignatius told her? Oh God. What did that mean? Was my dad in danger? Did they know where he was, too? Primal urges swelled in my mind—I had to get out of here. I had to find Dad. I couldn't let anything happen to him.

"Oh, don't look so dismayed. We've known your identity for quite some time. It's in everyone's best interest that you remain anonymous for as long as possible. We wouldn't want other interested parties meddling in our affairs or trying to capture or coerce you, would we?" Her smile reminded me of a spider eyeing a freshly trapped fly. "But if you wish to see the doctors freed, then I suggest you cooperate. I would hate to have your name associated with their deaths. The media has never been kind to you, has it? How quickly do you think they would turn on you again?"

I shuddered, my long tail swishing back and forth as rage like hellfire surged in my veins. My third eye told me she wasn't bluffing. She'd do something to them—even kill them—if I fought back.

The man with the shackles paused, eyeing me apprehensively for a second before he dared to come closer. One good punch and I could've blown his head right off his shoulders.

Part of me really wanted to.

"Can you hear me?" Drake yelled. "You need to get out of there! Right now!"

But I couldn't. I couldn't just turn my back on this now. Whatever this insane woman had to do with Ignatius, I didn't know. And it didn't make any difference.

Saving those people was all that mattered right now. They were facing death because of me, and I couldn't abandon them.

"Just get on with it, would you?" I growled low. "You keep wasting time like this and I'm gonna get bored. Do international terrorists have a review site? You know, like *Yelp*, only for insane criminals who like butchering innocent people so they can try to talk me to death? I'd like to leave a review after this: slow service, overly chatty, bad shoes—stuff like that."

Her eyes narrowed. I must have struck a chord. Oops.

"Take him," she commanded.

The guy with the fancy shackles obliged. I curled my lip, showing him some jagged teeth and following him with my ethereal, glowing eyes as he locked one cuff around my right wrist and then quickly moved around to fix the other end to my left. The thick metal chain that ran between the two heavy cuffs clattered as I straightened, studying them for a second or two— if only so Drake could see them through his micro-cameras. Maybe he could tell me more about them later.

They didn't feel strange or any different than regular metal. I should be able to snap the chain with one firm tug. I was kind of counting on that, actually.

"Now." Dr. Livingston's spiffy heels clicked over the stone as she came closer. She gazed up at me, the corners of her mouth curling into a knowing smile. "Why don't you tell all those meddlesome Americans to withdraw? I'm sure they're very close—listening to every word, correct? They won't find the doctors here. But if they wish to know their location, then they should do as I request. We wouldn't want their efforts to interfere with our meeting."

Standing on her toes, Dr. Livingston plucked the device stuck to the scales right next to my ear. I flinched and hissed, watching as she held it into the moonlight and smirked. "Or perhaps I should just tell them myself." She held the device to her mouth. "If you wish to receive the location of the hostages, then remove your forces from the area. And please, do not take me for a fool. I'll know if you comply or not."

A jolt of panic shot through me as she dropped the device onto the ground between us and crushed it under the toe of her pointy stiletto. I couldn't communicate with Drake now. There was another device on my lower back, somewhat hidden amidst the ridge of spines that ran from my neck to the end of my tail, but I didn't know if he could hear anything with that one. Could he even track my location now?

"These governments." She sighed wearily, as though the whole thing bored her. "They do love their illusions of superiority, don't they?"

Aaand here came the grandstanding evil genius speech. Great. I'd just assumed villains only did that kind of thing in comics and movies, but then Headmaster Ignatius had done it. Now I suspected it really was a thing. Too bad Drake was probably missing this.

"Oh, but you're above all that, right?" I muttered as I rolled my glowing, dragon eyes. "Let me guess—you've found a higher power. A path to greater enlightenment and sovereignty. Oh! And all I have to do is pledge my allegiance to you and I'll get all the wealth, power, and fame I've ever dreamed of. That sound about right?"

Once again, her eyes narrowed dangerously and her lips thinned. That probably should have been my first clue to stop. Double oops.

"Hard pass on all that, by the way. Can we just fast-forward to the part where I refuse, you do a maniacal laugh, we fight, and I roast you and all your cronies like rotisserie chickens?"

From behind her, one of Dr. Livingston's armed henchmen gave a whistling signal. Her smirk returned, curling over her beautiful features and igniting wicked dark fires in the depths of her eyes. "Of course," she purred as she stretched out one of her slender arms to motion some of her men behind her.

They parted like an armored curtain, making way for one extremely unlucky kid who looked like he might be about my age or a little younger. Honestly, it was hard to tell. His filthy, ragged clothing hung off his bony, emaciated frame as he shambled forward. His wide, frightened eyes stared at me through shaggy black bangs caked with grime. He wasn't even wearing shoes.

Then I realized what he was carrying.

Cradled in his trembling hands, a slender, gold-tipped cane made every nerve in my brain fire at once. My pulse hit turbo speed as a blinding mixture of panic, confusion, and uncontrollable terror buzzed through me like electrical current.

Oh God. That was... I mean, it looked like it. But how? Agent Kirkland assured me numerous times that it was safe. How had Dr. Livingston gotten ahold of it? And when?

"The Scepter of Time." The words left my lips in a shaking gasp.

Dr. Livingston's smile widened. "Oh good, I see you remember. Now, hold still. We wouldn't want any mistakes when so many lives hang in the balance, would we?"

Every muscle clenched as I watched the ragged-looking kid stumble toward me, holding that wicked cane out like he wanted Dr. Livingston to take it. She drew back and scowled, snapping angry words at him in a foreign language. Spanish, maybe? I couldn't tell.

Run—I needed to run. Right now.

But what if I did? What would happen to those doctors? Would this crazy woman make it look like it was my fault if they died?

I couldn't run. I was a lot of things—but no one would ever accuse Koji Owens of being a coward. I didn't run from a fight.

Then Dr. Livingston pointed at me. Or rather, at the shackles on my wrists.

The boy blinked between us, face going deathly pale, and then finally took a few more shaking steps closer to me. His knuckles went white as he gripped the cane fiercely, body trembling and breathing frantic. He pointed the golden tip right at the shackles.

Wait—she wasn't going to use the cane herself? Why? Why would she want someone else to…?

Oh. Oh no.

Kirkland was right. Handling that cane—the totem of time—must have a side effect. It had done something to Headmaster Ignatius that had eventually killed him, and she wanted no part of it. That had to be it. It was the only reason I could think why Dr. Livingston would be pushing it off onto someone else. Instead of getting her own hands dirty, Dr. Livingston was using this kid like a puppet.

"Coward." The word slipped past my snarling lips as I showed her my teeth.

Her mask of cold collectedness cracked for an instant. A spark-like wrath flashed in her dark eyes as she glared up at me. "Do not test me, boy. The kur may have chosen you, but I see your unworthiness."

Kur? That was part of the phrase Oceana had taught me to activate my full-dragon form. But what did that have to do with my totem choosing me?

Before I could even open my mouth to ask, the boy carrying my former-evil-headmaster's cane suddenly drove the tip of it into one of the engraved runes on my shackles. The totem scale set into the doorknob-sized round handle on the other end of the staff glowed to life, filling the air with a hum of power and a radiant golden light. I hissed and drew back. The boy with the cane did the same. And that's when I saw it. Something was wrong with his eyes. They were glowing brightly—shining like molten bronze in the dark.

The shackles suddenly constricted, snapping tightly around my wrists. I pitched back, roaring in dismay as the runes began to ignite with that same glowing golden light that seeped from the time totem scale. The light spiraled around the dark metal band, blooming to life in the dark of the jungle night. And every time another symbol lit up, the shackles seemed to get heavier.

I snarled, fighting to stay on my feet as the growing weight dragged my hands closer and closer to the ground.

No. Freaking. Way. This wasn't happening. I would not go down like this!

I bellowed, fighting back and flexing every muscle. I beat my wings as I thrashed, pouring every ounce of power I could muster into breaking free as I pitched and flailed. The sky rippled with crooked fingers of lightning.

Nothing worked.

My knees hit the ground with a terrace-shaking *THUD*.

H-How? How could these shackles contain me? What were they?

I couldn't move. The shackles pinned my arms to the earth. I ... I couldn't break free.

Oh God. What was happening?

The boy yelped and threw down the staff. It clattered across the stone and rolled to a halt at Dr. Livingston's feet. She bent down and wordlessly picked it up, completely ignoring the boy as he cried out frantically in that foreign language. Then he turned and ran. None of Dr. Livingston's armed guards bothered to stop him as he barreled past, bounding down the steps of the terrace and out of sight.

He was gone in two seconds.

And I was left alone with Dr. Livingston and her goon patrol.

"Ah, yes. That's better. On your knees like the servant you are," she purred as she came to stand over me, her bemused grin lit by the shining light that shone from the shackles. "It's useless to resist them. So far, the Bonds of Time have proven to be unbreakable, and totem-wielders far stronger than you have already tried and failed."

A whistle from her crowd of henchman made her pause, glancing back with a nod. She licked her lips like a hungry wolf as she crouched to look me in the eye. "Your friends in the American military have withdrawn. They've abandoned you. So much for heroism."

I turned my face away, refusing to look at her. She thought she had me pinned. Fine, I'd just let her go on thinking that for now. But I seriously doubted these magical chains would be able to hold my full-dragon form. And once I knew the doctors were in the clear, I'd remind her exactly who she was dealing with.

"It's just as well. The power of the kur was never meant to serve any human country or crown. You were not meant to be brought to heel like some glorified dog of war." She traced a finger along one of the spines that bristled from my forearms.

I jerked away from her touch and growled.

I could hear that menacing smile in her voice without having to look at her. "You are far more than you realize. You were hand chosen by them—selected from millions to harbor a spirit of chaos and become a kur yourself. How fortunate you are."

"I-I don't know what you're talking about," I rumbled through clenched teeth.

Her smile dimmed. "I know. Dear Fyurei told you both very little, didn't she? The silly girl explained only the very basic usage of your powers, nothing about what you truly are or what your presence means for the human world. She still aspires to defy her own destiny. Such a waste." Her tone took on a curious edge. "Tell me, do you know where she is? All alone without her darling father to guide her. Such a shame."

Fyurei? She was... she was talking about Madeline.

Groaning and shaking against the pull of the chains, I dared to look at the mad doctor. My nose wrinkled. My body thrummed with power as I pulled against those bonds with all my strength. They didn't move a single inch. "I'd rather die than tell you anything."

She chuckled softly. "Don't worry, Koji. Your death won't be necessary." She leaned in a little closer. "Not yet."

# CHAPTER 13

O kay, so things were not going as planned. Again. Nowhere in all those carefully coordinated Navy SEAL briefings was I supposed to be taken prisoner by an insane archeologist doctor woman, bound in magical shackles, and abandoned by the military to face certain doom alone.

But here we were.

My summer vacation had just reached a whole new level of suck.

And Livingston was still performing her classic supervillain monologue.

"Did you really think this power was a gift? A stroke of generosity from the universe for you to use as you please?" The doctor shook her head with another soft laugh. "Don't be juvenile. The totem scales are not some child's fairy tale or a radioactive insect. The spirit that lies ensnared within each scale is, in many ways, the very essence of inevitability—of destiny itself. It is one of the spirits of chaos sent into our world with a singular purpose: To make a path."

A path? Good grief, what in the world was she talking about? Nothing she said made sense. Madeline hadn't said anything about spirits or paths. But I didn't feel my third eye tingling—Dr. Livingston wasn't making this up on the spot. Whatever nonsense she was raving about was true.

She stepped back a few paces, putting more distance between us as she held the cane up to consider it in the flashing light of my storm overhead. I bit down hard, trying to will some of my power to lash out at her. One bolt of lightning—anything! But the storm overhead rumbled indifferently. Oh no. I... I couldn't control it.

"You are not a hero, Noxius." Dr. Livingston spat the name as though it were something disgusting. "You are a host. Your human soul is a temporary contamination to the spirit that now inhabits you. And every time you call upon him, every time you become Noxius and use his power, a little bit more of your spirit is eaten away—replaced with his. Slowly, you're becoming something far better: you're becoming *him*."

My breath caught. She wasn't lying about that, either. My totem was... *devouring* my soul? How was that even possible?

"Surely by now you've noticed it?" she continued, seeming to enjoy my complete horror. "Little by little, the strength of your will is crumbling, being overtaken by his. Soon, you won't be able to control him any longer. Your every thought will become his—regardless of what form you take. That is why you must come with us now. Only we can help you make this transition. We will help you embrace your destiny, Koji. Your sacrifice will be the first step toward a better world."

I was still hung up on the whole "your totem is eating your soul" thing to register anything else. Was that why I'd lost it during the training exercise in Nevada? Had that been the spirit of chaos inside my totem taking control?

I clenched my fists harder and shook those thoughts away. Now wasn't the time. I had to get out of here. Now.

Steeling my nerve, I glared back at her. No way was I going to let her see how that speech had rattled me. "You said if the military backed off, you'd let the hostages go. You gonna keep your word, or stand there and try to preach me to death?" I grunted as I gave another violent thrash against the shackles.

They still didn't budge.

Dr. Livingston gave a resigned, almost annoyed sigh and didn't answer. Turning, she slowly stalked a few more paces away before turning to hold the cane up—

—and drove the golden tip against the stone slab of the terrace beneath us. A flash of golden light strobed in the night, making the shackles on my wrist vibrate strangely.

Then it hit me.

Crippling, searing pain shot through my body. Every muscle contracted at once. My spine curled and my eyes felt like they might pop out of their sockets. I couldn't think. I couldn't move. My mouth flew open, but nothing would come out. I couldn't even scream.

The pain vanished as suddenly as it hit, leaving me in a trembling heap on the ground as I gasped and wheezed for breath. Oh my God. What the heck had she done to me?

Shakily, I lifted my head to glare at her.

Dr. Livingston sneered down at me, the wind snatching at her hair as her eyes glowed with that eerie golden light. "Normally, I would utilize a surrogate for such a thing. But I must say, watching you writhe at my command is too satisfying a prospect to resist. Shall we go again?"

I opened my mouth, intending to make another snappy retort. Something about her cane not matching her shoes. Before I could muster the words, she rammed the cane down again.

Another flash of light sent a fresh wave of agony scorching through me, resonating from the shackles on my wrists. It stole my breath and I reeled, flopping onto my side while my whole body shook out of control. My wings lay sprawled on the cold stone, limp and useless. I managed a garbled, frantic scream as every nerve in my brain seemed to fire at once.

When it passed, all I could do was lie there as my muscles spasmed and shivered. My vision tunneled in and out. Was she going to torture me to death?

No. Not if I could help it. I still had one ace in the hole. I just hoped the doctors were already safe because I couldn't put this off any longer.

Wheezing, I pushed myself back onto my hands and knees and drew my wings in close. Then I shot her one more, vengeful snarl. She was about to seriously regret ever meeting me.

Desperate anger kindled in my chest as I flicked one last, desperate look down to the totem scale glowing on my wrist, nearly covered by the shackles. Don't fail me now.

"I... offer my soul... to the power of the kur."

The words, now that I knew their meaning, were like poison on my tongue. She was right. Using my totem was killing me. Or devouring my soul, rather. Same thing, right?

Power and energy roared through my veins, surging through every part of me like a wildfire in my blood. Just a few more seconds. Then it would be over.

Another surge of crushing, paralyzing pain shot through me so suddenly, I couldn't even tell if it was Dr. Livingston using the scepter or something else.

It didn't matter. My heart stopped with a jolt. The cold stone pressed against my skin as I dropped limply to the ground. And everything went dark.

Pitch black darkness—cold and complete. A tingle of discomfort worried my chest and the trickle of something warm and wet oozed down the side of my face. Blood?

Slowly, my eyes focused. I blinked, staring around the inside of a car lit only by the pale haze of moonlight. The sterling glow bled through the shattered rear passenger window beside me, sparkling over the jagged edges of the splintered glass.

Geez. Why did that look so familiar? And why did my jaw hurt so much? Freezing—why did it feel like I was freezing? It was summer still, wasn't it?

Wait a second… had I been here before?

My halting, frantic breaths hung in the air like puffs of white fog as I squinted through the hole in the fractured window. Up a steep white snowdrift, the dark silhouette of a bridge stood out against a clear night sky.

That looked familiar too. But why?

Something frigid touched my foot and I jerked, ignoring the intensifying pain along my jaw as I looked down. Water—there was water inside the car!

It rose higher by the second, making my legs go numb as I kicked and thrashed. But I couldn't get out. I was strapped into a weird seat.

Oh God. It looked like a car seat. And my arms and legs looked way too short, as though I'd been shrunk. The more I looked around, the faster my heart pounded.

This was… this was *that* night. The crash. When Mom…

I dove against the straps of my seat, reaching desperately toward the front seat where a slender female figure slumped over the steering wheel. With the front of our car nearly submerged where it had crashed right against the steep, snowbound riverbank, every second brought more of the icy water pouring in through the smashed windshield. Mom's long black hair swirled in the rising inky current and her arms hung limply at her sides.

"MOM!" The voice that tore out of my throat sounded tiny—like the frantic wail of a little kid. I screamed and pitched, managing to pry one of my arms free of the straps. But my hands were too little to work the clasp to get out of my seat. I couldn't get free.

"Mom!" I cried out to her again. "Mom, wake up! Please! Answer me!"

My tears were warm against my cheeks. They blurred my vision as I fought for every breath.

Meanwhile, the cold water kept rushing in. It rose higher, submerging the base of my seat and making my chest seize with pain. Cold—too cold. I couldn't stand it. It hurt.

So, I screamed. I screamed until my throat was raw.

My teeth chattered as I lost feeling in my legs. My body trembled and shivered out of control, making my hands even clumsier as I clawed at the buckle between my legs.

It was no use.

The water kept rising, numbing my waist, then my chest. I couldn't take it much longer. Everything grew hazy as my head lolled against my chest. My eyes fluttered. My heartbeat slowed. Why did I feel so tired? Maybe if I just slept, if I let the exhaustion take me away, all this awfulness would go away.

Maybe it was just a bad dream.

"*Koji.*" The sweet, soft voice called so quietly I barely heard it over the constant rush of water still filling the inside of our car. "*My sweet boy. It's okay. Don't be scared.*"

I... I wanted to look up. I wanted to see my mom's face. I needed to. Just one more time, I wanted to see her smile crinkle the corners of her soft, dark eyes. I wanted to feel the press of her lips against my cheek. I wanted to remember her smell and the feel of her hand holding mine.

But the cold—it hurt too much. I couldn't keep my eyes open anymore. I was fading. Everything was slipping away into a cold, final silence.

And the only sound left was the softest of whispers: the sound of her voice.

"*You're going to be okay. Mommy loves you.*"

Something cracked against the side of my head, scrambling my brain and knocking me into a semi-conscious delirium that made my vision spot and slowly come back into focus. I blinked hard, swallowing against the stinging heat in my throat that felt like I'd swallowed a mouthful of crushed glass. The noise of my storm had fallen silent and streams of moonlight bled through the dissolving clouds. I glared into the scowling face of a man in black fatigues. One of Dr. Livingston's gun-toting henchmen.

Great. This again.

He brandished the butt of his rifle like he was going to hit me again.

I bared my teeth and gave a deep, thundering growl as I shifted. If he tried that again, I'd make him eat that gun. Literally. I'd ram it right down his throat and—

I couldn't move my legs or wings. They'd been tied with thick metal cables, pinned in place like I was a piece of cargo being prepped for transport. Not good.

"Ah, there you are. Welcome back. Perhaps I should have mentioned before," Dr. Livingston called in a bemused, almost teasing tone. "The Bonds of Time will not allow you to utilize your full-kur transformation. My apologies."

Yeah. She could take that fake apology and shove it.

"Now, lie still. As expected, it seems your crime-fighting counterpart won't be joining us. No doubt you warned her off. Or your military friends are insisting she stay out of it." Dr. Livingston gave a flourish with her cane, gesturing for the goon brandishing his gun in my face to back away. "No matter. She will submit to us sooner or later. And unlike you, she lacks the confidence to act on her own."

I groaned as I tried to flex against my bonds. I could snap a few measly metal cables, right? I'd broken tougher things than that. But the more I tried to move, the harder it was to breathe. Everything hurt. My joints were on fire. My bones ached and I couldn't stop shaking. My head pounded and my muscles twitched with lingering spasms of pain.

"She'll be much easier to lure in now, I'm sure, now that we have you. Fyurei, as well." Dr. Livingston's smug laugh echoed in the night.

I should've just kept quiet. Now wasn't the time to mouth off. If she hit me with that totem-torture again, I wasn't sure I could take it. But that laugh—it hit a nerve in my medium-well-cooked brain.

"The only... th-thing you h-have... is... awful taste in f-footwear."

Agony exploded through my brain again. I let out a garbled cry as everything went gray. My arms and legs went numb as a broken, ragged, desperate sob tore from my throat.

This was it. The end. It had to be. I couldn't... I couldn't survive it again. Kill me—why didn't she just freaking kill me?

Dad... I wanted my dad. I wanted him to help me, to save me from this.

The swell of scorching pain stopped so suddenly, I let out another sharp noise of relief as my whole body went slack. I lay, limp and helpless on the cool stone, with my brain still swerving somewhere between consciousness and death.

The movement of a large dark shape eclipsed the shafts of silvery moonlight. Then a flash of brilliant blue light broke over the jungle ruins an instant before I heard another piercing cry. A roar of challenge.

I knew that sound.

She appeared like a blue-scaled angel, materializing from the stormy skies with her scales shining like chips of pearlescent sea glass and her slender wings flapping gracefully. Her golden eyes glowed with wrath as she snarled down at Dr. Livingston and her collection of armed henchmen.

She let out another shriek of fury and spread her arms wide, summoning a burst of power that bloomed in the night like the rising of a neon blue sun. Behind her, the dark shapes of aircraft streaked by. A-10s—two of them zoomed overhead with an earth-shaking roar that kindled a fiery vengeance in my blood.

"O-Oceana," I breathed her name hoarsely. She'd come for me. And she'd brought the freaking cavalry.

# CHAPTER 14

I had no idea how she'd gotten here, who tipped her off that I was officially in over my head, or how she'd even found me in this godforsaken jungle. And right then, I didn't care. Oceana was here.

The report of gunfire popped and barked all around me, mingling with the *whump-whump-whump-whump* of helicopters that seemed to come from all directions at once. Then came the deep growling *brrrrrrrrrrtt* of A-10s hammering the ground with more artillery as they roared past. Every second drove my pulse faster and faster as panic whipped my mind into a frenzy. Setting my jaw against the splintering, piercing pain, I lifted my head to search the sky until I saw the gleaming shape of Oceana still hovering just above the ruins. My heart lurched, half with hope and half with sheer desperation. Free—she had to help me get free—right now!

She didn't know that Dr. Livingston had the scepter. If she used it to open a portal and summon another giant monster, it would probably take both of us to bring it down.

But Oceana didn't look my way. Her molten gaze stayed focused on the groups of black-clad terrorists still firing at her as they shuffled from one hiding place to another. The glowing power of her element filled the air with the smell of sea salt as she snapped two long tendrils of water like the tongues of a bull whip. They crashed over the ruins, smashing rocks and boulders

aside, and dragged Dr. Livingston's henchmen out of their hiding spots two and three at a time.

Well, that is, until the good doctor strode out into the open
with the scepter held high. The golden tip glowed like a star, just
like it had when Headmaster Ignatius used it to open those portals before. This was about to get extra nasty.

"You dare to toy with me, little girl?" Dr. Livingston snickered, her expression crazed as she gripped the scepter with both
hands and started to draw out the shape of a circle of golden
light in the air.

Oh no. Here we go again.

"Oceana!" I wheezed hoarsely, gritting my teeth against the
pain as I tried to flex against the cords that bound me up like a
Christmas tree about to be tied to the roof of some family's
minivan. Nothing cool at all about that, by the way.

Oceana hesitated, but only for a single second. Then her
eyes narrowed. Her lips drew back into a feral snarl of pure
rage. Her hands snapped into fists and her whips of water vanished instantly into mist.

Another flash of blinding white-blue light lit up the dark
like a nuclear blast. I cringed away, unable to shield my eyes,
until it faded. Squinting and blinking through the spots that
danced in my vision, my jaw dropped as the shape of a gracefully massive blue and silver dragon spread its wings to the night
sky. Its long, slender neck arched and its webbed paws flexed,
talons glinting like huge, curled chips of diamond. The translu-
cent fins that ran down its spine flared as it hissed and rose up,
letting out a booming cry that sent the rest of Dr. Livingston's
goonies running like a bunch of scared jackrabbits.

Holy. Crap.

Oceana had gone full dragon.

She dove toward the earth and landed with a boom that sent
me bouncing over the stone.

Dr. Livingston wasn't laughing anymore. She drew back,
gaze cutting to me with a look of defiant venom. "Touch me and

I end him," she screamed, thrusting the point of the scepter in my direction. "You stupid little child—you love him, don't you? So what would you do for love? Bargain for his life, perhaps? Surrender now and I'll consider sparing him!"

I cringed, preparing for the worst. Maybe she'd fry me and end it right there. Or maybe she'd drag it out, just so Oceana had to listen to me scream. I shut my eyes. Whatever happened, I didn't want to see it coming.

A sudden, sharp cry made my eyes fly open again just in time to see Dr. Livingston dangling from Oceana's jaws. My dragoness ally had snapped her up, cane and all, and now she tossed her back against the earth with a gory *SMACK*.

I winced. That had to hurt.

The cane clattered out of her grasp, rolling across the stone until it stopped only a few feet away from me.

Dr. Livingston started to crawl toward it, her movements jerky and desperate. Our gazes locked, and for a fleeting moment, I got a clear look past that shattered veneer of collected calm into the true frenzy boiling underneath. She really was out of her freaking mind.

Baring her teeth as blood oozed from the corners of her mouth, she tried to drag her injured body over the ground. Her hand stretched out, fingers spread to grab the cane. Her fingertips brushed it.

A giant dragon foot mashed down on top of her, pinning her to the ground like a cat with a captured mouse. Oceana lowered her head slowly, massive nostrils puffing dragon breaths over the mad doctor's face. Oceana's voice boomed in a monstrously deep tone, echoing over the ruins like a wrathful draconic god.

"*I... do not... negotiate.*"

It didn't take long for the SEALs to show up and take Dr. Livingston and the few of her hired humans that had survived into custody. Perfect timing, too. As soon as they had that crazy doctor in cuffs and held at gunpoint, Oceana's four minutes were up. Her full dragon form burst in a shower of silvery light, leaving her standing before me in the more humanoid form I was used to seeing.

Boy, was she a sight for sore eyes—literally. My eyes felt like two rubbery, overcooked hardboiled eggs in my skull as I lay on my side, blinking owlishly up at her.

Her legs wobbled as she walked close enough to envelop us in her gleaming wings. She began running her hands down my side until she got to some of the cables tied around me. Her expression crinkled, straining with exhaustion as she wrapped her hand around them. She didn't have much time left. After going full-dragon, she only had a few minutes in her half-dragon form before her power disappeared completely, and it wouldn't come back for a full day after that. But instead of running to hide, she stayed. Oceana broke my bonds one by one like someone popping the tags off a new piece of clothing. Then she got to my wrists... and the shackles.

Those wouldn't be coming off so easily.

"Y-you gotta get out of here," I managed in a weak, cracking voice. "You'll c-change back soon."

"Hush," she scolded. "I'm not leaving you here like this."

"But—"

She shot me a silencing glare that might've singed my eyebrows clean off my face.

I snapped my mouth shut.

Glaring down at the shackles again, her brow crinkled as she ran a hand over them. "I-I... I don't know if this will work. But I might be able to break them open with ice."

Ice? Since when could she use a power like that? "B-been holding that one out on m-me, eh?"

Her lips thinned. "Well, it's sort of... new. I think my powers are growing."

My heart sank, seeming to crush in on itself like a soda can under someone's foot at those words. Her powers were growing and she didn't know why. But now I did. It was because her totem's power was growing, devouring more and more of her. Crap, how was I supposed to tell her that?

The moonlight caught on some of the shining aquamarine scales along her cheek as her jaw stiffened. Soft blue light radiated from beneath her hand, lasting for a second or two before she drew back with a frantic huff. She was pushing it now. She had minutes, maybe seconds left before her power was gone.

But it was just enough.

Ice burst from the locks on the shackles, shattering the metal with a *crack*. The glowing runes on the shackles went dark. They dropped off my wrists and fell slack on the stone with a clatter. I let out a weak, whimpering breath.

I was... free.

The places beneath where the shackles had been were raw, burned, and bleeding—but it wasn't my blood. It couldn't be. It was *gold*.

Oceana and I looked up at the same time, staring at one another wordlessly. I knew we had to be thinking the same thing. What the heck was that? Was it because of the shackles? Or because of what Dr. Livingston had done to me with the scepter? Or... something else?

Whatever the case, we couldn't talk about it now. Not here. And not when her de-transformation put her power at risk.

Helicopters buzzed overhead, touching down or dropping rope ladders to deposit more troops on the ground. They searched the ruins with flashlights while the choppers panned massive beams of light around for any more of Dr. Livingston's men that might still be hiding. SEALs were locking down the last of the survivors and prepping them for transport.

We had to get out of here, find some place out of sight.

"Can you stand?" she asked, her tone softer.

"Yeah." I set my jaw and prepared to try. I got about five feet before my legs buckled and I dropped back to my knees. Every muscle ached, and I groaned.

Oceana seized my hand and guided my arm over one of her shoulders, hauling me to my feet so I could stagger along beside her out of the open and into the cover of the jungle. We barely made it past the tree line before my legs gave out again, nearly sending us both sprawling down a steep hillside. That was as far as I could manage, and she wasn't going to be able to carry me in about thirty seconds. So we found a place amidst the ferns and boulders, at the base of a big tree, to collapse into a big scaly heap.

With so many soldiers still running around, I knew it wasn't good enough. Just one glimpse of her transformation would sever her bond with her totem. And we couldn't risk that.

I wrapped my arms around her, dragging her down against my chest and enveloping us both inside my leathery wings. She tensed, her hands on my chest like she might try to push away. So I shut my eyes tightly and pushed my forehead against hers. "It's okay," I groaned, my teeth still clenched against the lingering pain that made every breath seize in my chest. "I... w-won't peek."

"Koji." She relaxed and wrapped her arms around my neck, hugging me tightly. As she shifted back, her body shrank in my embrace, becoming smaller, softer, and lighter. Her scales melted away, leaving the skin that brushed mine soft and smooth.

"You are the biggest idiot in the entire world, Koji Owens." Her human voice trembled as she put her hands on my scaly cheeks. "I was so worried. What if I'd been too late? What if they'd taken you away? Or killed you? How dare you try to do something like this without me!"

My mouth twitched as I fought back a smile. Opening my eyes, I relaxed against the trunk of the tree and let my arms fall limply back at my sides. My wings flopped uselessly against the soft, damp earth, stirring up leaves. "Th-they couldn't kill me. I'm s-super tough."

"No, you're super stubborn. Not even close to the same thing," she fumed quietly.

"D-Debatable."

She huffed and went on scolding me about being reckless and sending her weird, vague text messages. But I could barely hear it. A faint, high-pitching ringing steadily began to drown out everything else. Darkness closed in. And whether it was from exhaustion, pain, or a side effect of using my totem for this long, I couldn't shake it off.

I was fading. Slipping away.

I could barely make out Claire's frantic voice screaming my name as my head dropped to my chest, my gaze landing on one of my arms draped at my side. There, on my wrist, the single white scale that granted me all this incredible power looked a little dimmer than usual. Was it fading? Going dark?

Or was this the end?

# CHAPTER 15

Okay, okay. So I wasn't dead. Melodramatic, I know. Sorry.

I startled awake to a jolt of hot, stinging discomfort in one of my legs. My eyes flew open and everything snapped into focus as I glared at Agent Kirkland. Stooped over my monstrous half-dragon form, he drew back the taser he'd just used to zap my leg. Seriously? Tasing me? Not cool.

"He's back," Kirkland panted, glancing sideways at Claire.

She sat, huddled against my side with her beautiful sea-green eyes wide and haunted. Tears glistened on her flushed cheeks as she gripped one of my giant scaly hands.

"I'd punch you for that," I slurred angrily, still weaving in and out of consciousness. "But one hit and I'd knock your head clean off your shoulders."

Agent Kirkland didn't respond. Grabbing a big, chunky radio from his belt he started talking as his eyes scanned the jungle around us. "Misty-74, this is asset ground team. I've got him. Ready for extraction."

"Copy that," a voice replied.

Shrugging out of a heavy black tactical jacket, Agent Kirkland draped it around Claire's shoulders and carefully guided her away from me while I staggered to my feet. Good grief—she wasn't even dressed. With a dainty matching set of pink silk pajama shorts and tank top, it looked like she'd probably gotten straight out of bed to come to my rescue. The only thing she wore that was kinda-sorta-maybe suitable for being outside in the middle of nowhere in a dark jungle were her boots. Except, er, they were snow boots.

She eyed Kirkland distrustfully, edging away from him with her mouth pressed into a thin frown. I knew that getting mixed up with the FBI or military was the last thing in the world she wanted. So coming here now, getting involved, revealing her identity to these people—well, that was a pretty good indication of how much she didn't want me to die.

She'd exposed her most precious secret to save me.

Dang. I really owed her now.

No one said much as we waited on our extraction. A few guys from the SEAL team arrived and shepherded us to a nearby helicopter, and in a matter of minutes, we were landing on the deck of the warship in the middle of the ocean. I didn't see any evidence of Dr. Livingston or her men, and the more I thought about it, the more anger kindled to life deep in my chest.

Anger at Agent Kirkland and the rest of the stupid FBI.

This—all of this—was *their* fault.

I waited, biting down fiercely on all the things I wanted to say, until I'd been left alone in a small room aboard the warship to change back. My body shuddered as my power withdrew, soaked back into the totem scale strapped to my arm. Every scale that melted away, every second that bound my elemental power back into that bracelet, sent a fresh flood of agony through me. The deep wounds on my wrists looked like someone had slashed my skin open with a dull knife. They bled, dribbling crimson droplets down my hands to drip on the floor. Thankfully, my blood looked normal again. A small relief.

Very, *very* small.

I snatched the door open and cocked my fist, taking a wild swing at Agent Kirkland as soon as I saw him lurking outside.

He ducked just in time and my punch sailed through the air, sending me stumbling.

"YOU!" I yelled as I staggered and prepared to take another swing.

He blocked my blow and sidestepped, whipping me around into a restraining hold with my arms pinned at my back. "Koji, you need to take a few deep breaths," he warned in a low, unsettlingly calm tone.

"You did this!" I wheezed as I struggled, tears welling in my eyes. "It's your fault! You knew the scepter was gone! You knew someone stole it! And you didn't tell me!"

A tinge of frustration sharpened his voice. "Breathe, boy."

"I-I almost died because of you," I panted hoarsely. Shutting my eyes, my chest constricted with every ragged breath I took. I couldn't keep this up. My head was already spinning. "And now Oceana's caught up in this, too. And it's all your freaking fault! You knew you were sending me in there with the risk that they'd use that scepter against me. That's why you wanted me involved!"

"Koji, listen to me. I had no idea the artifact had been stolen," Agent Kirkland insisted.

"Bull—"

"Mr. Owens, I suggest you get control of yourself right now," he spoke loudly over me. "As soon as she produced it, word was sent to verify if it was a duplicate. We realized the one we had in our possession was a fake—a well-crafted forgery. Someone switched them out without us noticing. We don't even know when it happened."

Crap. He was telling the truth. Stupid third eye.

I bowed my head, my chin trembling.

"But we have the real one back in our custody now. And that's thanks to you and Oceana. You prevented what could have been a deadly, large-scale disaster if Dr. Livingston had used it in another major city," he continued, gradually easing his hold on me now that I'd stopped fighting back. "I know this doesn't feel like a victory, but it is. We have her and the artifact now. This could lead to real answers."

"What... what about the doctors?"

He hesitated, and then released his hold altogether. "I'm afraid only two of them were found alive. They're in critical condition. But that wasn't your fault, Koji. Dr. Livingston seemed to know a great deal about our plans. She was one step ahead of us from the onset. And, based on what we found during the rescue, it looks like many of hostages were used experimentally. She never had any intention of setting them free."

My heart gave a hard, wrenching thump. "You mean... she used the scepter on them?"

"I really can't say." He put a hand on my shoulder, slowly turning me to face him. "The two survivors will be interviewed as soon as they're able. We should know more then. For now, let's just take our victories where we can and be more cautious in the future." He cleared his throat, straightening a little. "I think now would be a good time to move you, Drake, and your parents into protective custody. Oceana and her family as well."

I shook my head and jerked away. "No. You do that, and my dad will know. He'll know about everything!"

Agent Kirkland studied me, his light blue eyes searching my face as though he were trying to gauge whether or not he could talk me into changing my mind. No way. Not gonna happen.

"Koji, the situation has changed. I think maybe it's time for him to know."

"NO!" I yelled again. "I get to decide that, okay? *Me!* That was our deal. You don't tell him anything, got it? I already ruined his life once. I'm not doing it again! Not like this!"

He didn't reply. He didn't have to. I could read the disapproval on his face without him having to tell me how stupid, childish, and reckless I was being.

It didn't matter. This was my call—not his. Dad was going to figure all this out sooner or later. And it would inevitably rip what was left of our family apart. He might even hate me for it. I'd done a lot of lying, sneaking around, and risking my life behind his back. It was too much to forgive. I mean, how could he ever trust me again after all that?

He wouldn't.

"Very well," Kirkland replied at last. He motioned down the hall behind me. "You need to go to the infirmary before we debrief you and return you to your *vacation*. I will have Agent Carrie arrange an alibi for your injuries."

My shoulders sagged. Deep inside, a creeping sense of disappointment and fear seeped into the foundation of my soul. I sort of wished he had fought me harder on it. My resolve wasn't exactly ironclad. I knew this was a mistake. Kirkland was right—it was time to come clean.

I just wasn't ready.

I barely had a relationship with Dad now, and crushing what remained of it was too much. It put a hard knot in my throat and made my whole face screw up just thinking about it. If Dad disowned me over this, or quit trusting me, or started treating me like a stranger—I didn't know if I could take it.

Without him, I'd be alone.

I'd basically be an orphan.

Claire sat next to me in the briefing room as the leader of the SEAL team went over the details of our mission. He described what had happened, what had gone wrong, and what we should be mindful of on future missions—things that I couldn't bring myself to listen to right then. I had a pretty freaking good idea what went wrong. Besides, none of what he said had anything to do with the hostages, which was the only part I cared to hear. I guess they weren't going to talk about that until they had finished collecting all the info they could.

When the meeting was over and the SEAL guys filed out, Claire, Kirkland, and I were left alone in the briefing room. Awkward didn't even begin to describe it. The guilt souring in my gut made me want to vomit. I'd never meant for her to get caught up in this. It was my mess—my problem—not hers.

I just didn't know how to even begin telling her that.

"Miss Faust, we've made arrangements to take you back home. You may rest assured that we will be taking full precautions to ensure your identity as Oceana remains classified." Kirkland stood first and started for the door. "It seems there is a strong possibility that there are more than a few traitors within our organization."

I snorted. "Gee, ya think? Someone stole the Scepter of Time right out from under your nose and you didn't even know it."

His pale eyes narrowed dangerously, like he didn't appreciate me reminding him of that. "In light of that, I have made the executive decision not to share your identity beyond the immediate team. Agent Carrie Bates and I are the only ones with that information. Not even the SEALs involved know the full extent of the details surrounding the artifacts you wield. I intend to keep it that way."

"What about my parents?" Claire's voice sounded small and afraid as she got up to follow him. She'd tucked herself into Kirkland's big coat like a turtle hiding in a shell, only her head poking out to gaze up at him with a fretful expression.

"As with Mr. Owens, the decision about telling them is entirely up to you." He sighed as he reached into the pocket of his black blazer and pulled out another sleek, thin cellphone like the ones Drake and I had. Our secret, untraceable line. He held it out to her with a softer, more earnest expression. "This is how we can contact you and how you can reach us if you need anything. It's a highly secured line. No one can trace it."

Claire's hand shook as she reached out to take it. "Thank you."

"Mr. Owens, I'll be back to collect you in a few minutes," Agent Kirkland added as he held the door open and guided her from the room.

She gave me one last terrified look before stepping into the hall after him.

I didn't even say goodbye. I should've said something—anything—to let her know she'd be okay. Kirkland would look out for her. Her parents wouldn't find out unless she wanted them to. Her identity was safe.

But she was gone and it was too late.

The door snapped shut. Crushing silence closed in around me, letting loose all the thoughts and worries that had been forced to wait while I focused on other things.

All the stuff Dr. Livingston had said buzzed through my brain like a swarm of angry hornets. My totem wasn't a blessing. It wasn't my ticket to superhero status. It was more like... a terrible, horrible, twisted, double-edged curse. I needed my totem's power now more than ever to keep the people I loved safe, but that same power was killing me—eating me alive from the inside out. A little piece of my soul was the price of their safety every time I used it.

Burying my face in my hands, I tried to keep breathing against the panic clenching at my lungs. I couldn't lose it. Not now. I had to keep it together. Claire didn't know what the totems were doing to us. I still had to tell her. Not now, obviously. Once things had cooled off, I'd find her, apologize for dragging her into my mess and outing her secret identity, and find some way to tell her.

I just had to hang on until then.

Looking at the bandages wrapped around my wrists, a weak laugh broke past my lips. I'd needed quite a few stitches and was definitely going to have some nasty scars. How was I going to explain this to Dad? Hopefully Agent Carrie could come up with something good, because my skills at deception when it came to my dad were pretty lousy. Frankly, it was a miracle he hadn't already figured out I was Noxius.

Out of nowhere, realization hit me like a punch to the throat. I knew someone else who had marks on their wrists exactly like the ones I was probably going to have.

Madeline.

I'd noticed them in passing during art class last year. She had identical, albeit much more faded scars on her wrists in the same place. At the time, I hadn't thought much of them. We hadn't been close enough for me to ask about something that personal. But now...

My stomach dropped and I sucked in a sharp gasp as I sat back in my seat. Did that mean Dr. Livingston had tortured her, too? How many times? And why? To force her to use her powers? Or something worse?

Those thoughts set rage like cinders sizzling over my tongue. Dr. Livingston had to pay for that—she *would* pay. Even if I had to make sure of it myself.

# CHAPTER 16

Drake was freaking out when I arrived back in the FBI suite aboard our luxury cruise ship. He rushed me as soon as I walked in, face blanched and eyes wide and haunted as he looked me over in horror.

"Koji! Are you all right? What the heck happened? They won't tell me anything!" He flashed Kirkland a scorching glare. "After she stomped my camera all I got was a grainy video feed from your tail cam and a GPS location."

"I'm fine," I lied, hoping the exhaustion in my voice would keep him from being able to tell. I mean, sooner or later he'd catch on. But maybe I could buy myself a few hours of sleep before I had to rehash everything for him.

Heh. Yeah, right. Like he'd ever let me off that easy.

Drake gave an exaggerated eye roll. "*Fine*? Are you kidding me? Have you even seen yourself? You look like someone tried to beat you to death."

Fair enough. I hadn't seen my reflection, but I didn't need to. No doubt I had more bruises than an old banana. There were already deep purple marks marking my skin where the cords had tied me down. One side of my jaw was tender to the touch, so I probably had a nice shiner forming there. I didn't even know where that one had come from. The guy boxing me in the face with the butt of his gun, maybe? Usually trivial stuff like that didn't leave marks thanks to my extra-tough dragon skin. But maybe the shackles had weakened me.

Or tonight I was just on the world's most epic unlucky streak.

"That's the story we intend to sell to your parents," Agent Carrie said as she came over to hand me an ice pack for my face. "Considering your record, its believable to say you stuck up for Drake in an altercation at the ship's video game lounge."

I groaned at the thought. This had another long-winded Dad speech about actions, consequences, and responsibility written all over it. "Can we at least say I won this time?"

Agent Carrie laughed. "Of course. But please, try to keep the rest of your injuries covered as much as you can. Long sleeves."

"And if his dad wants to press charges?" Drake arched a brow.

I sighed and turned away, ready to leave all this FBI crap behind me for the rest of my natural life. But no way that was going to happen. "He won't. I'll talk him down. It's fine. Let's just go."

Drake didn't argue, and no one tried to stop me as I trudged from the room and started the long trek back down to our level of the ship. Neither Drake nor I said a word as we walked the halls. It was almost four in the morning, so the only people roaming the ship were staff members, early risers on their way to one of the fitness clubs for sunrise yoga, and a few hardcore partiers who'd probably spent the night in one of the many lavish clubs.

I probably should have showered. I stank of sweat and I was covered in dirt and dried blood. All I could think about was sleep, though. The doctors at the infirmary on the warship had given me a little bottle of painkillers for the injuries on my arms. I gulped down one of them before kicking off my sneakers and crawling under the blankets. I curled into a ball under the fluffy down comforter. Thanks to the ice pack, half my face was pleasantly numb already. I was counting on the meds to take care of the rest.

"Hey, uh, Koji?" Drake was standing right next to my bed.

I popped an eye open to stare drowsily up at him. "What?"

His mouth scrunched. Running a hand through his shaggy surfer hair, he looked away with his brow pinched in a scowl. "I... I just think you should know... I was the one who called Claire, not the FBI."

I opened my other eye. "*You* called her? Wait, how did you even know she was Oceana?"

He gave a shrug. "You texted her. I mean, I knew you guys had to be keeping in touch somehow. And after we lost contact, everything started spiraling. They found all those doctors dead. I'm sorry. I hacked your phone account and looked at all your messages. Wasn't hard to figure out which one she was. Especially after that last message you sent. Pretty sure even the idiots at the FBI could've figured that one out. Good thing I encrypted your data, right?"

It was hard not to be impressed. Drake's skill of seeing stuff he wasn't supposed to never ceased to amaze me. Still. He'd contacted Claire—prompted her to get involved. I couldn't just let that one slide.

"She's terrified, you know," I grumbled, my hands instinctively drawing into fists under the blankets. "Her life's already complicated enough and you gave away her secret."

He hung his head a little. "I know. I really am sorry. I was just, you know, worried. I didn't know what was gonna happen to you. And I know we joke about who'll tell your dad if something goes wrong, but Koji, you're like my only friend in the entire world, you know?"

I let out a deep exhale and relaxed. "It's okay, Drake. Really. It sucks that Kirkland and the others know who she is now, but if you hadn't called her, then—" My voice caught. I shut my eyes and tried to keep my tone steady, indifferent, and like I wasn't about to have a full-on mental breakdown. "It's just, you know, probably a good thing you called her."

His bed creaked as he sat down and started shucking off his shoes, tossing them one at a time into the far corner of the room. "I've got a lot of work to do when we get back. I don't think the FBI realizes yet what all this suggests."

He was right about that.

"We're talking enemy infiltration into the military, FBI, and probably the CIA too. Compromised top-secret information. I mean, they stole a crucial, heavily guarded artifact most people didn't even know existed without anyone even noticing. Not to mention this 'terrorist' organization is unlike anything anyone's ever seen. Members from every country, every race, every possible background pulling strings for a cause we don't even understand." He sighed and flopped back onto his bed. "But the Wi-Fi here sucks royally and I left all my hardcore gear at home. So I guess I have no choice but to ride out the rest of the cruise playing backup to your alibis."

"Yep. Now shut up, I'm trying to sleep."

He chuckled weakly as he switched off the lamp between our beds. "Goodnight, dragon breath."

Dad was *pissed.*

Big shocker there. I managed to avoid him for almost two full days—thank you, motion sickness—but when he saw me at our fancy dinner on the last night of the cruise, his eyes nearly bulged out of their sockets. It'd been a while since I saw him get so angry that the little vein on the side of his temple stood out. Hello again, old friend.

It took a lot of explaining to talk him down. Team effort. Honestly, it probably wouldn't have worked except that Drake took most of the blame. He wove a tale of made-up debauchery, claiming that we'd found a couple of other guys and started a little mock-tournament in one of the video game lounges, playing for whatever pocket change people had on hand. After things got heated, especially since he kept on baiting our made-up adversary by using cheat codes and glitches to win every time, the guy snapped, and I leapt heroically to Drake's defense.

It sounded ridiculous even to me. Dad seemed to buy it, though. Anyway, it kept me from getting grounded, so I wasn't about to complain.

Shifting in my seat, I scratched at the collar of my button-down shirt. Dad had insisted on it and the tie, saying nice clothes were required if I wanted to enter the extra-fancy dining room. I didn't want to, but it was our last night on the ship, so I tried not to complain. Might as well make the best of it. Besides, everyone else was dressed up, too. Dad had dusted off one of his nicest suits and Ms. Collins wore a fitted, deep blue cocktail dress. Even Drake wore a freshly ironed button-down, although he'd drawn the line at wearing a tie.

I had to agree. Ties sucked. But I wasn't willing to risk my dad's wrath over it. Ms. Collins was a lot more lenient when it came to letting Drake decide what he was going to wear.

I seriously needed to invest in some bigger shirts, though. I'd barely gotten the wrists of this one buttoned over my bandages. Thankfully, doing that effectively hid them, so I didn't have to worry about Dad asking about anything other than the swollen, angry purple bruise on my jaw.

"And you're sure you feel okay, Koji?" Ms. Collins glanced between Drake and me, visibly concerned. Her gaze hung on Drake a few seconds longer, however. Her lips pursed slightly, and I noticed he was actively avoiding meeting her stare.

Uh-oh. Was she better at figuring out when he was lying?

A cold sweat shivered over my skin and I cleared my throat, hoping to distract her from using any more of her borderline Jedi-mom-mindreading-powers on him. "Uh, yeah. I mean it hurts, but I don't think anything's broken." My forced laugh cracked and died in my throat. "Guess I should be glad he didn't hit my nose."

"I'm surprised none of the staff stepped in," Dad mumbled around bites of a T-bone steak he'd ordered with a side of lobster.

Drake was still staring down into his food, avoiding his mom's deception radar. "It was over pretty fast. For being so gangly, Koji can pack a punch. Even I was surprised. Two hits and the guy backed off."

At least that part wouldn't be hard for Dad to believe. I'd only been in a fistfight once before. Well, that he knew about, anyway. Giant monsters and crazy headmasters didn't count. I'd held my own in a brawl back in my freshman year against an older guy almost twice my size who had been bullying me for months.

Come to think of it, that was the last time I'd seen that little vein appear on Dad's forehead.

"Well, Koji, that doesn't get you off the hook with me," Dad warned. "If you see that boy again, I want you to apologize."

"You too, Drake," Ms. Collins said.

We both nodded in unison, knowing full well that would never happen since, you know, that guy didn't exist.

Dinner dragged on with servers bringing out several courses of delicious meal options. It took me a while to make up my mind. Their gourmet burgers were stacked high with Wagyu beef and melty sharp cheddar cheese. The stuffed chicken marsala was served over garlic parmesan truffle mashed potatoes with a side of fresh green beans. They even had a South African barbecue platter of sliders with pulled pork, brisket, and peri-peri chicken.

I couldn't decide. So I just picked all of it and ate until I felt like I might puke. Next to me, Drake sat licking barbecue sauce off his fingers from the ribs he'd gotten. Across the table, Dad and Ms. Collins were in their own world, talking quietly and sipping on glasses of wine. Occasionally Dad said something that made her giggle and cover her mouth.

Then it was time for dessert.

There were just as many options to choose from on the dessert menu, including a full ice cream bar. I'd only just begun pondering how many toppings I could pile into one bowl of vanilla ice cream when a pair of waiters approached our table. One stood back, positioned behind Ms. Collins where she couldn't see, holding an ice bucket with a bottle of champagne and two slender glasses.

The other held a single slice of intricately decorated cake. The top was decorated with strawberries, curled chocolate shavings, and a pair of hearts molded from white chocolate. Was it just me, or was that a really fancy piece of cake?

I glanced around, but no one else seemed to be getting cake like that at their table.

All of a sudden, my stomach dropped.

I whipped around in my seat just in time to see Dad pull something out of his blazer pocket...

A small jewelry box.

Oh. My. God.

My body flashed hot and cold. Everything from my neck down went completely numb. I couldn't think. I couldn't even breath. I sat frozen, staring in mute horror as my dad pushed his chair back from the table and got down on his knee. Beside me, Drake had gone as stiff as a corpse in his chair.

The entire dining room went silent.

Ms. Collins glanced around, confused until Dad opened that box. Her eyes went wide and her lips parted like she might say something. But all she managed to do was look back and forth between my dad and the glittering diamond ring he held up.

Dad gazed up at her, eyes misty as he gently took one of her hands. "Amelia, I... I know it hasn't even been a year, and... and we've talked about taking things slow. But I can't stand it anymore. I can't go another day without asking." His voice trembled and halted, brows drawn up in a look of hopeful desperation.

Under the table, my hands curled into sweaty, shaking fists. Sick. I was going to be sick.

"Will you marry me?"

A collective gasp and flurry of whispers went up around the dining room. Everyone seemed to lean in, ducking and dodging to get a better view. A few people even took out their phones and started snapping pictures.

Ms. Collins sat completely still, her mouth open and her eyes searching Dad's face. She took a breath, about to say something.

"NO!" The word exploded out of me in a shout.

Now everyone was staring at me, instead.

It took less than a second for my dad's surprise to morph into a look of pure parental rage. He started to speak, but I didn't even let him get started. I didn't need to hear him explain to me why he was right. Not this time.

"Are you freaking kidding me with this?" I yelled, shoving my chair back and snapping to my feet. My face burned. Everything came bursting to the surface at once and I couldn't stop it. "You go from basically ignoring my entire existence so you can hang out with your new girlfriend, to dragging me on this stupid vacation where I can't even sleep at night because I'm trying not to have a panic attack because guess what, remember that whole thing where I can't swim because I watched Mom die when I was little? Yeah. That's *still* a thing. Thanks for asking, by the way." My face twitched, vision skewing in and out of focus as I start backing away from the table. "And now you're asking her to *marry* you? And you don't even give me a head's up about it? I mean, what the actual *hell*, Dad?"

"Koji." Dad growled my name like a warning. "You need to—"

"No!" I shouted again, louder this time. "*You* screwed up this time, not me! This is your fault! What happened to us being a team? What happened to you even giving a crap about me at all? I'm just supposed to shut up and pretend like everything's fine so you can be happy? Meanwhile, my whole life is turning to total shi—"

"KOJI!" he bellowed in his thundering Dad-voice.

I snapped my mouth shut, blinking hard against the tears that welled in my eyes. My jaw wouldn't stop quivering. Out—I had to get out. Now.

So I turned and bolted straight for the exit without looking back.

# CHAPTER 17

I made it all the way to our room before I threw up.

I burst into the bathroom and slammed the door, scrambling to lock it before I fell onto my knees in front of the toilet. I retched until my insides ached. Beads of cold sweat ran down my forehead and shivered along my spine.

When it was over, I flopped back against the wall and tried to breathe. My mind raced, but I couldn't remember anything I'd said. All I could see when I closed my eyes was Dad's furious glare and Ms. Collins's pasty look of shock.

What had I done?

I buried my face in my hands as my chest shuddered with a sob. I couldn't do this anymore— pushing stuff down and pretending it didn't matter. It did. It freaking mattered a lot.

And I'd never felt so alone in my entire life.

My dad acted like he didn't want me around anymore—at least, not like before. He just wanted me to keep quiet while he went on with his life, acting like Mom had never existed at all. I was basically an unwanted memento at this point.

Madeline had ghosted me and wouldn't even answer my messages.

Claire was terrified and probably furious with me about getting her involved.

Drake would undoubtedly be angry about what I'd just done.

More innocent people were dead because of Noxius.

Oh, and let's not forget that my totem was slowly killing me.

I hid my face in the crook of my elbow, gasping and biting down hard to keep from making any noise as more sobs seized in my throat. All I wanted to do was go home. I could have. It would be easy break out of here, shift forms, and fly back to New York. Then I could lock myself in my room. Or pack a bag and go to my grandparents.

Dad would probably send me there after this, anyway. He'd want me out of the way so he could patch things up with Ms. Collins.

My pocket buzzed and vibrated suddenly.

Reaching down, I dug my normal phone out and wiped my eyes so I could look at the screen. I had a new message.

It was from Claire.

CLAIRE:
Are you okay?

I hesitated, wondering if she was asking because of how we'd parted ways so abruptly after the botched mission in Colombia... or if her third eye was tipping her off to my epic mental breakdown. At last, I typed out a quick reply:

KOJI:
No.

She answered immediately:

CLAIRE:
Need a plus one?

With a deep, shaky exhale, I sank back against the wall.

KOJI:
It's not that kind of problem. Life
stuff. My dad sucks. He just proposed to
Drake's mom. Like, totally out of the
blue. He never said anything to me about
it.

CLAIRE:
Wow. I'm so sorry. Can you try talking
to him about it?

KOJI:
Yeah, well, I kinda did already. I lost
it in front of the whole dining room.

Understatement of the century. Lost it?
I'd pretty much gone full psycho in
front of the whole ship. I'd embarrassed
Ms. Collins too, which made me feel
worse. It wasn't her fault. Judging by
the look on her face, she hadn't known
what Dad was planning, either.

Before Claire could reply, I started typing again.

KOJI:
I'm such an idiot. Lately everything I
do blows up in my face, like my whole
life is one giant mistake. I'm really
sorry about dragging you into that stuff
last night. Drake told me he was the one
who contacted you. I never meant for you

to get involved or to put your life in
danger.

CLAIRE:
Koji, it's fine. I'm not mad at you.
Honestly, it's kind of a miracle I haven't been found out before now. It was
going to happen sooner or later. I would
have been way more upset if I'd shown up
and you were already dead because you
didn't ask for my help. No more solo
missions, okay? I can't lose you like
that. We have to stick together.

I tried really hard not to read too much into that. Really, I
did. On the one hand, I knew things were different between us
now. She'd already said she loved me. But that was after I'd
given up on liking her. She'd fallen for Noxius first, and I didn't
know what that meant when it came to regular, average me. Was
Koji without the dragon-totem really enough for her?

And then there was Madeline…

I knew I cared about her. Even now, more than six months
since I'd last had any contact with her. Our connection had always felt more organic—more real. But was it one-sided? How
long was I supposed to wait before I finally gave up that she ever wanted to see or speak to me again? I mean, sure, there was
the issue of the FBI looking for her. Before, she'd always found
ways to sneak me messages in ways no one else could detect.
She'd even given me my totem right under her father's nose.

I eyed the toilet, wondering if I was about to reunite with it
as a new, harrowing realization made my stomach clench. Did
Madeline know what the totems were doing to us? She'd been
helping her dad, which probably meant she was also working for
Dr. Livingston. And Dr. Livingston had hinted that Madeline
hadn't told Claire and I everything. So she *had* to know, right?

But, seriously, how could she not mention that teeny-tiny downside to Claire or me? She'd held that one, extremely important fact back. Why? If she really cared about me, then why wouldn't she tell me that my totem was killing me?

I rubbed my jaw, probing gently at the sore spot where my bruise was still healing. Then I finally typed out a reply.

KOJI:
No more solo missions. I promise. Hey, when I get back there's something we need to talk about. Think we can meet up again?

CLAIRE:
Sure. Usual place?

KOJI:
No. Central Park/Glen Span Arch. Tuesday @ midnight. You like waffles, right?

CLAIRE:
Ummmmm yes. Are we going somewhere to eat?

KOJI:
Yep. No pajamas this time.

CLAIRE:
Har har har. So funny. NOT. :P Take care of yourself.

Drake didn't come back to our room until hours later. By then, I was doing the best fake sleeping impression I could muster, lying on my side facing the wall with the comforter pulled up to my nose. He didn't say anything as he took his stuff into the bathroom, showered, changed, and climbed into his own bed. When he turned off the light, I heard him sigh deeply. But it wasn't a happy sigh. More like a "tomorrow is really going to suck and I'm already dreading it" sigh.

I could relate. Dad hadn't come to chase me down, meaning he was so furious he had to cool off before he could even stand to look at me again. Not good.

I tossed and turned all night, my thoughts racing between what a giant steaming pile of manure my life had become and how I was going to break the news to Claire about our totems. I hadn't even told Drake yet. But since she was a victim too, it only seemed right to tell her first. I didn't even fully understand what it meant to have something eating my soul. Would my lifespan be cut short? Dr. Livingston hadn't gone into detail, and now I was sort of wishing I had let her prattle on and grandstand for a little longer. Maybe Kirkland and the other agents at the FBI could get more out of her. No doubt they'd be interrogating her about everything.

Early the next morning, I finally gave up on sleeping and went to take a shower. I took my time going through my morning routine—washing my hair, running my electric razor over my chin and neck, and brushing my teeth. As the steam cleared from the cramped little bathroom, I finally got a good look at my reflection. Yikes. The bruises on my face had turned yellow and green, which I knew was a good sign. They were healing but still looked gruesome. The bruises around my arms, torso, and legs from the cables were still deep purple. They'd take longer to heal.

My gaze was drawn to the scar in the center of my chest. A portion of gnarled, rough, discolored skin in the shape of a hand. Madeline's hand. The doctor had promised that it would get better. After a year or two, they said I might even be able to have some laser procedures done to make it less obvious.

I swallowed hard, staring at it for a long time as that moment played through my head. Six months... Somehow, it felt longer than that. The look on Madeline's face as she lay delirious in my arms, combing her fingers over my cheek, was burned into my brain, leaving a scar all its own. No amount of cosmetic surgery would be able to erase that.

I emerged from the bathroom dressed in another long-sleeved hoodie to cover my bruises and bandages and a pair of khaki shorts. Today we'd be arriving back in Miami, staying overnight in a hotel, and then starting the long trek back home with an early flight back to New York with a layover in Atlanta.

Drake sat on the edge of his bed, his platinum hair rumpled and already dressed to go in jeans, flip-flops, and a T-shirt. He didn't even look up as I walked by to cram all my toiletries back into my suitcase. Awkward didn't even begin to describe it. Judging from the dark circles under his eyes, he hadn't slept much, either.

Fine. Someone had to clear the air here. It might as well be me, since I was the one who'd started it in the first place.

Sitting down on my bed facing him, I took a steadying breath. "Listen, Drake, I'm really—"

"Don't," he interrupted.

I frowned, slowly looking up to meet his gaze.

"Don't apologize, okay? You were right," he continued, hesitating to chew on the inside of his cheek for moment. "I mean, it's fine that your dad wants to marry my mom. That's not the problem. He seems like a good guy and Mom is nuts about him. But *that* was an epic fail. Totally not the way to do it— without even talking to us about it. We're not little kids. So, I guess... I just want you to know that I get it. I understand."

I leaned forward to rest my elbows on my knees, letting my head sink lower. I'd hadn't even considered that Drake was in the same situation I was. Well, sort of. He'd been caught off guard, too. He must've been too shocked to even say anything, and then I went nuclear and stormed off before he could even get a word out.

I rubbed at the back of my neck. "Well, still—I'm sorry for going off like that in front of everyone. I should've... ugh, I don't even know. I've just been trying to let it roll off for so long. He hasn't dated seriously like this since Mom, and I figured at some point he'd cool off and remember I existed. Guess not." I quirked my mouth and hesitated. "Is your mom okay?"

He shook his head slightly. "Hard to tell with her. We all left the restaurant not long after you did. Mom was pretty upset, so I tried hanging around nearby while they stepped out onto the deck to talk, but it was really awkward. They weren't going to talk about it in front of me. So I took a walk, you know, to clear my head and stuff. Then I just came back here."

"Dad didn't say anything to you, did he?"

Drake shook his head again.

I wasn't about to hope I'd get off that easy. He'd have plenty to say to me later. No doubt about that. "You think they'll break up?" I asked quietly.

"I don't know."

A soft knock on our cabin door made us both cringe and exchange a wary look. Oh no.

Drake got up to answer it while I sat, stiff and too petrified to move. A low voice murmured quietly to Drake. My stomach flipped and spun, sending shivers of anxiety through all my fingers and toes. I didn't have to look to be sure. It was definitely Dad.

When the door closed again, I risked a quick glance up. Drake was gone and my dad was now the only other person in the room. I gulped and looked down again. Maybe it was better not to say anything at all at this point. Silence might be safer.

Drake's bed lurched as Dad sat down and cleared his throat. "We need to talk, son."

Talk? Yeah, right. This was doomed to be one of those instances where he talked—a lot—and I got to sit there and look humiliated.

"I get what you're going through, Koji. Things are changing. You're changing. You've been moodier than usual lately, and we haven't really taken the time to sit down and discuss it. And I guess that part is on me. We should've had this talk a long time ago." He clasped his hands, weaving his fingers together. "But let me be very clear, and I need you to hear me when I say this: your behavior last night was completely unacceptable. You embarrassed me, and worse, you embarrassed Amelia. No amount of teenage hormones justifies that."

Um. *What?*

I gaped at him, hoping that I was hearing this wrong. I was misunderstanding. I had to be. No way my dad was trying to say my being upset was just because I was... *hormonal?*

"So you're going to apologize to Amelia, do you understand? And when we get back home, you're going to be grounded until school starts back. I want a different attitude from you starting now."

He kept talking, but I couldn't hear much after that. My pulse roared in my ears like the crashing of ocean waves. How could he try to shift all the blame onto me? Had he even heard any of the things I said? Didn't he get how much it hurt to have him treat me like this?

"Koji? Are you listening?" He must've noticed I wasn't paying attention to his self-righteous parental speech anymore.

"Yeah," I snapped. "Yeah, I am. *You're* the one who isn't listening. If you're gonna ground me, then fine. Whatever. But you *know* I'm right. All I'm doing is telling you a truth you don't like. Everything you've done since you and Ms. Collins got together has been one selfish, jerk move right after another. And you know what? I'm sick of it. If this is who you are when she's around, then I don't want anything to do with her anymore."

I regretted those words immediately. It wasn't Ms. Collins's fault. I knew that. She'd never been anything but nice to me and it wasn't fair to drag her into it. It was too late now, though.

My dad's face flushed with anger as he stared me down, probably trying to rein in his temper before he spoke again.

I didn't give him the chance.

Standing up, I snatched my backpack off the foot of the bed and flung the door open. "Just go back to ignoring me like you were before. At least now I know what role I'm supposed to be playing in all this. I'm just the troubled, hormonal outsider wrecking your perfect new family," I growled before I left, slamming the door behind me with a *bang*.

# CHAPTER 18

Dad didn't try talking to me again for the rest of the trip. No one did, actually. Drake stayed immersed in his phone, cruising his social media accounts and probably hacking more FBI confidential files— nothing new there. He kept his headphones on, loud techno music thumping away in fast, muffled rhythms, so I didn't even bother trying to talk to him.

Not that I felt much like chatting.

Ms. Collins and Dad stood stiffly next to one another at the airport, not holding hands or saying much beyond an occasional whisper. She wasn't wearing the shiny engagement ring. Did that mean she'd turned him down? Because of me?

I couldn't deny the aching, rotting sense of guilt that ate away at my insides just thinking about that. They'd been so happy before. And I had... well... basically wrecked everything in the most catastrophic way imaginable.

When we arrived back in New York, everyone loaded into our car with me squished in the backseat, as usual. We drove Drake and Ms. Collins back to their house. Dad helped take their bags in and lurked by the door just long enough for him and Ms. Collins to exchange a few words and an awkward hug. As he turned away, I couldn't help but notice the way she stared after him. Her soft, light brown eyes lingered on him, her lips pressed into a thin, worried line. It didn't take a genius to see how much she liked him. Maybe she even loved him.

Dad loved her, too. He wouldn't have asked her to marry him otherwise.

And I was ruining it.

The drive back home was painfully quiet. I stayed sitting in the backseat, staring down into the pages of one of my comic books in the hopes that Dad wouldn't try to strike up another discussion. I wasn't up for that yet.

Thankfully, I guess he wasn't either. He didn't say a single word all the way home. With the radio on low and both hands on the steering wheel, he kept his gaze locked forward.

The sun had just begun to set as we pulled onto our street. As soon as the car was parked, I bailed out and took my bags inside, stopping only to unlock the front door. I needed some personal space. Dad probably did, too. We'd never had fights like this before—ever. I didn't know what to do next. I didn't know how to fix it or what to say. Could it even be fixed? Or was this how things were going to be from now on?

Upstairs, my room was exactly the way I'd left it. *Dragon Age* and *Pacific Rim* posters hung on the walls, all with corners coated in pinholes and tape because of how many times I'd moved them. My desk was crowded with empty soda cans and wallpapered with the little numbered stickers the movers always put on our stuff when we had to relocate to another base. There wasn't a single piece of furniture in our house that didn't have at least four of those stickers somewhere on them. All my action figures were still arranged in battle poses on my shelves, and there was a pile of clean laundry heaped in one corner, hoping to be folded.

Home sweet home.

I shut the door and dropped my luggage on the floor. Stumbling over to my bed, I kicked off my shoes and prepared to take a much-needed nap. Or maybe I'd just go to bed. It was late, after all, and I hadn't slept well since we'd gotten on the stupid boat days ago. Even now that I was finally back on dry land, it still felt like I was rocking and swaying every time I closed my eyes. How long would that last?

As I flopped facedown onto my mattress, something crunched against my face. I lifted my head, glaring down at what looked like a little white sticky note positioned right in the middle of my pillow. I peeled it off the fabric with a frown. Who would be leaving me notes like this? No one had been in the house since we left, and I hadn't noticed Drake leaving anything there...

My heart hit the back of my throat.

There were only two words written on it, printed in neat, feminine letters. I knew that handwriting right away. Just like I knew exactly who had left this note and what they wanted me to do next.

Even if all it actually said was *Hot chocolate?*

I'd become exceptionally good at sneaking out after becoming a superhero. Part of the job, I guess. With my favorite sneakers back on and my pockets loaded down with both of my phones, my wallet, and enough cash to get a cab, I sat waiting while Dad went through his bedtime routine on the floor below. He trundled around in the bathroom for half an hour before everything finally got quiet. Cracking my bedroom door open slightly, I dared to peek down the stairwell.

His bedroom door was shut and the crack underneath it was dark. He'd gone to bed.

I gave him another half hour before I dared to creep to the big, circular window next to my bed and slowly push it open. The night wind picked up as I scaled the moonlit rooftops. After all the times I'd spent scurrying in and out of my house this way, I'd found it necessary to have all my potential escape routes memorized. You never knew when the FBI was going to bust your door down, after all.

I used a fire escape at the far end of an alley that ran behind our row of houses to get to street level. With my hood pulled up and my hands in my pockets, I started down the sidewalk to the nearest big intersection. The coffee shop wasn't that far, and I could've easily walked the distance. But I wasn't taking any chances of someone on the street seeing me coming.

Flagging down a cab, I squeezed my phone in my hand as the glittering night cityscape slipped past. My foot wouldn't stop tapping. Nervous? Ummm. Yeah.

When I spotted the place, my throat went dry. Positioned on a street corner, the cozy two-story coffee shop wasn't somewhere I hung out normally. Coffee wasn't really my thing. But I'd been before—a little over six months ago.

I leaned up to hand the cabbie the cash for my fare as he sidled up to the curb, bounding out before he'd even come to a complete stop. Standing in the glow that radiated from the shop's wide windows, I tried not to hyperventilate. Was she really here?

Had Madeline finally come back?

I burst through the door in a breathless frenzy, looking around the mostly empty seating area on the first floor. A couple sat together right by the window, leaning together as they sipped their drinks and talked in quiet voices. Another couple near the back were both staring at their phones, and a guy tapped away on a laptop in the far corner.

She wasn't here. Or, at least, she wasn't on this floor.

The barista standing at the counter smiled, seeming totally unfazed by my stammering as I ordered one hot chocolate and stood near to wait. If I ordered something, no one would ask any questions about why I was here, right? Besides, a little sugar might help calm my frazzled nerves.

I carried the warm mug up the steps to the second floor, my heartbeat accelerating with every step. At the top, I stopped and slowly scanned the tables and chairs. A few other patrons were scattered about, sitting on the sofas reading or working on laptops.

But Madeline wasn't here, either.

Was I too late? Was this a trick? A setup? No—that couldn't be it. I knew her handwriting.

So where was she?

My head still spun with questions as I made my way over to the table where Madeline, Drake, and I had sat together after seeing a movie. I couldn't explain it. It just felt wrong to sit anywhere else.

I came to a screeching halt, almost spilling all of my hot chocolate, right in front of the table. My eyes widened. Deep in my chest, my heart gave a painful, fretful twist.

There was another sticky note on the tabletop.

It took everything I had not to fling the mug aside and dive for it. Plucking the little white note off the table, I held it up to the dim light with my hands trembling. Two more words were scribbled on it in Madeline's handwriting:

*Next door.*

I left my untouched mug of hot chocolate on the table and sprinted headlong back down the stairs. Back in the chilly evening air, I turned in a circle as I tried to figure out where to go next. Next door? But which way? On one side of the shop, a little mom-and-pop-style deli restaurant was already closed for the night. That couldn't be it.

I whirled around, jogging down the sidewalk a few yards to see what was on the other side.

With a stoic, old-school front of gray stone and one wide window trimmed out in hand-painted gold filigree, the second-hand bookstore sat hunched between its much larger neighbors. The paper sign on the door was flipped to the OPEN side. Oh God. This had to be it.

Madeline had to be in there.

I still had the sticky note clenched in my hand as I sped for the door. A big brass bell jangled overhead, announcing my arrival as I stepped inside. Immediately, the snug, gloomy atmosphere of the bookshop seemed to swallow me whole. There was no one else in sight—not even behind the counter. I wound my way through the labyrinth of massive bookshelves that spanned from floor to ceiling. Each one was packed with more books than anyone could've read in a lifetime. There were heaps of more books stacked on the floor and piles of them arranged in corners. The farther in I went, the more the air smelled of that musky, old-paper aroma.

With no lights apart from a few dimmed lamps and ancient chandeliers, heavy shadows fell over corners and narrow walkways between the shelves. Lots of places to hide. I'd have to search every square foot of this place if I wanted any chance of finding—

"Koji." A quiet female voice breathed my name.

I froze. My whole body relaxed with one heavy, quaking breath as my heart pounded in my ears. The note slipped out of my palm and fell to the floor. Turning around slowly, I looked behind me.

She was standing only a few feet away, gazing up with those wide, stormy blue eyes. That was one of the only things I recognized about her now.

Even dressed in an oversized knit sweater that swallowed her frame, I could tell she'd lost weight—pounds that with her petite build left her looking disturbingly frail. Hadn't she been able to eat? Or had she been forced to beg or steal for food to survive all this time? Her jeans were dirty and ripped at the knees, and her ragged sneakers looked a few sizes too big. Had she just swiped all those clothes from a second-hand store? Or a dumpster? Her cheeks were sunken and her skin seemed dusky, caked with a lot of makeup that wasn't anything I'd ever seen her wear before. A disguise? Well, if so, then that explained the hair, too. She'd cut it off at her chin and dyed it an orangey shade of red.

But it was still Madeline.

I surged forward, wrapping my arms around her to drag her in against my chest. She stiffened at first, not moving as she sucked in a sharp gasp. Then, gradually, her arms found their way around my neck and she hugged me back. She buried her face against my shoulder.

"I was afraid," I admitted hoarsely. "I was *so* afraid you were dead."

"I know," she answered in a broken whisper.

"I messaged you. I called you so many times. You... you never answered."

She squeezed me harder.

"The FBI have been all over me trying to find out where you are. And then Dr. Livingston—"

She jerked back suddenly, seizing me by the elbows with a crazed look of terror in her eyes. Her hands slid, inch by inch, down my arms until they got to my wrists. I guess she could feel the lumps of the bandages hidden there under my sweatshirt, because she immediately pushed back my sleeves to see. Her fingers grazed the bandages, halting over my totem bracelet that peeked out from under one of the gauze wrappings.

When she looked at me again, fresh tears streaked her heavy eyeliner and mascara. "S-She got to you," Madeline whimpered. "Oh God, Koji. I... I'm so sorry. I should have been there! I should have..." Her voice broke, shoulders tensing as her face screwed up.

"Hey, it's okay. I'm fine," I murmured, trying to sound as comforting as possible while I gathered her in close again. "Shhh. Look, I really am okay, I promise. Everything is going to be—"

"No." She put her hands against my chest, holding me at a distance. "No, it's not, Koji. And we don't have much time, so you have to listen."

I frowned. "Wait, does that mean you're going to disappear again?"

She put a hand over my mouth and seized the front of my shirt, dragging me deeper into a narrow passage between two of the bookshelves. Hidden in the heavy shadows of a cavern of old books, Madeline began to explain. "I know you don't understand, but please—you don't know how dangerous these people are."

Grasping her wrist, I pulled her hand away from my mouth so I could whisper back. "No, you're right. I don't understand. Where have you been? If you needed help, if you needed a safe place to hide out, you could've asked me to—"

She cut me off again. "I can't be close to you. Don't you understand? They want *all* of us, Koji. You, me, and Claire, too. It won't work unless they have all the totem-wielders. And now my face has been all over the news. They already know who you and Claire are—where you live and how to get to you. Not knowing where I am is one of the only things still holding them back."

"What are you talking about? Who are *they*?" She wasn't making any sense.

Her eyes darkened, as though every speck of hope had just been snuffed out at once. "It's not that simple. This isn't one of your comic book stories where the villains all dress in matching uniforms. This is real, Koji, and they are a real evil."

"So tell me, then. Dr. Livingston is the one running the show, right? She was the one who started this, who gave your dad the totem of time and... did this to you." I slid my hands down, taking one of her hands in mine and pushing back the sleeve of her baggy sweater to reveal the scars around her wrists. The same ones I would have after my wounds healed.

Her jaw tensed and her gaze went steely. "She didn't start it. But she intends to finish it."

"Finish what?

Madeline looked into my eyes, seeming as haunted and ter-rified as she was exhausted. When she finally answered, her voice was barely more than a hushed, desperate whimper. "To merge our worlds."

# CHAPTER 19

"Hey! You kids better not be foolin' around back there." A gruff voice cracked over us like thunder. At the far end of the aisle, the bent silhouette of an old man leered at us through the gloom.

I blushed, releasing Madeline's wrists with a start, and stammered like a moron, "O-Oh! No, uh, we weren't doing anything like tha—"

The old man didn't care enough to even let me finish. "We're closing up. If you're not buyin' nothin' then go find somewhere else to do that," he barked before waddling back into his labyrinth of books like a cranky old troll.

It wasn't until he'd disappeared that I noticed Madeline was practically hiding behind me, her eyes wide and body trembling with fear as she gripped the back of my shirt. "Oh God. He saw me. I… I have to go," she whispered.

"Yeah," I agreed and seized her arm firmly. "And you're coming with me."

"But—Koji—no!" She squirmed, trying to wriggle free of my grip.

I shot her a silencing glare. "You're not disappearing on me like that again. Don't worry, I know somewhere we can go."

Her expression sharpened, going cold with a look of distrust. "There's nowhere I can go that they won't find me."

"Not true," I snapped and started dragging her down the aisles of bookshelves to the door. With my other hand, I snatched my phone out of my pocket and sent a series of quick messages. "Dr. Livingston knows about all that stuff that happened between your dad and the Fausts, right?"

Madeline was still trying to get free, pushing and tugging at my hand as we burst out of the bookshop's front door. "Yes, but that has nothing to do with—"

I spun on her suddenly, pulling her in close enough that I could stare her down with our noses only an inch or two apart. "For crying out loud, Madeline. Just this once, would you shut up and let me help you? I'm not stupid. I know what's at stake here. You've got to trust me, okay?"

Her furious little snarl broke, shattering into a look of shock and bewilderment. It only lasted a moment. Then she bowed her head in defeat, mouth scrunching unhappily. "Fine."

My third eye sense prickled. She didn't trust me. Somehow, that stung a lot worse than I expected. Now wasn't the time to call her bluff, though. We needed a safe place to talk and finally figure all this out. She was holding back a lot of valuable information about the totems and Dr. Livingston. And I was 1000 percent over this cloak-and-dagger, I-can't-tell-you-because-it-would-put-you-in-danger charade. She knew how all this crap was connected.

And I knew of one place we could go that Dr. Livingston and her cronies might never look.

A tiny part of me knew this might be a terrible idea. It had the potential to blow up in my face in a truly catastrophic and life-altering way. There wasn't much of a choice at this point, though.

It was this or say goodbye to Madeline forever, accepting that she was living like a hobo and apparently starving to death.

Her grip on my hand intensified as I led the way through the perfectly manicured gardens behind the palatial Camridore-Faust residence. I wondered if she even knew where we were. Her pale, haunted expression might've just been from terror that Dr. Livingston would somehow find her.

I got my answer as we climbed to the top of a tall ironwork lattice covered in flowering vines that stood along one section of the mansion's massive outdoor lounge. Claire had warned that since the lawsuit began, her parents had really cracked down on security. The perimeter fence had signs posted every ten feet warning that all trespassers would be prosecuted, and the property was being monitored by cameras. Maybe it was justified, but it seemed a little paranoid to me.

If we followed Claire's instructions, though, we could slip in and out without any being the wiser. That was the plan, anyway.

Scrambling to the top of the lattice, I helped Madeline up the last few feet before we crept down the length of the roof to a wide picture window at the far end of the second story. Warm light trickled through the edges of the closed curtains. We couldn't see inside. Was this the right one? It had to be. Crap, I hoped it was.

My heart hammered, making my fingers tingle as I knocked on the glass—just three soft taps.

The curtains snatched back so suddenly I nearly tripped backward and fell off the roof. Geez!

Claire's wide-eyed stare panned between Madeline and me, her expression going pasty with shock. Crouched beside me, Madeline looked just as startled to see her. Whoops. Guess she'd never been here, after all.

"Hurry, before someone sees," Claire whispered as she opened the window to let us in.

Madeline quickly ducked inside first before I fell in after her—literally. One of my shoelaces snagged on the window and I landed in a heap on the carpet. For crying out loud. Stealth really was not my thing.

"Smooth," a familiar voice snickered. Drake reclined on a sofa in the small seating area, watching us with a wide, cattish grin.

"How'd you beat us here?" I grumbled as I got to my feet and retied my shoe.

"Well, for starters, I didn't take a cab." He chuckled again. "I also probably didn't trip as much as you did."

"Oh, stop it, Collins. You've only been here for about two minutes." Claire shot him a look as she shut her window and drew her curtains closed.

He pulled a fake pouting face and shrugged.

The only one who didn't seem to be enjoying the banter was Madeline. She stood at my side, looking around Claire's bedroom with her face still blanched and afraid. Swallowing hard, she met Claire's gaze for half a second before looking guiltily down at the floor—almost like she expected someone to start yelling at her.

I put a hand on her shoulder. "It's okay."

Madeline's brows drew together, clumped locks of her coppery colored hair falling to cover one side of her face. "How long has Drake known?" she asked in a small, trembling voice.

"Since the holiday festival last year," he replied evenly. "Relax, I know how to keep a secret. And if we're baring all our biggest and baddest ones tonight, then you should probably know that I'm the one who handles all his technical and communication stuff when he has to fight as Noxius."

Claire arched a brow, looking just as surprised as Madeline for a moment. "You're working for the FBI?"

He snorted and rolled his eyes. "Please. They're basically working for *me*." His sharp, cognac stare flicked to Madeline. "So, you found her."

She tensed, taking a small step back behind me.

"Yeah." I swallowed hard. "And we all need to talk. No more secrets—not between us."

"Koji, please, I-I... I can't." Madeline's voice caught.

"Why don't you boys give us a minute?" Claire spoke suddenly, crossing her arms. "My bedroom's next door. You can wait there. Just don't leave my suite, okay?"

Drake took his time getting up, stretching, and ambling out of the room. I followed, my stomach flipping and swirling with anxiety as I dared to take one last look back over my shoulder at the two girls. Were they seriously about to talk? About what had happened between their parents? My throat went dry just thinking about it. This could not end in a fight—not now. Not when I'd finally convinced Madeline she could trust me.

Claire must've been reading my emotions again because she cast me a small, gentle smile and nodded slightly.

I let out a breath and nodded back. I trusted her. She could fix this. Maybe. Hopefully.

Shutting the door to Claire's bedroom, I tried not to be extra weird about staring around in wonder. I'd never been in a girl's bedroom before. You know, because of the whole never-having-had-a-real-girlfriend thing. Drake, on the other hand, was already lounging in the velvet clawfoot sofa positioned at the foot of the king bed, scrolling away on his phone.

So, I took the opportunity to look around—in a non-creepy way.

The whole room had a surprisingly warm, cozy feel to it with dark wood furniture, the decor in earthy tones of hunter green, deep maroon, and gold. Overall, it was every bit as elegant and expensive-looking as you'd expect. But little hints of her personality were hidden here and there, incorporated so seamlessly her parents had probably never noticed. A slender wooden wand leaned up against a marble bookend on one of her shelves. An intensely beautiful and detailed painting of a young woman leaning into a crooked wooden staff as she floated above a circular pond probably looked mundane to her parents. Pretty—but nothing special. Only, I'd seen that painting before. It was a piece commissioned for a famous author and painted by Kuniko Y. Craft. Totally geeky. But, like, covertly geeky.

Even Claire's nightstand looked like it might buckle under the weight of all the books she had piled there. I recognized a few of the titles: *Sabriel*, *The Goblet of Fire*, and... was that seriously the *Silmarillion*? The rest were a mixture of epic fantasy, Dan Brown bestsellers, and a few biographies of Renaissance masters. Interesting.

"Having a good time snooping over there, stalker?" Drake baited. "Gonna peek in her underwear drawer too? Or read her diary?"

I snapped upright and shot him a venomous glare. "Don't be gross. I was just seeing what she was reading."

His smile was undeniably smug and Grinch-like again. "Suuuure."

"Did you know she was into fantasy stuff?"

He gave another one of his classic I-don't-care shrugs. "No. Unlike you, I've never been obsessed with her."

"I was never obs—"

"Oh, please," he interrupted with a groan. "Before you drag me down *that* river in Egypt, at least give me a lifejacket."

"What?"

"De-nial." He paused, glancing up from his phone. "So what's with Madeline showing up out of nowhere?"

I wandered back to sit down next to him. "I don't know. But she's terrified, Drake. She knows a lot more about this than she ever let on. I couldn't let her just run off again—not without telling all of us what's really happening here." My mouth quirked, jumping involuntarily into a sour pucker. "Also, there's, uh, a few things I haven't told you and Claire. So I figured we should just get everything out in the open at once."

Drake perked up. "What are you talking about? What haven't you told me?" he demanded.

I shook my head. "Not yet, okay? I'll… explain in a minute, when they're finished."

We didn't have to wait long. After about fifteen minutes, the door opened and Claire and Madeline appeared long enough to chase us back into the small living room attached to Claire's bedroom suite. Not really a big shock that the princess of Saint Bernard's had a huge, royal-looking setup for a bedroom. Honestly, I was surprised she didn't have her own kitchen and home gym, too. Maybe she did in a different part of this massive house.

Claire insisted on letting Madeline use her bathroom to take a shower and change into some clean, borrowed clothes. It was good, I guess, that they seemed to be getting along. Or at least Madeline wasn't putting up a fight anymore. She drifted along in Claire's shadow, not saying anything and avoiding eye contact.

While Drake and I waited around, Claire ran out of the room to get food. She came back with her arms full of potato chip bags, bottles of sports drinks and sodas, and a stack of small white boxes with gourmet sandwiches inside. I could've done a swan dive into all that, but Claire insisted on waiting until Madeline was back so she could have first pick.

"Koji, do you think she's been starving this whole time? I didn't want to say anything, but she looks awful. And she wouldn't say where she's been sleeping or where she's been getting anything to eat," Claire fretted as she arranged all the snacks on the coffee table.

"I didn't ask, but I'm glad you're helping her."

Claire's brow crinkled with a worried frown. "I know she's not really my sister. We aren't actually related. But, Koji, she's completely alone in the world now. She has no one left. The people who are looking for her probably want to hurt her. She's obviously terrified, and I can't just stand by and do nothing. I can't let her go on like this."

"*We*," I corrected, keeping my voice quiet. "You're not alone in this. None of us are. That's part of the reason I called everyone here tonight. If we're going to figure this out, or even survive it, then we have to start working as a team."

"So what are we going to do about her?" She blinked at me hopefully, like she was counting on me to have some grand master plan.

Spoiler alert: I didn't.

I gnawed on the inside of my cheek while I pondered that. "Let me figure something out, okay? First, let's just hear what she has to say about Dr. Livingston and what they tried to do to me in Colombia."

I could tell Claire didn't like that answer. She wanted a plan—now. Unfortunately, none of this had even been on my radar as a remote possibility. I hadn't heard a single word from Madeline in over six months. And I'd been under the impression that the FBI and military had things under control when it came to crazy people using the time totem to maim, kill, and destroy.

So much for that.

No one said much else until Madeline emerged from the bathroom, dressed in some of Claire's jeans and a clean sweater that fit her much better than the last one had. Her hair was still damp as she came over to sit down in one of the plush wingback chairs, gaze fixed on the floor. She didn't hold anything back when it came to the food, however. As soon as Claire offered, Madeline grabbed two of the sandwiches and a blue sports drink and started gulping them down.

"I guess I should be the one to start," I mumbled as I rubbed the back of my neck. It only seemed fair since I was the one who had called this impromptu meeting of the Saint Bernard's World Saving Totem Club.

"No," Madeline spoke up suddenly. She still chewed on a bite of sandwich as she curled her bare toes into the white shag rug anxiously. "I'm the one who should go first."

"Where have you been all this time?" Claire blurted as she sat down on the sofa between Drake and me. "After I carried you to the power plant, I left to get some medical supplies to treat your injuries, but you just disappeared. We've all been so worried about you."

Madeline bowed her head, hiding her face behind her hair again. "I know. I'm sorry. I didn't have a choice. I trashed my phone and went back to the school. I had a bag stashed there stocked with things I might need if I had to run."

"You had a go-bag hidden at the school?" Drake sounded impressed.

She fidgeted with the cap to the sports drink. "I learned early on how to survive like that—moving fast and leaving no trace. They taught me how. I knew there might come a day when I had to get away from them, if I ever got brave enough to try. So I'd already gotten all the supplies I needed. You know, passports, IDs, cash—that sort of thing."

"Who?" I demanded, surprised at the frustration in my own voice. I wasn't angry at her, but I wanted to get to the bottom of it all. I needed to find out who had done this to her and make sure it never happened again. "Who taught you all of this? Your dad?"

Madeline seemed to shrink as though she were caving in on herself. "Some. But mostly Dr. Livingston. Her people taught me. And that's why I can't stay here—why I can't be close to any of you. They trained me, and they'll know how to find me if I mess up or get sloppy. I can't take any risks. Not now, not when I'm so close."

"So close to what?" Claire's tone was much gentler.

Her mouth screwed up. Her chin trembled. After nearly a minute of sitting there while she swallowed and fought to blink back tears, Claire was the first one to bolt from her seat to crouch on the floor at Madeline's feet. She grasped her hands, petting them gently. "It's okay, Madeline. You're safe here. And whatever happened, whatever you did before, we're not angry at you. We just want to help."

Madeline wiped her eyes on her sleeve as she sniffled. "That's what you don't understand about Dr. Livingston. God, you don't know how dangerous that woman is! If I say too much, if I tell you everything, she would hurt you more. She'd do anything to you to find out."

Now Drake was leaning in too. "To find out what?"

When Madeline looked at me, a cold pang of realization hit me square in the gut. An instant before she said it, I got a creepy, tingly feeling on the back of my neck. I knew what it was. She'd told me before—sort of in passing. At the time, I'd been too distracted by other stuff like her dad's murderous plans to comprehend what she'd said. But I knew it now. I felt it like ice-cold fingers brushing up my spine an instant before she said it out loud.

"Where the totem of earth is hidden."

Seconds ticked by in numb silence as we all sat, staring at one another. A million thoughts raced through my brain as my hands slowly drew into sweaty fists. Madeline had found it? How? When? Is that what she'd been doing this whole time? Where was it? Could we get to it first? Did Livingston really not know where it was?

"Before my father set out that night to attack the Philharmonic, I guess a part of me knew I wouldn't be coming back. They'd been operating out of a stronghold beneath the Hudson Bay."

Drake's jaw dropped. "A secret base *under* the Hudson? You've got to be kidding."

"I wish I was," she muttered. "It's gone now. They were preparing to flood it or blow it up while we were making final arrangements. Looking back now, I don't think they ever expected my father to be successful. I think they expected him to die. It was a cover so no one would be suspicious about the explosions or commotion from them destroying that place. Before we left, I stole some things. Just in case."

"Like what?" I pressed.

She rubbed at one of her forearms. "Data. All of it I could get access to at the time. Everything they had on the possible location of the earth totem, all their research from the experiments they'd done on me with the scepter."

My mind frazzled at that last bit. It was true, then. They'd done *experiments* on her. With the scepter—probably like what they'd done to me. That had to be how she'd gotten those scars. Had they done that to her just to see what would happen? To see if she could be controlled?

My heart hammered against my ribs as I bit down hard against all the things I wanted shout. I could've put a fist through Claire's wall. I wanted to put a fist through Mr. Ignatius's coffin—or Dr. Livingston's skull. I'd have settled for either. Her father was just as guilty as the evil doctor. He'd let this happen.

As she continued, I had to sit there and keep listening. "I took everything I could and ran. I don't know if they even realize I took it. I have to assume they do. And what's worse is I don't know if Livingston has figured out where the earth totem is. They were desperate to catch Koji. I can only assume that's because of his third eye. Maybe they were hoping to use him to find it."

"How could *I* be of any help to them? It's not like I know where it is," I growled as I fixed my glare on the toes of my shoes. I couldn't stand to look at anything else right now. "Being a walking lie detector doesn't do anything to—"

"It not just lies you can sense, Koji," Madeline corrected, her voice still trembling as though she were afraid of me, too. "You have the gift of discernment. You can sense intent and deception of any kind. In time, you'll be able to detect it even from things like writing or objects."

"Like I can with emotions in messages," Claire whispered in awe.

She nodded. "You've had your totem longer, so your third eye has had time to manifest more strongly. The longer we have our totems, the stronger our third eye gifts become, and more of our elemental abilities will awaken. Koji would be able to discern things written in historical texts—to guide them down the right path to find the totem."

Great. Just freaking great. I groaned and dropped my face into my hands. "Well, that explains why she tried to fry me into submission."

"I'm... so sorry, Koji." Madeline whimpered.

I couldn't reply. I wasn't upset with her, of course. It was a lot to take in. And, honestly, we hadn't even gotten to the good part yet. Now seemed like as good a time as any to drop that bomb.

"So, I guess all that happens because the spirit inside our totems is devouring more and more of our souls, right? We get a fun boost of power while it's eating us alive from the inside out? That about the size of it?"

"WHAT?" Drake and Claire gasped in unison.

The secret was officially out.

# CHAPTER 20

Madeline didn't reply. She didn't have to. One look at her utterly crushed expression, the tears streaming down her face, said it all. Dr. Livingston hadn't lied—I knew that much. But I'd sort of been hoping she was holding out some crucial facts or details that might give me even the smallest shred of hope.

Nope. It was every bit as bad as it seemed.

Claire staggered to her feet, backing away as she reached under the collar of her shirt to pull out the religious medal she always wore on a long, shimmering golden chain. Fixed to the back, the pearlescent white scale for her totem looked exactly like the one on my bracelet. She stared at it in horror. "S-so we just transform in front of one another! That would fix it, wouldn't it? If we see each other transform, we'll lose our bond with our totem and it won't be able to—"

Madeline cut her off. "And who will fight the monsters that Dr. Livingston can still bring into this world? What you saw my father do with the Scepter of Time barely scratches the surface of its capabilities. He wasn't trying to destroy an entire city or raise a whole army of those monsters. But he could have, and now Livingston might. We are the only thing standing in her way, and the only thing she needs to achieve her goal."

"No," I protested. "The FBI got the scepter back. They have Livingston in custody right now. She's done."

Madeline's eyes fixed me with an empty stare that felt like I was looking into the infinite abyss of a black hole, as she replied, "She's never done, Koji. You may have interrupted her plans and forced her into the open, but no one can hold her. Her agents stole the scepter once. They'll do that and more again without batting an eye."

"So tell us then." Drake cut straight to the chase. "What does she want from all this? What's her endgame?"

"Her goal is *their* goal. The spirits of chaos. The kur." Madeline's whispering voice halted, knuckles going white as she twisted her fingers in her sweater sleeve. "And what they want is *us*."

"Us?" I barked in disbelief.

"Human beings," she clarified. "Specifically, our souls. Our spiritual energy. It's what they feed upon—what they need to survive. Our totem scales were sent here eons ago, not as some benevolent act to grant us supernatural power, but as probes. A test to discern if our spiritual energy was what they required. As our own souls are devoured, we *become* them. More specifically, we become their harvesters."

Oh God. This wasn't real—it couldn't be. Stuff like this didn't happen in real life! No. Way. This was a nightmare. It had to be.

Fortunately, while I was having an internal meltdown, Drake still seemed able to maintain a rational train of thought. "But the creatures we've seen summoned with the scepter aren't like Noxius and Oceana or even you. They didn't have those kinds of powers. They were mostly just big, dumb animals."

"You're right," Madeline agreed. "The scepter opens portals between our dimension and theirs, but only for a tiny fragment of time. It isn't long enough for anything with complex consciousness to pass through. What you've seen transported into our world are what Dr. Livingston calls lesser-kur. They're the equivalent of rodents or insects in their world—sentient but largely unintelligent. She theorized that's what the kur survive on while they search for new worlds to feed upon. It's enough to sustain them, but only for so long."

"So I've almost gotten killed fighting the equivalent of interdimensional cockroaches? Fantastic. Just freaking great!" I burst out of my chair and started pacing the room, trying to walk off my boiling rage.

"Not helpful, Koji," Claire warned.

I stopped and struggled through a few deep breaths. "S-Sorry. I just... I don't know what I'm supposed to do now. I don't want to keep a power that's killing me, but giving it up gets more people killed? I mean, is there any scenario here that doesn't end with someone dying?"

Madeline opened her mouth like she was going to answer and then closed it again. Turning her face away, I finally heard her mumble, "I don't know. Dr. Livingston's only goal is to bring the true kur here. That's all she ever researched or talked about."

"Why, though?" Claire had her totem scale pendant squeezed in one of her hands as she stared earnestly down at Madeline. "Why would she want to do something that would ultimately kill her, too?"

Madeline's head dipped lower as she murmured, "She believes letting the kur devour your soul makes you immortal within them. Almost like you become one of them, I think. It goes back to something she found during one of her archaeological expeditions in Egypt a long time ago. She guarded all that information very carefully. I might have managed to swipe some notes about it in the data I took, but I don't know for sure."

"Do you have that data with you?" Drake's amber eyes glinted like he was busy formulating his own plan.

"Well, yes, but—"

"Show it to me."

"It's heavily encrypted."

"Good thing I'm not a moron, then." He offered a crooked smirk and held out a hand. "Trust me, okay? If I can hack a few top-tier classified FBI databases from my phone, I think I can handle a little encrypted data."

Madeline jerked back slightly. "See, this is what you don't understand! The FBI, CIA, military, president—whoever—you can't trust them," she snapped, her tone desperate as she flashed a hysterical glance around at all of us. "That's what I mean—what you *have* to understand. You can't trust anyone now. Dr. Livingston has accomplices in every country. Her network is incredibly deep and fiercely loyal. They're ingrained into every government, military, police force, community—everywhere you can possibly imagine. There's nowhere she doesn't have eyes and ears, just waiting for orders."

"That's how they got the Scepter of Time back," I realized aloud.

"Yes," she confirmed. "It's only a matter of time before she is free and armed with the scepter. So I have to move now—I have to get to the totem of earth before she does."

I gulped. Agent Kirkland had mentioned his suspicions about a traitor in the FBI who helped swipe the scepter. If this was true, then it was way worse than just one mole. Unless...

"What about Agent Kirkland?" I asked. "Is he one of her followers?"

Drake shook his head. "No way. I went through everything from his personal phone and email records to his high school report cards—he sucked at Algebra, but he's no traitor. Carrie's clean, too. And was a phenomenal volleyball player, as it turns out."

"I'm sorry, but can we get back to the evil organization trying to destroy the world, please?" Claire urged. "How did your father get caught up with someone like Livingston?"

Madeline froze, seeming paralyzed in her seat for a moment. Then, in a soft, broken murmur, she began to explain.

It wasn't as bad as I'd thought.

It was much, *much* worse.

The more Madeline talked, the more she divulged about everything that had happened with her father and Dr. Livingston, and the more I felt like I was going to throw up again.

The good news was Madeline seemed to already know everything we did about what was going on with Dr. Livingston and the FBI. She even knew about her dad passing away, which was weirdly a huge relief. With no idea how I could possibly break that news to her, I'd been struggling to figure out the right time to bring it up—especially since it was apparently his exposure to the Scepter of Time that killed him. Tough topic to crack.

But Madeline already knew about that... and a whole lot more.

All this had begun a long time before I'd even moved to New York—or before we all started high school. For Madeline, it started after her mom passed away when she was five years old. Losing his wife was more than Gerard Ignatius could take. He'd lost his mind, driven to a state of insanity over getting revenge on the Fausts. And Madeline... well, she was just an innocent kid caught in the crossfire.

"For a long time, it seemed like nothing more than chance that we met Dr. Livingston," she explained quietly, drawing her legs to her chest. "Father always had an affinity for collecting historical artifacts—particularly ones that have to do with ancient religions, mythology, and the occult. He said he liked finding little bits and pieces of the same imagery and themes that seemed connected despite being from completely different times and cultural backgrounds. He would get this smile whenever he found something new. He used to say that the greatest irony of mankind is despite how far we think we've come, all we've really done is gone in circles."

Madeline sighed and quirked her mouth thoughtfully. One of her hands brushed along her sleeve to pause at the place under her sweater where her own totem scale was fixed to a golden cuff around her upper arm. "After Mother died, collecting things became more than an hobby. It was an obsession. He'd take me out of school for weeks and drag me all over the world to different auctions to search for new artifacts to add to his collection. We were at an auction in Cairo when he spotted my totem scale."

"How long ago was that?" Claire asked, her gaze flickering in my direction. It didn't last for more than an instant, but that brief glance was more than enough for me to see the traces of worry crinkling her brow. That concern twisted in my gut like a hot knife, too. If using our totems slowly ate away at our soul, and Madeline had been chosen by her totem way before the rest of us, then how much of her soul had been eaten away?

How much longer did she have until…?

My brain throbbed, throwing the brakes on that train of thought. I couldn't stand it. I couldn't even think about that.

Not yet.

"Ten or eleven," she answered. "It was in a collection of ancient Egyptian ceremonial pieces being auctioned by a private party." Her expression dimmed with cold resolve. "As it turned out, that private party was hosted by Dr. Livingston. She'd located the first totem scale and placed it at various auctions on high reserve. It was her way of fishing for its wielder. She wasn't actually trying to sell it, she was just trying to expose it to as many people as she could in a controlled environment."

Drake was back to scrolling on his phone again, brows knitted with focus as his fingers danced over the screen. "Found it. Leifton Rare Antiquities Auction, six years ago. She even registered under her real name. Bold move. And your dad bought it for—whoa, *sixty thousand dollars?*" He blinked up at her in surprise. "Where does a school headmaster get that kind of cash?"

Madeline shrugged, but her jaw tensed as she swallowed hard. Life insurance from her mom? I couldn't bring myself to ask something like that. And honestly, it didn't matter.

"So you tried it on?" I guessed.

She bobbed her head once. "Yes. And when the bond was made, Dr. Livingston approached us immediately. She told my father about the totems, the kur, and how I had been chosen. She made it all sound so wonderful. Like... like I was special." She choked and covered her mouth, eyes squeezing shut as tears rolled down her cheeks again.

I took a stumbling step closer as the instinct to rush to her, to put my arms around her and hold her close, almost overtook me. But I hesitated. Something uncomfortable squeezed in my chest. Madeline had been keeping all of this from us—that the totems slowing killing us. And, sure, her reasons sounded good. But how could she not tell me? How could she not find some way to warn me sooner?

I looked down at the toes of my sneakers.

It took a few minutes of Claire whispering softly to calm Madeline back down enough that she could continue. Unfortunately, the rest of the story wasn't totally unexpected. Dr. Livingston was a black widow, spinning her silky lies and pulling those delicate strands to suit her plans. And Madeline had been a helpless little kid caught in her web from the start. Dr. Livingston had manipulated Gerard Ignatius, using his hatred for the Fausts to convince him to allow them to experiment on Madeline with the Scepter of Time. Because of that, they'd found ways to bind, torture, and control totem wielders like us. They'd used records and ancient texts to make devices like the shackles and then tested them out on Madeline. And her father had just stood back and watched while they tormented, scarred, and abused her for years.

Then they'd found another totem—the one for water. Claire's totem. Because of her third eye, Madeline had been able to sense who would be the one to wield it right away.

"Father was furious when it turned out to be you," she murmured, blinking tearily at Claire. "He didn't want you to be special the same way I was. He didn't want you to have your totem. He argued with Dr. Livingston a lot about it. But I—I was so relieved."

Claire drew back slightly. "Relieved?"

"Maybe it was foolish, but somehow knowing that my birth sister was also destined to be a totem-wielder made me believe that we weren't supposed to be enemies. I wanted to know more about you, to be close enough that we could work together and stop Livingston before she hurt anyone else. But I didn't want her to do those things to you that she had... already been doing to me. So, when they weren't paying attention, I took the totem and gave it to you. I had to be sneaky about it, of course. You could never know it came from me. And when Dr. Livingston and my father found out, they were absolutely furious. It was worth it, though." A hint of satisfaction glinted in her soft gray eyes as she smiled.

Claire smiled back. "I just wish I had known it was you sooner. We could have fought this together a long time ago."

Madeline's stormy gaze shifted to me with meaningful force. "We couldn't. Not until they discovered the air totem... and I found *him*."

I blushed and rubbed the back of my neck. "Uh, what, umm, what do you mean found me?"

"By the time we found your totem, my third eye sense had grown more powerful. I knew it the second you landed in New York. I followed you from your hotel a few times. I wanted to know who you were, what you were like, and if you might be someone I could trust. I saw you and it was so obvious right away that you were truly a good person." She hesitated, her cheeks flushing as she looked away.

I almost choked out loud. Seriously? Madeline had been following me around when I first got here? Oh no. She hadn't seen me doing anything stupid, had she? Like scratching myself, or picking my nose, or that time I accidentally got my foot stuck in the subway train doors and lost my shoe? Ugh. No wonder she'd acted all weird around me in art class. I probably seemed like a complete moron.

"Things between my father and Dr. Livingston had grown more tense by then," Madeline went on, still blushing. "She shared secrets with me, trying to drive a wedge between my father and me. I let her think it was working long enough to gain her trust so I could steal your totem and bring it to you. I knew she would never trust me again after that."

"But you knew the three of you would be able to stop your dad if he decided to go public and attack the Fausts," Drake finished for her, finally putting his phone aside.

She gave a small, resigned nod. "My father was aware of the danger of using the Scepter of Time. In all of Dr. Livingston's experimentation, it was impossible to hide the fact that using it came at a high price. It didn't matter to him, though. He was bent on revenge and at times, I wanted it, too. I wanted to be angry. I wanted someone to blame for my horrible life. I thought that if my mother had lived, then none of this would have happened. It was ridiculous. It wouldn't have changed anything. The totem would have found its way to me regardless. I was still destined to be chosen. We all were."

"So, can you sense who is supposed to have the earth totem?" Drake's voice had a curious edge. "Could we contact them now? Let them know the situation before, you know, we drop a life-sucking, dragon-power-giving, ancient artifact in their lap?"

"Not yet," Madeline admitted. "My third eye allows me to sense the location of totem wielders. Sometimes, it even gives me glimpses of their face—but only after I physically touch the totem itself. As soon as I touch the earth totem, I'll know who is destined for it."

"Then we've got to find it—*now*. If you give me that data, I might be able to help you find the earth totem's location," Drake insisted. "Or at the very least, I can dig out any useful information that we might be able to use against her. This is our chance to be one step ahead."

"I think I already know where it is," she replied. "Even without the data, I was able to pinpoint a few hotspots of her network's activities around the world. Those places are where I intend to start my search. And that's why I can't stay here—why you can't tell anyone you've seen me or try to contact me again. I have to wait for the right moment to take it, when their gaze is drawn elsewhere."

"Drawn elsewhere?" I didn't understand how she could possibly anticipate something like that.

"I wasn't joking when I said that they will take the Scepter of Time back." She leveled a steely, determined frown on me. "They'll free Livingston as well. I have no doubts about that. And when they do, that is when I must make my move."

I swallowed hard, knowing the answer before I'd even finished asking, "Why don't you let us help you? I could go with you. Two of us stand a much better chance of—"

"No," she cut me off sharply. "Once I have it, I'll have to go back into hiding immediately. They'll be searching for me more fiercely than ever. And they'll likely have new clues about where I am. It's going to be dangerous, and I won't... I won't put you at risk."

I was about to make a compelling, expert argument about how I was already at risk, but Claire spoke up first. "Please, at least stay here tonight. Just so we know you're safe."

Madeline stiffened, glancing around at us with a tense, uncertain frown. Finally, she gave a small sigh. "Okay. Do... do you have a razorblade I can borrow?"

Claire glanced her over warily. "What do you need that for?"

She pulled up the sleeve of her sweater, running her thumb over a thin, raised bump in the crook of her elbow. What the heck was that? Was there seriously something underneath her skin?

"If you want the data, then I'm going to need it," she said. "And probably some Band-Aids, too."

# CHAPTER 21

I volunteered to handle the razorblade. Not that I was any kind of pro with one or was all that comfortable with cutting other people open. I just wanted a few minutes alone with Madeline, and if this was the only way to get it, then so be it. Nurse, scalpel, please.

"Aren't you afraid your father might realize you're gone?" Madeline asked as she sat on the countertop next to the sink, watching my pathetic attempts to sterilize the small razorblade. Claire found one in her dad's shaving stuff and brought it along with a small first-aid kit without anyone noticing. I got the impression that her parents were totally clueless about a lot of the things she did. You know, like sneaking out to do dragon-superhero stuff. Maybe they didn't check in on her much? In a house this big, it wasn't all that surprising. They probably had staff that did all the cleaning and cooking, anyway.

"Not really," I admitted as I turned on the hot water in the sink and rinsed the blade. "Nothing grooms you for sneaking around like superhero business."

"He'd be upset, though." She sounded genuinely worried—like she was afraid her presence might get me into trouble.

I snorted as I put the razorblade down on a clean washcloth and cracked open the first-aid kit, removing some packets of sterile gauze. "He's already upset with me. And besides, this is more important. Okay, let's see that arm."

I expected her to roll up her sleeve. I guess if she'd still been wearing that old, too-big sweater, she probably could have. But this one was more fitted—closer to her size. Before I knew what was happening, Madeline pulled it over her head and stuck her bare arm out in my direction.

Heat tingled through my face, down my neck, all the way to my shoulders. Steam was probably coming from my ears. S-She'd just... taken her shirt *off*. Right in front of me. I'd never seen, you know, a real, actual girl in a bra before. I mean, not that it was any different than a bikini top. And this wasn't romantic.

But still. It was lacy. And purple. Had she been wearing that the whole time? Or was she was borrowing it from Claire? Geez, why was I even thinking about this? Gah! *Focus, Koji!*

I tried not to wheeze out loud as I stepped closer, taking her arm and forcing my shaking hands to steady. Crap. Not cool at all. Maybe she'd just assume I was nervous about cutting her open and not, er, anything else.

Like bras.

"So, uh, what is this? I mean, how'd you get the data inside your arm?" My voice tremored and squeaked, betraying what a complete nervous wreck I was.

"It wasn't that hard. Originally, I'd put it all on one of those small USB drives—but only temporarily," she murmured, avoiding my eyes as I wiped at the spot on her arm with an alcohol swab from the kit. "It's a microchip. The same kind they put in pets. With the right modifications, you can store a fair amount of data on them, so all I had to do was break into a vet's office and transfer the data before I injected the chip."

Wow. Breaking into vet offices? Saving stolen secret information onto tiny chips and injecting them under her skin? Madeline was apparently way more capable when it came to this international fugitive, hardcore Jason Bourne lifestyle than I was. Come to think of it, she was better than me at a lot of stuff. Painting. Ceramics. Winning arguments with Drake.

My chest constricted with a familiar pain. I'd missed her so much. I'd almost driven myself crazy worrying about where she was or if she was safe. Now she was sitting right in front of me.

So why did it still feel like she was a thousand miles away?

"This might hurt a little." Or a lot, depending on how bad I sucked at it. I kept my voice quiet, trying to focus on keeping my hands steady as I held the blade right above the small, raised lump in her skin.

"It's okay," she murmured. "I can handle it."

I bit down hard. I knew she could handle it. Duh. That wasn't the point. She'd been handling it—everything—by herself from the start. And now that I was here, wanting to help her, she'd refused to even talk to me. Months had gone by, and I didn't know what was happening to her or where she was. Now that she was here, I couldn't shake the feeling that when she disappeared again, either to steal the earth totem or to hide from Dr. Livingston... I'd never see her again.

I kept my mouth shut as I steeled my nerves, pressing in with the point of the blade and cutting a thin line in her skin. Blood trickled down her arm and dripped on the countertop, and I realize why she'd taken the shirt completely off. This was going to be messy.

It took a minute of working with some thin tweezers from Claire's bathroom drawer to finally get the chip out. It was no bigger than a grain of rice, and slick with blood as I dropped it into a little paper cup.

I gave her a gauze pad to hold against the cut. "I know things were bad between us before. Er, well, maybe complicated is a better word. Anyway, I just wanted to say I'm sorry about your dad. That he died, I mean." I stammered and stalled like a total idiot. *Way to go, Koji. Bring up her dead dad—that'll lighten the mood.*

"I wish you could have known him before," she replied, her voice so faint I could barely hear it. "He was so enthusiastic about life. He had this hunger for adventure and finding lost treasures. He'd spend hours reading to me from his books about ancient history and showing me where all the archeology dig sites were that he wanted to visit. He promised to take me on all those adventures to find those lost treasures together. I think that's why I hate Dr. Livingston so much. She took the most beautiful thing about my father and twisted it into something wicked for her own gain."

I put my hand over hers. "We're going to stop her, Madeline. I know you don't think we can, but we will. I never back down from a fight."

She met my gaze but didn't reply.

I took that opportunity to finish dressing her wound, applying a small butterfly bandage over her cut and wrapping it with gauze, just to be safe. It wasn't an expert job, but it would do. "You sure you're okay to stay here with Claire tonight?"

"Yes."

I sighed and started cleaning up the blood on the counter, tossing the razor and the rest of the tools into the first-aid kit once they were blood-free. "I'm glad you two are getting along better. I have to admit, I was a little nervous about bringing you here."

A smile brushed over her lips. "You thought we would argue over you? Like a love triangle with you caught in the middle?"

"W-Well, I, uh, no, not over me, that's not what I, uh... I mean, no." Halfway through my blathering reply, I realized she'd been teasing me. Her smile widened as she peered up at me, impish light shimmering in her soft gray eyes. Great. She'd gotten me good with that one.

But two could play that game.

Stepping in closer, I took her hands in mine and let my forehead bump gently against hers. I smirked and waggled my brows. "Maybe I should just sneak you into my house next time. You can make fun of me while I bawl in terror over whatever horror movie you want."

Okay, so it wasn't a very good attempt. Before, whenever I'd made my clumsy attempts at romantic gestures with her, she'd blushed and acted all flustered. It was totally cute. I only hoped my flimsy Koji-charms still worked.

Madeline stiffened, pulling her hands out of mine as she leaned away. "Koji... we can't do this."

I watched, frozen in shock as she drew back from me. My heart pounded as I struggled to figure out what else she might be talking about other than, well, the obvious. "I-I, um, I'm sorry. That was a weird thing to say. I didn't mean, you know, anything dirty. I suck at flirting."

She kept her face turned away as she picked up her borrowed sweater and pulled it back on. "It's not that. It's just too complicated. We can't be like we were before. We can't be *together*."

"O-Oh, well I get that you can't come back to school. At least, not until everything is—"

"That's not what I mean." The tinge of icy finality in her tone was impossible to miss.

Oh. So this was her way of letting me down easy.

My stomach dropped to the soles of my shoes. "Madeline, please, just hear me out. I know things are kinda messed up right now, but after we—"

Her gaze snapped up to fix me with a silencing glare. "*No*, Koji."

I stood, dumbfounded and barely able to breathe. I'd never seen that coldness in her eyes before—like all the light and warmth inside of her had been sucked out. Like she wasn't even human anymore.

Was this what her father and Dr. Livingston had turned her into?

It only lasted a few seconds. Then she sighed deeply and dropped her head into her hands. "I'm so sorry. I didn't mean to sound... It's not your fault, okay? You haven't done anything wrong. What we had, what you gave me, was so beautiful. It's a gift I will cherish forever. It was the first time in my life I've ever felt normal. But we can't do this anymore. Normal couple things, dates to the movies, hot chocolate, painting together—I can't do it, Koji. We can't be like that."

Despite my best efforts, I couldn't keep from sounding pathetic. "Why?"

"Because the instant I let myself become attached, the second I feel something for you, is the same moment that Dr. Livingston has leverage to force me back into the open. For years she used my father against me. I won't let her use you, too. Or anyone else, for that matter. I won't make myself vulnerable like that again."

Anger whipped through my chest like winds from a rising storm front. I glared back at her, searching in vain for the girl I'd fallen for somewhere behind that guarded, steely gaze. "It's not your job to protect me, Madeline."

"It's not just you I'm protecting," she snapped as she hopped off the counter and started for the door. "It's myself. It's Claire. It's whoever is destined to wield the earth totem. It's everyone else on the planet. No offense, Koji, but some things are more important than some childish fairy tale romance. And I'm not willing to risk it. There's too much at stake, even if you refuse to see it."

I. Had. No. Words.

No matter how hard I tried, I couldn't make a single sound. My throat tightened. The anger thrumming through me fizzled. My arms hung slack at my sides.

What did that mean? Was she breaking up with me? Was that even the right word? We'd never been a real couple in the first place, right?

Before I could piece together even one intelligent sentence, Madeline glanced back at me over one of her slender shoulders. I could have sworn I saw the tiniest hint of pain in her expression. "Give the chip to Drake. He'll know what to do with it. And watch your back, okay? If Dr. Livingston knows who you are, then she likely knows your family, too."

My brain was still too deep in a frantic reboot to respond.

"Once I have the earth totem, I will send it to you immediately, so be on the lookout," she continued. "But that's as much as I'll be able to do without risking exposing myself or the chosen wielder to Dr. Livingston's network. Will you deliver it to them—to the person the earth totem chooses?"

I sucked in a steadying breath and forced myself to say, "No."

Her eyes widened.

"Not unless you agree to keep this with you," I clarified, slipping the thin FBI secret phone from my pocket and holding it out to her. "It's a secure line. Untraceable. And the only one who can answer it is someone we can trust. If you get in a bad spot, if you need help, swear to me you'll call Agent Kirkland."

Madeline eyed the phone like it might be explosive. Then, slowly, she stretched out a trembling hand to take it. "Okay."

Something about that answer didn't sit well—probably my third eye tipping me off that she was fibbing. She had no intention of ever using that phone.

Fine. Whatever. That was her choice. She could cut me off, break up with me, and tell me to get lost. It didn't matter. I just wanted her to be safe. I wanted her to know she wasn't alone—that someone out there was still watching her back. And if she didn't want that to be me, then… okay.

At least I knew Kirkland wouldn't let her down. Not if he wanted to keep both his arms, that is.

I stood in silence, my mind still churning long after she'd shut the door and left me in the bathroom alone. Part of me knew Madeline was right. There was a lot at stake here. But how the heck was pushing down all emotion and refusing to feel anything at all better? Emotion was the only thing that had saved me from Dr. Livingston in Colombia. If not for that, Claire never would have been able to find me. And Madeline was the one who started this romantic whatever-it-was. She'd kissed me first. Now I was supposed to just let it go? Move on? Pretend it never happened?

I guess so. What other choice was there? I wasn't going to try forcing it. And I wasn't going to beg her to be with me. That wasn't the kind of relationship I wanted with any girl—one with me desperate to make her stay and always feeling like I wasn't enough for her.

There was no other choice, really. I had to figure out how to let it go. God, this was going to suck.

Picking up the cup with the microchip inside, I tried to ignore the frenzy of confusion still whirling through my brain. I told myself it didn't matter. She was afraid and convinced she had to protect everyone else on her own. That wasn't true—and eventually she would figure that out for herself. This involved all of us, and that's the only way we were ever going to stand a chance of stopping Dr. Livingston from using that scepter again.

Her network was vast, strong, and loyal, so ours had to be even bigger, stronger, and more dedicated. Either we did this together, or we might as well not even do it at all.

Claire and Madeline spoke in hushed voices as I left the bathroom. If they watched me go past, I never knew it. I kept my head down as I crossed through the bedroom to get back out into the small living area. Drake stood by the window, his fingers waggling with excitement as he held his hand out for the cup like a kid begging for candy.

"So? Everything okay?" he asked as he held the cup up to inspect the chip. "Aaah, so that's what she did. Clever."

I kept my answers short as I stepped around him to open the window. "Fine. Let's just go. I'm supposed to be grounded. If Dad randomly decides to check my room and finds out I'm not there, he'll probably ship me off to military school."

Drake gave a bemused, snorting chuckle. "You? In military school? You wouldn't last through the first set of push-ups."

"Nope," I agreed as I climbed out the window and waited for him to catch up before closing the sliding glass pane again. "As soon as I got a chance, I'd transform and leave."

His grin was wolfish and a little creepy. "And I'd delete your name from all their systems and databases so it'd be like you never existed."

"Why do I get the feeling you're the only one actually enjoying all this special ops stuff?" I sighed.

"Touchy tonight, eh? Still pissed at your dad?"

I shook my head. I really wasn't up to spilling the ugly truth that Madeline had just dropped me like a rotten tomato. *Splat*— Koji feels everywhere.

"I don't even know anymore," I grumbled.

"Well, listen, I'm not supposed to say anything, but my mom wants to sit down as a group and talk about everything that happened. She thinks it's important for us all to get a chance to say how we feel, or whatever."

I groaned and rolled my eyes. That was literally the last thing I wanted to do right now. I didn't even want to think about it—or any of the other ridiculous, overwhelming crap that was currently seeping into my already complicated life.

Drake didn't sound all that thrilled about it either. "I'll let you know when that's coming. Maybe we can drop another pot on your head and get out of it."

I cracked a smirk as we made our escape from the Faust residence and started for the street. "Been there done that. New school year means we need some new excuse material."

"Okay, no pots then." He rubbed his chin thoughtfully as we strolled the sidewalk for a few blocks before flagging a cab. "What if we say you got hit by a car? Or fell out a window? Or got mauled by a bear?"

"Dude, there are no bears in Manhattan."

"Okay. Mugged then?"

"For what? My cell phone with the broken screen? Or the ten bucks in my wallet? Oh, or maybe my sub sandwich punch card with three holes left?"

He laughed and gave me a shove as I climbed into the backseat of the cab first. It never failed. Drake had a knack for pulling my head out of whatever mess was currently smothering the life out of me. I wasn't even sure he realized it. Maybe it didn't matter if he did or not.

Maybe all that was important was that we stayed friends, no matter what happened.

"You know, I kinda figured the hero gig would involve way more chasing down purse-snatchers or guys in black-and-white striped sweaters robbing banks," he mused. I guess he wasn't worried about the cabbie overhearing us. Not that we were being specific enough for it to matter much. As far as he knew, we were just two dumb kids chatting about video games or something, right? Right.

"Yeah, me too."

"And way less parental manipulation. I mean, seriously, trying to spin all these alibis *and* save the world? Not that the alibis are working so well lately. You know, for a weird military kid, you get grounded more than anyone else I've ever known."

I couldn't exactly argue that—and Drake didn't even know about all the times I'd been grounded in the last year. Not that I was going to let him in on that information. He did not need to know that I'd been grounded for using Dad's work laptop to download mods for my video games. Mods that, uh, may or may not have been riddled with viruses. Whoops.

Quirking my mouth, I cleared my throat and stole a glance at him out of the corner of my eye. "Uh, so... just so you're aware... I gave Madeline my phone."

His brows shot up. "*That* phone?"

I nodded.

"And she actually took it?"

"Yeah."

He sank back in the seat a little. "Think she'll actually use it?"

All I could do was shrug. The Madeline I'd just talked to, the one I'd found hiding in that musty old bookshop, was a hollow shell of the girl I'd known before. It felt like I didn't know her at all.

And now it seemed like she'd put up this huge wall between us. A wall I had no idea how to get through, or around, or over, or... whatever. Ugh. Was I even supposed to? Was she right? Was it better this way?

Or was I just being an idiot?

Probably. Nothing new there, right?

# CHAPTER 22

There were only a few sweet, precious hours left until the first day of school.

I probably should have been more pumped for it. I mean, this was junior year. I was actually at the same school as last year—a special bonus treat for a military kid. I had friends. As in, more than one. Also, a bonus.

Too bad the very thought of going back to school made me feel like I was sitting in the doctor's office, trying to mentally prepare myself for some doc in military fatigues to ram a popsicle stick down my throat in the name of healing. Choking. Gagging. Flailing. All of that, but in a starchy uniform and tie.

It probably had something to do with the fact that Dad and I were still stalking around each other in the house like a couple of gunslingers. Tense didn't even begin to describe it. We hadn't eaten dinner at the same time in almost a month. We hadn't even said a word to one another beyond a barked question or command and mumbled reply.

This stalemate couldn't go on forever. I knew that. Eventually, he'd corner me for another father-son, heart-to-heart chat. I just had no idea what that was going to be like. Things were different between us—and not just because I'd ruined his marriage proposal. Things between Dad and Ms. Collins had cooled considerably. And I guess that was my fault, too. I'd ruined his first real, meaningful, and good relationship since Mom.

No wonder he hated me.

Drake had assumed I was joking about military school. But as the days wore on, and we still hadn't resolved anything, that possibility had me walking on eggshells and keeping out of sight, hoping he would just forget I existed altogether.

Everyone else seemed to be doing a good job of that, anyway. Why not jump onboard?

Okay, okay. So that was a little melodramatic. Drake and I still hung out whenever I got a chance to sneak out and break the rules of my grounding-sentence. We'd passed the late-night hours at his place while his mom was at work, working through the encrypted data Madeline had given us. Er, well, he was working through it. I was mostly just there for moral support. And Funyun disposal.

I was pretty good at that last part. Years of rigorous training.

Plus, you know, after everything with Madeline, eating my feelings helped to heal the wound of having my heart crushed like a snail under an eighteen-wheel truck. I'd decided to raincheck the top-secret waffle-rendezvous with Claire, though. Even if we were just friends and I'd never meant for it to be a date, it still felt wrong. I knew she had *those* kinds of feelings for me. And my brain needed a break from girls.

It needed a break from a lot of things.

Camped out on a beanbag chair on Drake's bedroom floor, I watched the ending battle on *Pacific Rim* and reveled in the epic awesomeness of giant robots beating the crap out of giant kaiju alien monsters. Drake hadn't moved from his seat in hours and leaned into his trio of computer screens while his fingers flew over his keyboards.

The sudden squeak of his rolling desk chair made me look up just in time to see him lean back, stretch his arms over his head, and yawn. "You better head back soon, yeah?" he said as he spun the chair around, pulling his headphones off to let them dangle around his neck. "Your dad'll be up soon."

I glanced down at my phone screen and cringed. 4:56 a.m. Yep. He was right. Getting to my feet, I shook the crumbs off my hoodie and started for the door. "See you at school," I murmured, already dreading the inevitable standoff whenever Dad and I left for the day. Maybe I could just leave for school before he got out of the shower and then—

"Hey, dude?" Drake called.

I paused in the doorway.

"You okay?"

A hard knot formed in the back of my throat. My hand—the one above my totem bracelet—clenched. Lately that leather band, infused with all its ancient power, felt heavier and heavier.

"Yeah," I managed. "Fine."

"I don't need a third eye to tell that's a lie, Koji."

I didn't reply. What was the point? I could tell him, but he already knew.

Stepping out of his room, I shut the door behind me and clapped my hand over my wrist, whispering that single, life-altering word: "Awaken."

The power of my totem scale sizzled to life.

I never had to worry much about being spotted leaving his apartment at this hour. Drake and his mom lived in a rougher side of town. Not bad, mind you, just not great and usually pretty quiet this time of night—er, morning. Granted, I didn't always go dragon to get back home. But I was in a time crunch and, let's face it, why run when you can fly?

It took about two minutes to make it from Drake's place back to mine, skimming the Manhattan skyline with my wings spread wide. I landed as gracefully as an eagle atop our house, gripping the rooftop with the long, curled talons on my reptilian feet. For a second or two, I just stood there. I couldn't resist. Before me, the entire city was spread out like a tapestry of slender, gleaming glass spires reflecting the golden light of the rising sun. This was my city. My kingdom. My responsibility.

My everything.

"Tsk tsk tsk," a familiar voice scolded.

I suffered a small cardiac arrest. Whirling around, I stared directly into the molten glowing eyes of Oceana. Her long blue and silver hair rustled in the morning wind, rippling like silk ribbons over her sleek, scaly form.

"You never learn, do you? What did I say about taking joyrides over the city?" A bewitching dragoness smile curled over her lips. "Do I need to hurl you into Central Park again as a reminder?"

I hung my head slightly, swishing my long tail. "I was a little late for curfew."

She stepped lightly past me, eyes fixed upon the horizon. "I'll say."

"What... what are you doing here?" I dared to ask.

She turned and fixed me with a meaningful stare. "I thought I should warn you that I'm coming back to school tomorrow."

I arched one of my dragon-y eyebrows. "Warn me? Planning on starting a food fight or something?"

She cracked a grin and shrugged. "Who knows. It was a nightmare getting my parents to agree to it. But in the end, they'd rather see me back in school than going to the press with a public apology for everything that was suffered by my birth sister and her family because of their lies and manipulation."

Okay. Wow. Now both eyebrows were up. "You're blackmailing your own parents?"

Her lips pursed proudly. "Just a little taste of their own medicine, really. Besides, it doesn't matter. I already sent the apology letter to the press."

I couldn't help it. I choked out loud. "Y-y-you did? After they already agreed to let you go back to school?"

"No," she answered simply. "Before that."

I wasn't sure what to say.

"After seeing her, I made up my mind." She paced to the edge of the roof, the wind filling the leathery membranes of her slender, blue-scaled wings. "I'm not going to be like them, Koji. I'm not going to play by their rules. Not anymore. No more secrets. No more lies, scandals, and self-righteous speeches. I want to be something my parents can't even begin to understand." Her eyes narrowed slightly, taking in the bright glow of the rising sun. "I want to be *real*."

A smile crept up my face and I didn't even try to stop it. Standing next to her, I put a hand on her shoulder and sighed. "For whatever it's worth, I like the real you much better."

She giggled and shrugged my hand off with a taunting smirk. Sinking down in a crouch, she spread her wings and prepped for takeoff. "So do I. Watch out tomorrow, Owens."

I nodded, raising my hands in mock surrender. "I've been warned."

Oceana winked, nodded, and took off into the sunrise like a shimmering, silvery-blue arrow. Part of me envied her. She was changing, but she was becoming something better. Or at least that's how it seemed to me.

And I... well, I just felt stuck.

Stuck and—LATE! Oh my God. So freaking late!

Clambering down the slope of the roof, I slapped a hand over my totem bracelet and bade it to sleep. As the last few hints of my scales melted away, I rounded the narrow ledge to my bedroom window. Cold sweat slid down the sides of my face as I pressed it open and stepped softly down into my room. One look around and my whole body sagged with relief. Whew. Everything was just how I left it. Dark. Quiet. A reasonably messy disaster, but hey, it's not like I was expecting company.

I turned back, clenching my teeth and wincing as I carefully pulled my window closed. The old hinges resisted, threatening to squeal and give me away. As the big circular pane slid back into place, I dared to let out a long, shaky exhale.

Aaand that's when Dad cleared his throat.

I whirled around, heart thumping wildly, to find my dad standing in my bedroom doorway with his arms crossed. All the blood drained out of my face. He was already dressed for work in his military "blues" uniform—a white shirt adorned with medals and a pair of pristinely ironed navy blue pants. As a pilot, he'd never worn that uniform much outside of special occasions. He must've gotten up earlier than normal to check it over.

That angry little vein was back, throbbing away, and I could practically see tiny burning villages crackling and smoking in his narrowed eyes. Peasants screaming and running for cover.

Oh God. I was about to die.

"Have a nice time?" he asked. The unnatural calm in his tone made my brain scramble. It reminded me a little of Hannibal Lecter from *The Silence of the Lambs*. That couldn't be good.

I opened my mouth, but nothing would come out. Not even a pathetic scream for help. Sirens blared in my head. My life was over. Military school, here I come. Drake was right, I couldn't do three push-ups without collapsing. I'd be dead within a week.

"I'd ask how long this has been going on," he continued, still using that creepily calm voice. "But after watching that display, I'm going to assume this is a regular part of your routine. So instead I'll ask this." His eyes went steely. "Where have you been?"

Lie—I needed a lie. A good one. Something he would believe that wouldn't get Drake in trouble, too. He'd undoubtedly cover for me, but I wasn't about to throw him under the parental bus of doom, too.

"Uh, I-I, umm." My thoughts tangled. *Come on, brain, don't fail me now.* Before I could stop it, I blurted the first thing that came to mind. "I-I've got a... girlfriend."

Great. He'd never buy that. Might as well start writing out my will.

Dad's brow knitted, like he was focusing all his parental mind powers on me at once to try and figure out if I was telling the truth. "A *girlfriend?*"

"Y-Yeah," I squeaked.

"And you've been sneaking out to see her?"

"Uh, well, she's... kind of high profile. So we can't exactly meet in public. Plus, I'm grounded still."

His frown deepened. "Well, on top of dealing with my son sneaking out past curfew while also under a grounding sentence, I now have to call her parents and apologize. So thanks for that, Koji. Thanks a lot." He rubbed his eyes. "Who is she? What's her name?"

I scratched at the back of my neck. "Well, uh, that's a little complicated. I don't exactly know her real name." Pearls of sweat rolled down the bridge of my nose. "It's...um, it's Oceana."

His scowl broke into a look of total shock. "You're sneaking out to see one of those monsters?"

"She's not a monster, Dad," I protested weakly. "After I met her at the whole Winter Ball thing and then she saved everyone at the Philharmonic, we... kinda sorta started hanging out." Oh, sweet Mary Mother of God, I hoped he was buying this. Never in my life had I needed some Drake lying backup like I did right now. "And I don't know her real name, but I do know that she doesn't always look like a dragon-girl. It's kind of like a suit—sort of. Anyway, she's actually really nice. And we hang out. At night. A lot."

I gulped, my sweaty toes writhing inside my sneakers while I waited on him to respond.

Seconds ticked by.

At last, he muttered what were probably a few profanities under his breath and shook his head, pinching the bridge of his nose. "Koji, superhero girlfriend or not, I'm not sure you get how serious this is. And to be perfectly honest, I'm at a loss."

Well, that made two of us.

"I was going to wait to bring this up this afternoon, but I guess now is as good a time as any," he said, and I got the distinct impression I wasn't going to like whatever came next. "I made an appointment for you with a therapist. Well, it's for both of us, actually. Amelia thought it would be a good idea for us to work through this with professional help. As much as I despise the idea, you've backed me into a corner. I don't know what else to do. So we're going—today after school."

All the feeling seemed to gradually seep out of my extremities, leaving me numb and tingly. Dad wanted us to talk with a therapist? Like, lying on the long couch, "it all started when I was born" kind of therapist?

Before I could even wrap my mind around that idea, he fixed me with a hard, dangerous look. "In the meantime, I'm going to be thinking of how to address this... sneaking out problem you seem to have. This will have consequences, Koji. I hope you're prepared for them."

My stomach dropped. Oh no. Frantically, I tried to think of what could be worse than being sent to military school.

"If I come in tonight and you aren't here, expect whatever those consequences are to intensify," he warned.

I managed a small, frantic nod.

Silence swallowed us again—that same awful, strained, angry silence that had been building up ever since that night on the cruise ship. It set my heart pounding in my ears, like waiting on a bomb to detonate or a doctor to break bad news.

Eventually, I knew that silence was going to break. And whatever came after would almost certainly be explosive. I just hope I survived it.

# CHAPTER 23

Going to bed wasn't an option. Not with the threat of mysterious consequences and attending therapy hanging over my head. I couldn't relax. So instead, I waited in silence, stretched out on my bed, until I heard Dad leave for work. Then I got ready for school.

A quick shower and shave were all I bothered with before I put on one of my Saint Bernard's Catholic School uniforms—a button-down shirt, tie, sweater, dark slacks, and dress shoes. Sadly, everything from last year still fit me. I hadn't gained any muscle or even grown. Not that I was all that worried about the height part. I was already six feet, so it's not like I was in dire need of any more inches.

A few pounds of muscle would've been nice, though.

By the time I got to school, a booming thunderstorm had settled over the city, bringing with it churning dark clouds, howling winds, and sheets of cold rain that stung my cheeks like needles. Naturally, the rain didn't start until I was already half-way to school and too far to go back for my umbrella. So much for my peaceful rooftop sunrise. The reckless, stupid part of me wanted to transform long enough to use my power to make the storm disperse. But what was the point? I was already drenched.

My shoes sloshed and my hair dripped as I stalked through the front door, wringing wet and cursing under my breath. I was a full hour early, and there were only a handful of other students milling around in the grand front foyer. Freshmen mostly. You could pick them out by their wide-eyed looks of terror. Boy did that bring back memories.

Thankfully, Drake was nowhere to be seen. I was in the clear. Otherwise, I'd have probably been subject to intense teasing for the rest of the day. I dripped a puddle trail all the way through the school's front entryway, down the first hallway past the headmaster's office, and down two more long halls lined with classrooms to the men's locker room. There had to be some towels in there, right?

I flipped the light switch on as I passed through the swinging door. I hadn't stood in a school locker room since my own freshman year PE class. I shuddered. Never again. Dodgeball had officially scarred me for life because being the tallest, skinniest freshman automatically made me everyone's favorite target.

The setup in the locker room was better than I'd hoped. There were stacks of clean white towels folded on a shelf next to the shower stalls and a few of those nifty swimsuit-spinny-dryer things on the far wall. Perfect.

With no one else in sight, I threw my stuff down and quickly stripped out of my wet clothes. I'd packed an extra shirt to keep in my locker in case of emergencies or mustard stains, so I put that on with my only semi-damp boxers and toweled off my hair. Then I got to work running each piece of my uniform through the swimsuit-dryer.

It didn't work as well as I'd hoped, but it at least got them dry enough I wouldn't be dripping anymore puddles through the school. Good enough.

I'd just slipped back into my dress slacks and fastened my belt when the sound of the door opening echoed over the white-tiled walls. Who else would be here this early? One of the coaches, maybe? I told myself it didn't matter. I was almost finished. All I had to do was put my tie and sweater back on and—

"OWENS." The unfamiliar voice boomed in the locker room.

I whipped around just in time to see Damien Blount storming toward me, face flushed and eyes blazing with fury.

Oh no. What now?

Before I could speak, react, or do anything, he grabbed the front of my shirt collar and slammed me back against a row of lockers with a *BANG*. The impact knocked the wind out of me, and my head cracked off the metal locker doors.

Claire's beefy maybe-ex-fiancé snarled right in my face, his other hand already cocked in a fist. "You slimy, arrogant, little—" He didn't even finish his insult before he swung. He punched me across the jaw so hard my head snapped back and smacked off the lockers again. The warm, coppery flavor of blood filled my mouth and stars winked in my vision.

"Did you think I didn't notice you ogling Claire all the time like a freaking stalker? Or that no one would tell me about you making passes at her when I wasn't around?" He narrowed his eyes as he yelled in my face, his whole body twitching like he couldn't decide if he wanted to rip my head off right away or beat me to a bloody pulp first. "I know about *everything!*"

Okay, I seriously doubted that. No way Claire had told him about our after-school-or-sometimes-during-school job.

Damien's knuckles blanched as he drew back again, prepping to take another swing. "You've been trying to get between us this whole time. Well, congratulations. She ended it. And now it's gonna cost you."

I should have been terrified.

Granted, Damien wasn't as tall as I was, but he at least had forty pounds of solid muscle on me. Not to mention he was on the judo team, and word around the school was that he might have national-level potential. So, there was absolutely no doubt in my mind that Damien Blount could break every bone in my body and fold me up like a cheap lawn chair.

But I wasn't scared. I wasn't even surprised or shocked anymore. I was... *angry.*

"Back off," I growled through clenched teeth. "I never touched her or said anything to her like that. I don't know where you're getting this, but you need to recheck your facts. Claire and I are friends—that's it. If you want to get pissed at someone because she broke up with you, go look in the mirror."

His eyes widened. For an instant, he seemed to freeze in place. So, I took that opportunity to punch back.

One hit right across the nose made him release the front of my shirt. Damien staggered back a step and I immediately rushed him, giving him a shove so I could put some more distance between us. If he came after me again, at least I'd have a little more time to prepare.

My chest heaved with ragged breaths as I glared at him, fists balled and braced for a brawl. He'd win, of course. I stood no chance of overpowering him. But I did not run from a fight. Not ever.

"Don't freaking lie to me, Owens." Damien gave an ironic, humorless chuckle as he brushed his fingers over his nose, smearing the blood that oozed from his nostrils across his chin. "Tabitha told me everything. How you were crushing on her from the start. How you're the only one she talks to now. I guess you thought taking her to dances and stuff was your big lucky break, huh?"

My temper flared. My vision went red. Tabitha sold me out? After I'd helped her reconcile with Claire? What the actual hell?

"Tabitha's an idiot," I fired back. "Or she's just jerking you around. I only did that stuff because she or Claire asked me to. I like someone else, moron." My boiling rage subsided a little at the thought, making my arms relax some as I forced myself to admit it out loud. "Or I did. It doesn't matter now. She dumped me."

Damien hesitated, blinking as his expression skewed with confusion. "What? Who?"

Pain stung at my chest and I was too humiliated to even look him in the eye. "Madeline Ignatius."

"You were dating *Madeline*?"

Ugh. For crying out loud. Twist the dagger, why don't you?

I shook my head and licked my teeth behind my lips, still tasting blood. "Sort of. It was casual. But... I really liked her. Then she ended it." I decided not to give him a timeline for all that. I didn't want to give away to anyone that Madeline was back in the city. Besides, it wasn't any of his business.

Thick, tense silence made the air between us seem heavy. I could sense him studying me, as though he were trying to figure out if I was lying or not. I guess I looked exactly as miserable as I felt because he finally let out a defeated sigh. "Great. Just great. Coach'll kick me off the team for this."

I flicked him a puzzled glance. Was he going to actually confess he'd attacked me? Or did he just expect me to snitch on him?

Clearing my throat, I dared to let my guard drop. I straightened and rubbed the back of my neck—anything to hide the way the adrenaline still had my hands shaking. "I... uh, I hit you back. So let's just call it even, yeah?"

He arched a brow dubiously. "Seriously?"

I gave a small nod as I turned away to start picking up my tie and sweater. Then I grabbed a clean towel off the shelf. "My dad's already royally pissed at me," I said as I tossed it to him so he could wipe his nose. "I don't need anything making it worse."

"Oh." Damien caught the towel, but he kept eyeing me up and down like he wasn't fully convinced. "Well, anyway, sorry about this."

I shook my head. "Don't worry about it."

"For the record, you hit pretty hard for, uh, someone who..." His voice trailed off like he was struggling to come up with a word to describe me that didn't sound insulting.

"Looks like Jack Skellington in a Catholic uniform?" I managed a half smirk as I quickly tied my tie and tucked it beneath my shirt collar.

He gave a snorting chuckle. "Sure, whatever." Then he paused, looking uncertain. "So we're cool?"

"Yeah, we're cool." I yanked my sweater over my head and picked up my bag and damp extra shirt. "I may trip Tabitha the next time I see her walk past me, though."

"Don't bother," he replied glumly. "I'll talk to her."

I'd already started for the door when he called after me again. "Hey, Koji?"

I paused and glanced back. "Yeah?"

"You talk to Claire sometimes, right?"

"A little," I lied like an absolute dog. But he did not need to know that most of our talks centered around superhero stuff.

"Do you, uh, do you think it's possible she has feelings for someone else?" His mouth screwed up, like he was bracing himself for my answer.

I could've lied to him again. It would've probably been the safer, smarter option given what we'd just been through. But Claire was already keeping a lot of secrets from this guy. And if he had any real feelings for her at all, then someone should tell him the truth, right? So he could move on? Claire had been pretty clear that she didn't have any feelings for him. So it was kinder to let him down easy instead of giving him false hope, right?

I had to look away. "Yeah. I think so."

Damien bobbed his head slowly. "I... I sort of figured that. I was hoping it was you because, otherwise—" His voice caught, mouth flattening into a hard, dejected line for a second or two before he seemed able to continue. "Otherwise, I can't compete. Not with someone like that."

"Someone like who?"

Damien hung his head, twisting the blood-speckled towel in his hands in frustration as he mumbled, "Noxius. Things weren't the same between us after he saved her at the holiday festival."

"O-Oh," I choked. "You, uh, you really think she'd fall for a half-dragon monster guy?"

"Come on, you were at the Philharmonic. You saw the battle. You know Madeline was one of them. Whoever the guy really is under that dragon disguise, he's human. And he's the one she wants." Damien balled the towel up and tossed it into one of the hampers at the end of the row of lockers. I could only see one side of his face, but even that glimpse of his profile was enough. I'd seen that look before—mostly from Dad whenever someone mentioned my mom.

Damien cared about her. He might've even loved her. But… he knew he'd already lost. She was as good as gone. And there was nothing he could do about it.

The rest of the school day passed like a dreary, rainy eternity filled with strangeness I could not even begin to fathom. My schedule was okay, I guess. I had all the basic core classes: Algebraic Connections, Environmental Science, English, Economics, blah blah blah. The only fun thing I had to look forward to all day was art class. Mr. Molins had invited me to join one of his graphic art classes with a bunch of seniors so I could start learning some Adobe and 3D rendering programs. I knew the instant I cracked open Photoshop and started practicing with the tablet and stylus that I was going to enjoy the challenge.

Unfortunately, that's where the good news ended.

Claire was right. Her reappearance at school had everyone stirred up from the second she darkened the doorway. When Claire's letter hit all the major news sites a little before lunch, rumors flew like trailers in a tornado. It went viral in seconds, and more than one person approached to ask if I'd heard anything from Madeline since she went to prison, or if she was really in the witness protection program now.

I only had two class periods with Drake—Economics and lunch. Claire was in my English class, but I was too much of a coward to even look at her. I shuffled to the back of the room and dropped into an empty row by myself. Tabitha was in my Environmental Science class, which was right before lunch. I couldn't decide if it was weirder that she sat down next to me in the back row or that she hung around to walk with me to lunch instead of falling in with a group of her friends.

"I'm so sorry, Koji! I guess I didn't do a good job of explaining things to Damien. It's all my fault—I should've been clearer," Tabitha pleaded as she trotted beside me like an excited puppy. "He was asking if you two had been hanging out and I said I just knew that you talked a lot and were really close. He must've gotten the wrong idea."

Yeah. No kidding. I had a brand-new, giant bruise on my chin to show for it.

"It's fine," I mumbled as I shuffled along with my hands in my pockets.

"No! It isn't. Please don't tell Drake—he'll be so angry," she begged. "You've got to let me make it up to you."

I forced a smile just so she'd let it go. "No, no. It's okay, really. I won't say anything to him. I promise."

Tabitha didn't look convinced, and she sat stiff and silent next to Drake for most of the lunch period. Honestly, I wasn't mad at her. It sounded like Damien had been grasping at straws—desperate for any alternative rival instead of Noxius—so him singling me out wasn't a big surprise. I was an easy and convenient target.

What was a surprise was looking up to find him sitting down next to me at the lunch table. Damien gave a small, half-hearted grin and shrugged as he plopped his lunch tray down and settled in.

Um. What the heck was going on? Since when did he sit with anyone who wasn't on the judo team? And why me?

Across the table, Drake stared at our new table buddy with his eyes as big as softballs. His chewing slowed, then stopped. While Damien and Tabitha exchanged an awkward greeting, Drake mouthed, *"Why is he here?"*

I rolled my eyes and shrugged. How was I supposed to know? Did swapping punches make us friends now? Like some weird judo rite of passage? Or maybe—and this was *way* more likely—he was just sucking up because he was still afraid I'd go squealing to a teacher or his coach about what happened.

Whatever the case, it made the rest of lunch painfully awkward. Drake kept his head down and didn't say much. Damien didn't either. Tabitha talked enough for all three of us, and I tried to at least look like I was listening as I shoveled handfuls of sweet potato fries into my mouth. If I was chewing then I had a valid excuse not to answer, right? Plus, you know, giving myself a delicious food hug did wonders for my current outlook on life.

At the end of the day, I had a bag full of homework and a growing suspicion that I'd somehow entered the Twilight Zone and was currently experiencing an alternate reality where Damien and I were friends, Tabitha was a nice person, and I actually stood a chance at making decent grades. Standing in front of my locker, I tried to wrap my mind around that while I crammed a few of my textbooks next to my notebooks and binders. I'd forgotten to clean my bag from last year, so I wasn't prepared when I pulled out my art journal from Mr. Molins's class—the same one shared with Madeline.

I swallowed, staring down at the frayed edges of the sketchbook. Why did I even have this thing anymore? I should just toss it. It's not like I was ever going to actually write an entire comic about myself as a superhero. Talk about lame.

I cringed as the voice of Josh, the covert FBI secretary, crackled over the intercom system, echoing down every hall in the school. "Koji Owens, please report to the headmaster's office. Koji Owens to the headmaster's office."

Great. What now? Had someone else seen my fight with Damien and reported it? Or had one of my teachers noticed my bruise and gotten suspicious? Either way, this couldn't be good.

Slamming my locker, I shouldered my spiffy uniform-mandated messenger bag and started down the stairs to the main office. I'd barely gotten in the door when Drake bounded to his feet and rushed to greet me. What was he doing here?

Off to the side, another familiar face stood by the door to the headmaster's office. She hugged a small brown leather instrument case against her chest. I had seen her from behind in class, but I almost didn't recognize Claire as I sat beside her. She had all her beautiful, soft golden curls wound into a braided bun with a few spiraling locks framing her face. It changed her whole appearance. Her faint, apprehensive smile sent a pang of worry through my chest. Why were we all here? Was this about Dr. Livingston?

Before I could ask, the door to the headmaster's office clicked open and Agent Carrie waved us inside with a similarly cautious smile.

Drake and I swapped a glance. He shrugged. I guess he didn't know what this was about either.

I barely got a foot through the doorway before the sound of a man's voice brought me to a lurching halt. Okay, this was definitely not good. Sitting in one of the leather chairs across from the desk, Agent Kirkland had his fingers laced together and a preoccupied, pensive frown on his lips. His gaze darted to each of us—Claire, Drake, and me—as we entered and stood close together like a flock of scared goats.

"I hope you guys had a good first day back," Agent Carrie spoke up as she shut the door. Her efforts to diffuse the oppressive tension in the air were painfully obvious. Nice try, though. Points for effort.

Agent Kirkland, on the other hand, cut straight to the point. He took a folded-up photograph about the size of a piece of paper from his pocket and spread it out on the desk. It was grainy and out of focus—probably because it had clearly been taken at night through a long-range lens—but the image was clear enough you could tell exactly who the two figures were. It was a shot of Madeline and me climbing into the back of a cab outside a familiar secondhand bookstore.

"Anyone want to explain this to me?" he demanded, his tone eerily calm and composed. "I thought we had an understanding about what you were supposed to do if you saw, heard from, or found a way to contact Madeline Ignatius."

I tensed. Claire shifted next to me.

Drake was the only one who seemed completely unfazed. "Sure. She contacted Koji to pass along some top-secret data. But she doesn't trust you—and frankly, after that hot mess in Colombia, I don't blame her."

Kirkland sat up straight, his pale eyes blazing like cold fires in the dim light of the office. "She is a threat to public safety. Need I remind you that she is responsible for the deaths and injuries of nearly fifty people at the Philharmonic?"

"And *you* have a mole in your organization that got a bunch of innocent doctors tortured and killed," Drake barked back. "It almost killed my best friend, too, by the way. So how about you climb down off your pedestal and get real with us for once?"

Kirkland pursed his lips, seething silently for a moment or two before he spoke again in a calmer, quieter voice. "Very well, then. Less than twenty-four hours after this photograph is placed in my hands, I was given notice that the artifact was stolen again."

"Th-the scepter?" I blurted with a wheezing gasp.

He nodded slightly. "Once again, we don't know how or when it was taken. And although Dr. Livingston remains in our custody, I am no longer confident that we will be able to keep her there should her... affiliates attempt to free her. Especially if one of them possesses a certain fire-generating totem scale."

"Madeline isn't a traitor," Claire snapped suddenly. "She hates Livingston, probably more than any of us. I felt it in her emotions when she told us everything. That kind of hatred isn't something you can fake."

Agent Kirkland breathed a long, heavy exhale as he stood. The leather chair creaked, and his shoes clicked off the hardwood floor as he paced back and forth in front of Carrie's desk. "You do realize the position you've put me in, don't you? I can't trust any of you to relay important information to me. I can't trust my own staff or superiors. And because of that, I can't even trust myself to make adequate decisions about how to keep more people from dying."

No one spoke for a long, uncomfortable moment. My mind churned at the prospect of having the scepter at large and in the wrong hands again. Crap. He was right. If we didn't start working as a team on this, it could go sideways on a much bigger scale.

I bowed my head as guilt sank into the pit of my stomach like a block of red-hot iron. "There's, um, there's something else you need to know," I murmured.

Kirkland's brows shot up. "Is that so?"

"I gave Madeline my secret phone," I confessed. "I don't know if she'll use it, but I made her take it. She's going to try to steal the earth totem soon. I don't know when, exactly, or even where she's going. But Madeline said she thinks she knows where it is and can get to it before Livingston. If she does, she's going to deliver it to me for safekeeping."

"Oh God," Carrie whispered. "You're sure you don't know where she is? Or where she might be going?"

"No." I stared down at the floor, my ears burning with shame. "I tried to get her to stay. But Madeline thinks she has to keep hiding. She's terrified of Livingston finding her. I said if she got in a bad place, if she needed help, to call you. You... you could help her, right?"

Carrie and Kirkland exchanged an uncomfortable, obviously uncertain glance. Great. So much for that.

"We'll certainly try," Carrie promised.

"If you get any tips or ideas about her location, please let us know. But only report it to me or Agent Carrie. Understood?" Kirkland added. "You mentioned she gave you data? Data about what?"

Drake was already taking off his backpack and digging through it for one of his many self-built laptops. "It's all heavily encrypted. I mean, pro-level stuff. But here's what I've gotten so far. You, uh, you might want to grab a seat. This could take a while."

# CHAPTER 24

I didn't stick around for Drake's entire presentation. A lot of what he'd found was just more detailed information about stuff I already knew, like the tests Dr. Livingston had done on Madeline with the scepter and her own totem. That was *not* something I was interested in hearing about. Anger like wildfire scorched through me as I listened to Drake describe it. All I could picture was a little, 10-year-old Madeline strapped to a metal table and experimented on like a lab mouse. It was too much. I guess Carrie and Kirkland could tell how much it bothered me, because neither of them argued when I excused myself and left the headmaster's office.

I told myself to let it go. Breathe. Don't think about it. There wasn't anything I could do now to change any of it, and Madeline didn't want me around to try to help her now. I needed to focus on normal life stuff. Yeah—that would help.

Standing before the front doors of the school, I watched the storm still raging full force outside. Ugh. Great. I'd really been hoping I could use the walk home to clear my head. So much for that.

Typing out a message, I let Dad know the storm had gotten too bad for me to chance walking. He quickly responded and told me to wait inside. He was already on his way home and would swing by to pick me up in a few minutes. We'd go straight to our therapist appointment.

If not for the fact that I'd already gotten soaked once today, I might've just opted to walk anyway rather than having to sit with him in the creeping afternoon traffic. The lineup of cars in the streets outside seemed worse than usual today. Maybe this much rain had things slowed down or there'd been a few accidents or something.

Regardless, it was going to be a long ride.

"Have you been sneaking off to fight bad guys without me again?" I almost jumped right out of my fancy dress shoes as Claire appeared beside me. Her smile was tinged with hints of worry as she studied my bruised chin.

"You know it." I snorted. "Can't have you stealing all my glory every time, now can I?" I decided not to tell her what had actually happened. The last thing I needed was to get caught up in more drama between her and Damien. We had enough to worry about.

"So, how was your first day back?" She sidled closer, joining me in staring out at the stormy streets through the glass window in the door.

"Probably not as bad as yours." I chuckled. After all, I'd only gotten harassed a few times about Madeline. I could only imagine what she'd been through. "Violin?" I tipped my head to where she still held the small instrument case in one hand.

"Actually, yes. And as far as first days go, mine was great," she announced. "It was really nice to be honest about everything. My parents wouldn't let me play anything except cello. I've always wanted to try the violin. So I bought one. I start private lessons tomorrow. Next, I think I'll start learning electric guitar."

"Yeah?" I stole a quick glance at her, unable to resist a half grin at the idea of watching her raging on a hot pink Flying V. Epic.

Claire was now smiling from ear to ear, clarity and energy sparkling in her sea-green eyes. "Yeah. I'm pretty excited. I wish I had been brave enough to do this a long time ago. I don't know if I'll be any good, but it's fun to try."

Well, at least one of us had enjoyed the first day back.

Through the pouring rain, I spotted a familiar car sliding to a halt right outside the school. My phone buzzed as I got a new message, but I didn't have to look to know who it was from. Dad was here. I had to go.

Shifting my backpack, I took a deep breath as I prepared to brave the weather. "Well, see you tomo—"

"I'm so sorry that she ended it, Koji," Claire interrupted suddenly.

My heartbeat skipped. She *knew*? Had Madeline told her about breaking up with me?

I was too afraid to look down at her again. I didn't want her to see it—how much it hurt to even think about. It was stupid, I guess. She could feel it because of her third eye, but still.

"You've been sad and confused since that day," she whispered. One of her hands bumped mine, like a subtle gesture just to let me know she was right there beside me. "And that night, you were..." She hesitated, her voice fading to silence. Then I felt her curl one of her fingers gently around mine to give my hand a small tug. "I wanted to burst in there. I wanted to scream at her that she was wrong. That she shouldn't do anything to hurt you like that. But I couldn't. I could feel her emotions, too."

My pulse thrashed in my ears as I shut my eyes tightly, struggling to keep my own emotions from breaking the surface. "What were they?" I just had to know.

"Anger. Regret. Sorrow." Her voice was so quiet I could barely hear her. "But most of all... fear."

"Do you think she ever loved me?" The question ripped out of me before I could stop it. It was a stupid, selfish thing to ask her. Claire liked me, maybe loved me. Asking her about another girl's feelings was a major jerk move.

But I couldn't help it. I needed to know. I had to.

Her hand slipped away from mine.

When Claire didn't answer, I looked down to see if I'd hurt her—or maybe she'd walked away. Instead, I found myself staring directly into her shimmering, worried eyes and felt like we were completely alone in the universe. She couldn't lie to me.

But more than that, I knew she'd never try.

"I don't know," she said. "I think the person she is now may not be anything like the Madeline we knew before. Either because of her exposure to her totem, or what Dr. Livingston did to her, or losing her father like that. It all takes a toll. And when I try to focus on her emotions, everything feels so tangled and confused. I don't think she even knows how she feels anymore."

I bowed my head as I pushed the door open. "Well... I guess that makes two of us, then."

Dad didn't say a word when I climbed into the back seat of the car. No way was I sitting up front next to him. Usually, he would've at least asked how my first day was, pressed me for details on what classes I was in, what my teachers were like, or if I made any new friends. Typical parent stuff. But he didn't even say hello.

With the radio down low to fill the silence, he kept his gaze trained forward as he pulled away from the school and merged into the slow-moving traffic. Thunder growled from the turbulent sky, momentarily drowning out the rhythmic *swish-swoosh-swish-swoosh* of the windshield wipers. I caught a glimpse of his face in the rearview mirror. The tired lines around his eyes seemed deeper than usual. Long day? Or was he just tired from sitting around trying to think up a way to punish me for sneaking out?

"What happened to your face?" Dad asked suddenly.

I flinched and focused my gaze out the side window. "Tripped going up the stairs this morning."

He didn't reply, and I had no idea if he could tell I was lying or not. Sadly, me tripping and giving myself nasty bruises wasn't exactly a new thing. Maybe he bought it.

The minutes dragged by almost as slowly as the traffic, and we didn't say anything else to one another until the traffic came to a complete stop near a big intersection. The downpour made it totally impossible to see what the holdup was. I could barely see the cars around us, let alone what was going on farther down the road.

"Good grief," Dad growled under his breath as he put the car in park and sank back in his seat. "Looks like we're going to be here a while."

With nothing better to do, I decided to get a jumpstart on some of my homework. I'd barely gotten through reading the first couple of pages in my economics textbook when the high-pitched squeal of a siren howled past. A cold chill surged up my spine. Emergency lights flashed through the rain and a loud horn blared in frantic warning for people to get out of the way. A firetruck?

I craned my neck to get a better look as the big engine muscled its way past, honking and waiting for everyone to clear a path. My eardrums throbbed in rhythm with the wailing of the siren. About the time the first one vanished into the stormy gloom, a second firetruck and an ambulance went past, weaving through the gridlocked traffic as fast as they could.

Not good.

Dad frowned. "Must be a wreck."

My stomach did a panicky backflip. "Y-Yeah."

Taking out my phone, my hands shook as I typed out a message to Drake:

KOJI:
Hey, can you check local emergency chat-
ter for info on a wreck near the school?

It didn't take him ten seconds to reply:

DRAKE:
Duh. On it. Just a sec.

I waited, squinting and trying to peer down the road past the gridlocked cars and sheets of rain. Overhead, the crack and boom of thunder made my heart jump.

My phone buzzed again.

DRAKE:
Three-car pileup. Two deceased on scene.
One car flipped with victims still
trapped inside. Emergency services can't
approach because the car hit a powerline
pole. Lines are down with live current.
It's going to take a few minutes for
them to get the power switched off.

A hard knot lodged in my throat as my heartbeat thudded in slow, hard beats that made my ribs ache. It was bad. People were dead. More were still trapped and might be hurt. And the emergency responders couldn't even get close enough to help them because of the power lines.

But I could.

Slowly, I lifted my gaze to the front seat where Dad was sit-ting, staring idly out the windshield and drumming his fingers on the steering wheel in time with the song playing over the ra-dio. Somehow, I had to get out of the car. I had to get out of sight. More importantly, I had to do both without Dad noticing.

Or at the very least, without him getting suspicious about what I was up to.

I only had one idea. It was a terrible, truly pathetic, extra-sucky one. But there wasn't time. This had to work.

"Hey, uh, Dad?" I called up to him as I slid my phone back into my pocket.

"Hm? What?"

"I, um, I gotta go to the bathroom."

He shot me an exasperated glare in the rearview mirror. "Kinda stuck here, son. You're going to have to hold it."

"I don't think I can."

He rolled his eyes and bent down, rummaging around through all the papers and junk in his floorboard. "Here, use this." He handed me an empty foam fast-food cup.

I stealthily unfastened my seatbelt, praying he wouldn't hear the click of the buckle and snap of the belt retracting. "It's, um, it's number *two*, Dad."

"You have got to be kidding me."

"I think I saw a gas station at the last intersection. I'll just go there and be right back." I gripped the door handle. "I'll be fast, I promise."

Dad shot me one of his best parental warning glares in the rearview mirror. "No. It's not safe for you to walk out in the street like that, especially in this weather. Stay in the car."

"But, Dad, I—"

"Koji, just hold it. You're almost seventeen years old, you can wait a few minutes."

Another ambulance blurred by, lights and sirens going full blast.

I set my jaw. This was going to get me in worse trouble, if that was even possible at this point. Freaking out during his proposal. Sneaking out. Just add blatant disobedience in the name of emergency bathroom breaks to the list.

"I'll be right back!" I yelled as I suddenly threw the door open and bolted out of the car.

"KOJI!"

Dad's shouting protests faded behind me as I took off into the pouring rain. I weaved through the other parked cars caught in the traffic jam as the cold rain soaked through my clothes and ran down my face. Fast—I had to make this fast. I needed a place to transform and then I could get down to business. Five minutes tops.

Maybe. Hopefully.

I ducked into the first alleyway I came across, sprinting past dumpsters and muddy puddles filled with floating bits of soggy trash until I couldn't see the street anymore. At least in this weather, I was pretty much guaranteed to be the only idiot standing outside. Also, I doubted anyone would be able to see me through the downpour. Good enough.

Time to let the dragon loose.

Raking back the drenched sleeve of my sweater, I clapped a hand over my totem bracelet. "Awaken," I commanded.

Power sizzled to life, surging through every muscle as I flexed my arms wide and let my head roll back. The warm, tingling heat of my element spread through me in an all-consuming wave. Black scales climbed my body, covering my skin and disguising my features. My legs twisted and warped, becoming more reptilian. My long, spiked tail swished. My wings unfolded to the stormy skies with a snap like crack of thunder and I let out a roar of satisfaction.

All right. Let's get this done.

I sank into a crouch with my legs coiled for takeoff.

"Koji? Koji!"

My heart stopped. Panic flushed through me from the top of my horned head to the tips of my clawed toes. Oh my God. Was that...?

I whirled around.

The silhouetted figure of a man jogged toward me, too far away to make out in the rain. But the closer he got, the more clearly I could see him.

And the more clearly he could see me.

He came to a staggering halt, staring up at my towering draconic form with his eyes wide and face completely blanched of all color. "K-Koji?" He faltered, voice catching as his chest heaved with frantic, sporadic breaths.

I stared back at him through the frenzy of the storm, watching the tears pool in his eyes and spill down the sides of his face.

"Hey, Dad."

# CHAPTER 25

We stared at one another through the pouring rain for what felt like forever. Dad didn't say a single word. His eyes searched me, brow drawn into a look of total anguish and fear. I knew that look all too well. It'd been burned into my brain on that night when the emergency responders pulled me out of my mom's wrecked sedan. It took four cops to hold him back as he cried out my name.

And now... that same brokenness made his chin tremble and mouth mash up into a twisted, bitter line as he gazed up at my draconic form.

"Go get back in the car," I insisted, my voice a soft growl above the whoosh of the rainfall. "I'll meet you at home."

Dad didn't reply, not even when I strode past him. I got a running start before I took off into the storm. Thunder crackled overhead, making my heart jolt in my chest as I ground my jaw. He knew.

My dad knew I was Noxius.

It didn't take long for me to deal with the car wreck. A few downed power lines were nothing for my totem-powered strength. I yanked them away, looping the sizzling cables over the top of the tilted pole so they weren't near the wreckage or sitting in any pools of water. The firefighters and paramedics gaped in awe as the live current snapped and zapped at my scaly hide. The contact stung, but not enough to make me let go. I could stand way worse than that.

With the cables cleared, the emergency crew rushed in without hesitation. I saved them some trouble by wrenching off the car door so they could get to the pinned passengers—a frantic young mother and her two little kids still buckled into their car seats.

Standing over the upturned vehicle, my wings outstretched to give them some shelter from the rain while they worked, I looked up when one of the policemen began waving traffic through in an effort to clear the gridlock. Dad's car rolled by slowly, but I couldn't see him inside through the rain.

Maybe that was for the best.

I didn't need to be able to see him to sense his gaze on me like the heat wafting from an open oven. There was no talking my way out of it this time. No alibi or carefully crafted lie could ever cover this up.

I had no choice but to come clean.

"Noxius!" one of the firemen called out as he jogged over. "Thank you for your help."

I forced a dragon-y smile and nodded. "No problem."

"No one's heard anything about you since the Philharmonic. We weren't sure you were even still around. I have to admit, it's comforting to know you've got our backs. Makes us all sleep a little better at night." He smiled and stretched out a hand, offering to shake.

My heart sank. After an awkward moment of just standing there like a moron, I remembered to shake his hand. My huge scaly palm all but swallowed his, and I was careful not to crush his fingers before letting go.

I didn't know what to say, though. The people of this city were counting on me—I knew that. But actually hearing someone say it to my face while I was in this form? Last year, everyone screamed in terror at the mere sight of me. Now I was a figure of hope.

Only, according to Dr. Livingston, I wasn't. Not really. This power wasn't meant to be used for good. It was meant to destroy.

I was an interdimensional weapon of war.

Those thoughts buzzed around and stung my mind as I took off into the pouring rain and headed home. My heart pounded with slow, hard thumps that sent waves of panicked chills all the way down to my toes. Dad would be there, waiting for me.

And he knew.

The storm made for decent cover as I descended into the alleyway between our house and the next one. Tucked out of sight right next to the dumpster I'd fallen into the very first time I transformed, I covered my totem scale and bade it to sleep. In a matter of seconds, all my draconic power melted away. I was me again. Regular, normal, pathetic me, standing in the cold rain.

By the time I got to the front door, my pulse stammered and stalled in a wild frenzy as I struggled to stay calm. Now wasn't the time to get hysterical. I had a lot of explaining to do. Dad was bound to be furious. I'd been lying to him about all this for a long time, after all. Stay cool, Koji. Just keep calm.

Opening the front door as quietly as possible, I crept inside and quickly pressed it closed.

The sound of the TV drifted in from the living room.

That's where I found Dad.

He sat on the sofa, bent over with his face in his hands, as a news anchor in a poncho on the screen prattled on about Noxius's brave efforts in rescuing victims of a serious car accident. I took a few more cautious steps into the room, then lurched to a halt. Dad sucked in a sharp, stammering breath.

Oh God. Was he... *crying*?

My mouth screwed up.

I stood in my drenched preppy school uniform, dripping a puddle onto the hardwood floor, as I wrestled with what to do. Leave? Stay? Say something? What could I even say?

Suddenly, Dad whirled to face me. Maybe he'd spotted my reflection in the TV screen or something. Or maybe he'd heard me desperately trying to breathe past the hard knot in my throat.

He bolted to his feet, face red, eyes bloodshot, and cheeks still wet from tears as he stared into my eyes.

I shivered, half in terror and half from the chill of being soaking wet. My stomach flipped and swirled. My breath caught as I tried to choke out words. "D-Dad, I—"

He rushed me. Throwing his arms around my neck, Dad gripped me hard as he broke down. All I could hear were his ragged, broken breaths as he managed to sob out two words: "My son."

I couldn't hold it in anymore. I squeezed him back and buried my face against his shoulder, unable to stop the tears that welled in my eyes. He put a hand on the back of my head and kissed my hair. And for a long time, we just stood that way.

Every emotion poured out of me at once. All the fear about almost dying in Colombia, the worry about Dr. Livingston, the pain about being rejected by Madeline, the anxiety about Dad's relationship with Ms. Collins, and the despair over being replaced by her and Drake as the sole focus of his attention. I hadn't wanted to admit how much it all terrified me. It was too much. I couldn't handle it by myself. I needed help.

I needed my dad.

"I-I'm... s-so sorry," I cried as I gripped the back of his shirt. "I s-should've... t-told..." I couldn't get the words out as I trembled, choking on every breath I tried to take.

"It's okay, Koji," Dad said softly as he petted my hair. "I'm here. I'll always be right here."

Sitting next to me on the sofa, Dad took the news about my secret life as a superhero pretty well. He only cussed a few times, and not even at me. They were just general exclamations of parental terror when I told him the gritty details about my battle at the Philharmonic and my latest mission to Colombia. I spared him some of the more gruesome stuff, and I didn't give up Oceana's real identity. Until she was comfortable with it, I didn't want to out her to anyone else. Madeline, though? Well, I had to own up to that one. Especially after she'd been the one to burn her handprint into my chest.

Other than those few outbursts, Dad sat quietly and listened until I was done. His expression stayed pensive and grim, but he didn't seem angry. Frustrated, but not upset. So far, so good. Maybe I'd come out of this without being grounded for the rest of my natural life.

"So, let me see if I've got this straight," he said, leaning to rest his elbows on his knees as he pinched the bridge of his nose. "You left the cruise ship by helicopter, flew to a Navy warship to rendezvous with a group of SEALs, battled this Dr. Livingston woman and were nearly killed, then returned? In one night?"

I gnawed on the inside of my cheek for a second. "Um, well, yeah. Basically." Okay, so when he put it like that, it did sound a little unbelievable. "I can go transform again really quick if you don't believe me."

He shot me an exasperated look. "Of course I believe you. I'm just struggling to rationalize why the FBI chose to leave me out of all of this. My only child, who is still a minor, is risking his life to fight an international terrorist organization, and they left me in the dark?"

"Yeeeah, well, actually that part was sort of my fault," I confessed. "Agent Kirkland said it was my choice. I didn't want to tell you because... because, well, I was afraid you'd want me to get rid of my totem. That you wouldn't let me fight. And I can't just leave Oceana to do it all on her own."

"Do her parents know about all this?"

I shook my head. "It's her choice if she wants to tell them."

Dad let out a heavy sigh as he sat back and ran his hands through his hair like he might start ripping out fistfuls of it in frustration. "I don't know what to say."

"I don't either." I sighed, too.

"And this power is... slowly eating you alive?" he asked.

"Yeah." I hung my head. Here it came: the demand that I get rid of my totem immediately. No way he'd want me to keep my totem now. Shutting my eyes tightly, I bit down hard against that scorching pull deep in my chest—a rage like hellfire I could barely contain. That heat, that anger, it wasn't me. It was the kur. I knew that now.

And I had to keep it under control.

"But if you give it up, there's no one besides Oceana to fight this Livingston person if she decides to attack again?"

I gulped. "Well, um, there's Fyurei. But she's been a little unreliable lately. And the military helps some too, but you've seen how that can go. They're no match for another crocodile monster—not unless they want to blow up the surrounding city too."

Dad didn't say anything for a few minutes, leaving me to sit in numb, petrified silence as I watched his expression flicker between anger and deep thought. At last, he looked at me. His eyes searched mine, almost as though he were trying to find something hidden deep inside me. Noxius, maybe? Or some evidence of my totem slowly sucking my soul away?

"Okay." His tone was strangely calm.

"O-Okay?" I stammered, not sure what that meant.

"Whatever all this means, whatever's happening—I don't understand it fully. And I don't know what to do about it, or if there's anything I can do. So you've got to tell me what you want," he clarified, reaching over to take my hand and squeeze it firmly. "Tell me how to help you, Koji."

I opened my mouth, but nothing came out except a stunned, breathy squeak. He wanted to help me? Seriously? He wasn't angry? Or upset? Or determined to get rid of my totem?

It took a few seconds to process that. And while my brain struggled to deal with that revelation, the noise of the TV filled the silence with a breaking news bulletin.

Dad and I glanced up at the screen at the same instant.

A somber-faced female anchor sat behind the sleek glass desk, staring right at the camera and probably giving crucial details. But I couldn't hear it. I couldn't think. I couldn't even breathe.

The headline at the bottom of the screen made everything in my world come to a screeching halt: *DRACONIC MONSTER SUSPECTED IN VATICAN MUSEUM HEIST.*

"That wasn't you, right?" Dad gripped my hand harder.

My voice came out as a hoarse, panicked whisper. "No."

"Oceana, then?"

Slowly, I pulled my hand away from his and reached for my cell phone. No sooner had I taken it out of my pocket, then it buzzed with a new message notification.

DRAKE:
She found it.

All the blood drained from my face as I sat, gaping back and forth between my phone and the TV screen.

"Koji?" Dad leaned in, probably noticing how I'd suddenly gone as pale as a corpse.

I snapped my mouth shut. Everything had gone numb except for the feel of my phone in my hand and my own heart pumping wildly.

"Son?" Dad coaxed, his tone tight with concern.

"No," I answered at last. "Not Oceana. It was Madeline. She…" My voice cracked as I sucked in a steadying breath and looked up at him again. "She found the earth totem."

# ACKNOWLEDGEMENTS

Special thanks to Keith, Kyle, and Luke for their expert advice on all things military!

\* \* \*

Thank you to my wonderful agent, Fran! I'm continually thankful for all your hard work and support!

\* \* \*

Thank you to the folks at Owl Hollow Press for their enthusiasm and work making this series the best that it can be!

\* \* \*

Thank you to my wonderful family for all their love and support! You guys never fail to make me feel so blessed and humbled to have you in my life!

**NICOLE CONWAY** is a graduate of Auburn University with a lifelong passion for writing teen and children's literature. With over 100,000 books sold in her *DRAGONRIDER CHRONI-CLES* series, Nicole has been ranked one of Amazon's Top 100 Teen Authors.

A coffee and Netflix addict, she also enjoys spending time with her family, practicing photography, and traveling.

Nicole is represented by Frances Black of Literary Counsel.

Find her online at www.authornicoleconway.com and here:

### #WINGS | #SPIRITSOFCHAOS

CPSIA information can be obtained
at www.ICGtesting.com
Printed in the USA
LVHW040438270123
738005LV00003B/300